BISCUITS with BLANCHE

THE SAVAGEST AGONY AUNT WHO EVER DIED

MIKE LAWSON

Contents

Blanche • 5

January • 13

February • 51

March • 79

April • 100

May • 127

June • 153

July • 182

August • 210

September • 228

October • 248

November • 263

The Coup • 274

For the biscuits who followed the rules

BLANCHE

I was in the first-class cabin on the upper deck of a BA 747 from Jamaica to London when I choked on a custard cream, lost consciousness, and died somewhere over the Bermuda Triangle. It was New Year's Eve 1999 and I was in my prime. When the murderous biscuit got lodged in my throat the bitch of an air hostess half-heartedly performed the Heimlich manoeuvre on me. She was evidently more concerned about creasing her scarf and smudging her make-up, that she'd put on with a trowel four hours earlier, than bringing me back to life.

Cilla, you know the one, Scouse, buck teeth, awful voice, she was my partner in crime. Cilla was unconscious after downing a bottle of White Lightning in our hotel room before we left for the airport. Then she had the obligatory champagne to give the paps a photo opportunity in the airside bar. She staggered up the aircraft steps and greeted the cabin crew with her usual cheery 'Fuck off.' She had a reputation for loving the finer things, but she was never happier than when she was scoffing a Frey Bentos Steak and Kidney pie and washing it down with a bottle of cheap cider. Even when the Senior Cabin Crew made an announcement for a doctor she didn't flinch. When we landed in Heathrow, myself now a corpse, she stood up, collected her two hundred Benson and Hedges from the overhead locker, stepped over my lifeless body, and fucked off into the daylight.

We'd been in Jamaica as Cilla was filming a Wish You Were Here special. She got fired when the showrunner walked in on her doing a shot of Lenor and a line of Daz all White. We still had a bloody good time though. Reminiscing about how we met and the adventures since. Inseparable for the best part of forty years, we were forever having quarrels, she got very jealous of my friendship with Princess Di and I couldn't stand how she idolized Thatcher. We'd only just got talking again before the trip;

she'd sent round a team of naked butlers to apologise on her behalf, she knew all my weak spots.

I won't hold back just because I'm dead. Me mam always said I had a gob like the Mersey Tunnel, which is ironic as we lived in Salford. Not the rough part, but not the nice part either, if it did have any nice parts in the '40s. No need to try and imagine it, just look at a picture by Lowry, although he wasn't very good at staying between the lines. What a life I had; my only regret is that I didn't outlive Thatcher. I did meet her a few times in the living life but never crossed paths with her in this ghostly one. Mind you, would I be able to tell the difference, dead or alive she had no heart. She's why I ended up residing At Her Majesty's pleasure.

Anyway, I was stuck on that aircraft for eleven years. Flying around in an aluminium tomb. It was enjoyable to begin with, I could never have dreamt of travelling the world when I was growing up. The furthest I'd been until I was ten was Fleetwood. I was twelve when we went to Scarborough, I thought it was a whole new world. The only downside of being onboard was the passengers. You could have made a Channel 5 documentary on the falling standards of the social classes the way some of them behaved and dressed. I find it inconceivable what the girls wear now: a size 18 squeezed into a size 10 boob tube, rolls of skin spilling out over the sides. You can hear the fabric screaming from the strain: mutton dressed as shite. People used to make an effort to travel, wear their Sunday best. Now they chuck on the first thing they find on the floor, you're very lucky if it has a crotch.

I loved nothing more than having a sneaky rummage through the passengers' belongings. In the early days I just use to make things fall over, then I mastered the art of being able to move items. I once swapped a vibrator from the bag of a girl on a hen party, who were on their way to Malaga, with a Filofax of a businesswoman who was closing a multimillion-pound deal in the Costas. I thought the C.E.O would be furious, but she was grinning from ear to fanny when she returned a week later. You can get up to all sorts when you're an invisible spirit. I used to lift the latches on the galley stowages so on take-off the service carts would go hell for leather down the aisles. You should have seen the look on the air hostess's faces when fifty bags of salted nuts went whizzing past them on wheels. I was never a poltergeist, just bored and mischievous.

When I passed over, I had a choice: stay on earth as a bodyless soul until able to possess another human form or climb the stairs to the pearly gates and cast an eye over the shenanigans on earth. I chose the former. I'd spent the last forty years looking down on people so there didn't seem much point going up, plus it was over a thousand steps upstairs and I couldn't be arsed. Who'd want to put in all that effort to be greeted by a bunch of judgmental do-gooders? So, there I was, happily floating around this aircraft as a white mist until I found somebody suitable to inhabit to walk back into civilization. The trouble was this aircraft was no longer part of a luxury airline that had taken Cilla and me on our travels. It had gone tits up and was now part of a fleet for a low-cost carrier. The first-class cabin was reduced to only two rows of four abreast seats, dramatically reducing the chances of finding anyone half suitable to impose myself upon.

In the years I was onboard I never crossed the line and went into economy, it was definitely there though, I could smell it. The odour of working-class perspiration transported me straight back to Langworthy Road, to a time when me dad would fall through the front door after a day working at the Ford Factory at the Manchester Docks. I don't quite know what he did there, I was led to believe he was a professional alcoholic. I stayed up front with the stars in first-class, a few dead ones popped through in transit: Judy Garland, she was an awkward one. I had to hold her back from trying to overdose on a passenger's TicTacs, she thought they were paracetamol. She hadn't grasped the concept of being dead. I was in awe when Audrey Hepburn passed through on her way to the Seychelles, still very much a star, even in the afterlife.

I feasted on the gossip magazines that had been left behind in seat pockets and passed time devouring the in-flight movies. I was always fascinated with Hollywood and the stars of the big screen. Me mam worked in the Ambassador Theatre at the top of our street as an usherette. She'd let me slip in for free to keep me out the cold. I didn't like popcorn; me mam would give me a packet of custard creams to scran on instead. I always had a bounty of them in my handbag growing up, a sugary reminder of home.

The best times were when it was a quiet day and it was just the two of us there for the matinée: she'd let me play whichever film I wanted to watch instead of the advertised feature. I'd always choose a blockbuster starring Marilyn Monroe. I idolized her from the second she appeared in a slit sequined red dress and white feathered fascinator in Gentlemen Prefer Blondes. The next day I went to the chemist on the precinct and bought a bottle of peroxide and bleached my hair. I was only the kid in Chimney Pot Park with a platinum beehive. Me dad said, 'what've you done that for, you look like you've been at your hair with a knife and fork'. Bastard.

It was 1953, I was only ten, but I knew there and then that I'd be leaving Salford behind soon enough. I watched every film Marilyn was in after that and noted every lesson from her blockbuster How to Marry a Millionaire. And that is exactly what I did. Gone are the great Hollywood icons, replaced with a conveyor belt of reality tv contestants who couldn't string a sentence together without spelling it out in spaghetti first. Although, some of today's so-called stars are not much better. I've seen popstars lose their cool and control of their senses. A particular one who shan't be mentioned, as I'm not one to gossip, demanded a diversion to a Starbucks halfway across the Atlantic for a fair-trade Triple shot, Venti, Half Sweet, Non-Fat, Caramel Macchiato when the crew had run out of organic pixie milk. They had to be tasered and restrained for their own safety. Another leading actress wasn't much better, she used her crusted nipple as a bottle opener.

Something had to be done about the destruction of civilized society, the falling standards of social etiquette, wayward politicians, and Gemma Collins being a role model to the young. I couldn't bear to see the world so full of morally bankrupt people who couldn't give a rat's arse about how filthy their net curtains or front steps were. My mother had the shiniest step on Langworthy Road, she polished it every weekday and bleached her nets twice a month. She used to say, 'a window without a net curtain is an invitation for a peeping Tom.' She'd be shocked now if she could see the internet, everyone putting their every move they make online, checking in for a colonoscopy on social media with a matching selfie. I couldn't stand for it. It had to change, and I was going to be the one to make it happen.

I saw my chance to escape the aircraft when Sarah Ferguson, Duchess of York, boarded in the summer of 2011. It was the one and only time I crossed over the threshold into economy. She was taking Beatrice out the country to burn the toilet seat she'd worn on her head at William and Kate's wedding. I can only imagine it was an Aldi special buy. Beatrice was sobbing from the ridicule she got from the press. She was considering selling a picture of Charles at the reception seductively fingering an Iceland vol-au-vent whilst talking to Pippa Middleton to take the focus off herself. Camilla had been distracted doing the Agadoo.

I waited to seize my opportunity to escape. I had visions of going to the palace as I lurked underneath Fergie's porky possum, attending official engagements and meeting world leaders. Although I knew Liz had sent her to Coventry, I was still sure I could worm my way back in with the Royals. I just didn't realise she was now living as a recluse on the top floor of a high-rise flat in Salford.

It was only a short flight Fergie was travelling on, the Canaries. A cheap bucket and spade getaway. She'd paid for it by collecting tokens from The Sun. What she'd saved on the holiday she spent in the duty-free shop: a litre of whisky and a giant Toblerone stuck out of her pleather handbag. She'd scoffed the Toblerone by the time we'd reached the channel and had ordered a glass of ice to accompany her whisky from the hostess. This particular hostess was called Chantelle, had an orange ring of foundation around her neckline, a beak where her mouth should be (her lips had been inflated with Polyfilla), and a gold chain which hung loosely over her foundation-stained collar. The necklace spelt out her name in capitals, supposedly to remind her of who she was every time she looked in the mirror.

The flight was a bit turbulent as we edged out over the Atlantic and down towards Las Palmas. There were a few concerned looks from passengers, but I wasn't arsed, well you don't get bothered about much when you're dead. A few drinks had spilt with the rocking of the aircraft and it was a little difficult to walk in the cabin, but Chantelle had sales targets to meet and nothing was stopping her from earning her 5%

commission. She was up and down that cabin like a rat up a drainpipe. Smoke coming off the wheels of her cart. A passenger had asked for the airline's exclusive gift set: an overpriced miniature bottle of perfume which smelt like camel piss and came with matching soap and body lotion. Chantelle had none left but went to check the back galley to see if there was any more in stock. Another hostess, not important enough to be described, told Chantelle there was some in the overhead locker above 30C. She stumbled her way there, grabbing the passengers' ponytails to keep herself steady. As the plane rocked from left to right in the jet stream, Chantelle reached up and pressed the shiny metal button to open the overhead locker.

An avalanche of cheap duty-free products come tumbling out bashing Fergie, who was seated in the cheap seat below, on the head. It was a bottle of Northern, by Jane McDonald, that delivered the knockout blow. A musky perfume with a hint of mushy peas. Fergie's fuselage slumped out of her seat and fell into the aisle. Chantelle carried on, although she did think her cart hitting a speed bump back to the galley unusual. The other passengers didn't care about the unconscious woman on the floor, a few of them took selfies but soon got bored. I saw this as my Houdini moment. My chance to escape this monotonous tube of take-offs and landings. As Fergie lay unconscious, I used all my ghostly strength to inhabit her body. I instantly went from a svelte white mist into a menopause.

It was strange at first, getting used to the new rules of possession. I could see and hear everything from within Fergie's body, but I couldn't communicate with the outside world. She was very much in control of all her senses and actions until she had a couple of stiffeners. Then I would take over the conscious mind and use Fergie's body as if it were my own. Fortunately for me, she'd developed the habit of having vodka with her breakfast orange. I was normally in complete control by the beginning of This Morning. When the alcohol wore off, I'd go back to lurking under Fergie's skin and she would have a memory like she'd done ten shots of Sambuca the night before — hazy and regretful. She never knew I was there, but she did wonder where her sudden good taste in furnishings had come from. I got to quite like her if I'm honest;

maudlin yet hopeful.

On entering Fergie's flat, I had to barge the door open with her shoulder, it was blocked by a 50/50 mix of memorabilia of Budgie the Little Helicopter and pictures of Andrew, Duke of York. The pictures were faded and showed signs of heavy fingering. Liz (The Queen to you), paid for what she believed to be appropriate security for an ex-Royal: an incontinent corgi and a very aggressive swan guarded the entrance to the lift. The state of the furniture led me to believe that this may have been the epicentre of a civil war between Buck House and Boadicea Manor, the name of this council-clad tower block, the former claiming victory. A confidentiality agreement was placed next to her phone, a threat to Fergie every time it rang.

Those first few years I didn't do much, just stayed lurking beneath Fergie's consciousness taking in the world as it is today. It was worse than I thought. She was worse than I thought. Day after day we sat watching reruns of Jeremy Kyle and Judge Rinder; drinking cheap wine; Instagram stalking Kate Middleton; sobbing at The Yorkshire Vet; laughing at Women Who Kill; and putting on an evening gown and tiara to watch The One Show. Liz had left her with nothing, neither material nor mind.

The sight of the dregs of society airing their shitty laundry in public perplexed me. On one particular episode of a daytime show, Camilla took a lie detector test to prove to Charles that she hadn't sold his mother's crown at Cash Converters. A national disgrace that our royalty had shared the same stage as a man who was trying to find his mother through the DNA of a genital wart, the nuns had found it in the basket he'd been left in.

Time to pull my sleeves up and make a difference. If I could go from Salford to the West End via a few misdemeanours, anyone could. Time to shake up this flat, then the nation. First, I remodelled Fergie's den using Tesco clubcard points and threw away the pictures of Andrew, I just chucked them over the balcony. Then I placed an advert in the classified sections of the national press:

'Blanche of Tiller Girl fame, known for her intimacy with the Royal Family, becomes Britain's straightest-talking Agony Aunt. Clean up your marriage, shimmy up your lives and muzzle up your misery for the price of a stamp and bottle of gin. Write to Lady Blanche Mountbatten at ...'

It was a chore matching deliveries of gin to emails, it was bloody marvellous trying them all though. Some people just sent e-vouchers which I thought lacked imagination. I kept them but deleted the email. By the end of the week, I had the postman coming four times a day. The flat looked like a Royal Mail sorting office, gin and letters everywhere. In the end, I just chose the five letters/emails that had been delivered with the best gin from the most desperate of people. I find desperate people are the easiest to use, some would say manipulate. I wouldn't argue. Besides, a small and dedicated army can come in useful when one has a vendetta, and there is no grudge bigger than mine against a Tory. People often say, 'life's too short to hold a grudge.' Luckily, I'm dead.

January

Victoria Townsend
29 Hellbourne Close
Salford

2nd January 2020

Dear Blanche,

I've been imprisoned in my marriage for the last forty years. Every month has felt like a life sentence. We met back in the mid-70s when he had hair, and we were both slim. I was shy. I would hide in the middle of my girlfriends in the pub so no one would talk to me. I was at nursing school when I met him, Dave. I'd gone with three of my classmates into the city centre to celebrate our last day of the first year. It was a huge relief to us all that we'd got through it. The ward we worked on was run as a dictatorship by our matron, she'd taken a dislike to me for coming from South Manchester and not the posher North.

We went to a little pub at the end of Deansgate (it's long since closed), and that's when I met Dave. I was completely taken in by his confidence and his danger as he leaned on his motorbike outside the pub. He came over to speak to me and bought me a half-pint of lager. My fate was sealed. It was fun and adventurous in the early weeks and months, catching a moment together whenever we could. Escaping on his motorbike, lovesick teenagers. I suppose he felt dangerous for me, the girl who had always been top of the class. It gave me life. He gave me life. It didn't last long. He's been killing me slowly for forty years.

We married eighteen months after we met. Nothing fancy, a registry office and then onto the Legion for a few sandwiches that my Mum had made. Before the wedding, my dad said, 'You don't have to do this kid, it's not too late to turn back.' It was out of character for my dad. He must have been able to see Dave's true colours. Dave's not really a husband, just someone who shares facilities.

Things changed quickly after the wedding. He became short-tempered, he's stayed like that ever since. We used to drive round to his mother's in the nice part of North Manchester and he would make me wait outside in the car for hours at a time. I was pregnant. He must have been ashamed or resented me for having to trade in his motorbike for a sensible run-around. I dropped out of nursing school shortly after. We moved into a nice house which needed some work. Nothing major. A bit of modernising. My parents lent us the money for a deposit. He never thanked them.

We had three children: Sharon, Nicholas, and William. Sharon and Nicholas came in quick succession and William was a surprise ten years later. Dave was a terrible father. He missed every first step, every first word, every nativity. He was either down the pub or recovering from being there. He was never short of money. He was a respectable tradesman, still is. You'd never have known he had a bit stashed away. I was forbidden to spend money on the kids, when I did it was like World War Three. He went away working one week to Scotland with the rest of his builder mates and took the plug off the boiler. The house was so cold I don't think the Christmas snow ever melted off the roof. I promised myself I'd leave him when the kids grew up. I never did. I looked into it, I looked at buying a house on my own, but I always stayed. There'd be a ceasefire long enough for me to change my mind. A few happy weeks would pass then normal service would be resumed.

We've spent eleven months out of every year (for the last twenty-eight years), not talking. I lived in hope that when we retired it might be different, that we could at least talk and travel. We don't.

I haven't lived, I've existed. Don't get me wrong, I've been there for him whenever he's needed me. I've worried about him when he's been ill. Fifteen years ago he nearly went into a diabetic coma, I rushed him to the hospital. I was worried sick. I called the kids to come. The two eldest did but the youngest refused. They'd fallen out two years before and hadn't spoken a word to each other since. Dave ended up in the hospital for three weeks with ulcerative colitis. He had most of his bowls removed and replaced with a colostomy. He's a martyr to it. He proudly shows it off under the loose-fitting t-shirts he wears, wanting sympathy. He lets his bag bulge with contents and stinks out the whole house before he will go and change it. He won't wear a colostomy belt to hold it in place either — people wouldn't be able to see it then. I live my life with a can of air freshener in my hand.

I hate him. I hate everything about him. I hate myself for not leaving him. I hate this beautiful house, a prison of unhappy memories. I hate the smell that lingers in each room. I hate that even now I still can't leave. I hate that I'm nearly seventy and it's too late to start afresh. Blanche, how can I escape?

Please help,

Victoria Townsend

Blanche
Boadicea Manor
Salford 6

Dear Victoria,

It is never too late to leave and start afresh. Have you ever heard of Stockholm syndrome? Judy Finnigan suffered with it dreadfully for years and she's seventy-two. Though she had an epiphany in the queue at the Little Shopper whilst she was waiting in line to buy a scratch card. Richard has asked for a divorce on the grounds that she's a functioning alcoholic. Judy granted him the divorce on the grounds he was a "wretched, overbearing, dominating, bastard of a chauvinist pig" who hasn't let her get a word out edgeways since the This Morning Christmas Special in '99. She hated him long before that mind. She plotted several attempts to finish him off: she once woke up early and greased all the edges of the floating weather map in the Albert Dock. She knew Richard was doing a special feature on it later in the day. Judy placed 2000 broken bottles under the surface of the Irish sea, ready to impale Richard when he slipped on the grease and submerge himself to his death. She was furious when the feature got cancelled due to adverse weather.

Have you thought about finishing him off? You could do it very subtly and slowly so as not to arouse suspicion. You say he's a diabetic? Put some extra sugar in his tea, leave his favourite sweets lying about the house or put an air bubble in his insulin injection. If that fails, a sledgehammer across the back of the head should do it.

There are lots of women who began their journey later in life. My good friend Liz Smith was in her fifties when she got her breakthrough role in a Mike Leigh film. She used to come to the bingo with me and Princess Di until they fell out over two fat ladies, they were sitting at the next table talking so loudly that we couldn't hear the numbers being called.

Di missed the call out of the number she needed for a full house. She marched over to the two fat ladies and shoved their bingo dabbers up their nostrils. Liz was mortified and made her excuses to leave muttering 'I always preferred Camilla.'

Victoria, it's simply never too late to up sticks and go. Think Shirley Valentine. It was whilst watching a rerun of that film late at night on Channel 4 that Di finally decided to leave Charles. She called me up and said, 'Blanche, I'm going to leave him and run off with a foreigner.' It was 1991 and she was staying in a chalet at Pontin's, Blackpool. She stuck to her word when she met Dodi. They'd planned to open up a little beachside cafe in Sharm El Sheikh. Alas, it wasn't meant to be.

So, Victoria, grab life by the colostomy bag and live it. Get packing and leave him behind. Get on that midnight train to Skegness and never look back. Failing that, you can take baby steps and join a few social clubs. Have a look in your local press. Build your confidence with some amateur dramatics or get fit in a ping pong tournament at the YMCA. Just get out of the house.

Blanche

Diane Abbott MP
House of Commons
Westminster

5th January 2020

Dear Blanche,

Is it really you? I don't believe it. How have you been? Are you well? I've not heard from you in so long that I thought you had passed away. I saw an advert in the Parliament Chronicle and thought it can't be, but Lady Blanche Mountbatten isn't a common name, is it? I'd only picked it up to do the sudoku. Jeremy is on at me to improve my maths. I don't know what to say — Thank you — I owe you everything. I have thought about you often over the years and always hoped we'd reconnect.

It must be twenty-three years since I last saw you and thirty years since we spoke properly. I'll never forget that day Blanche. You saved me from scandal. Thirty years Blanche. I've never forgiven myself for remaining silent as I watched them drive you, my honourable friend, away in the back of the police car. I wanted to help you, I really did. I would never have survived the scandal. If a black female MP were arrested for inciting a riot, the party would have ceased to exist. I've thought of you every time I've passed Trafalgar Square. I hear the noise of the riots and see the angry crowds so clearly. Your leadership of the People's Union Against the Poll Tax was inspiring. It was a privilege to be your secretary. That summer weekend I came to stay at yours in Brighton, I can feel the hangover just thinking about it. You were always mischievous; I can't believe we went skinny dipping in the dead of night.

I can still remember the day we met. It was that rally against Thatcher's proposal to scrap free milk in schools at the Hackney Empire (you never did tell me why it was so important to you). You walked on stage with such a presence that you had the crowd eating out of your hand. Beehive perfectly postured, every word spoken with uncompromising truth. You united the crowd in their loathing for Thatcher. It's because of you we hung on to free milk for as long as we did. I told Thatcher, 'No use crying over spilt milk,' When she left the Commons for the last time. I said that for you.

31st March 1990. Thousands came, Blanche. I don't know what you said to Kinnock to get him to cancel the Labour Party rally the same day, but it was genius. All those extra people came to march for you instead. Thatcher had no chance of survival against you. I suppose I'm writing to ask for your forgiveness and your help. Can you do it again, could you take down the Tories?

I know you didn't intend for the riots to get so out of hand with all the violence, although I suppose it was to be expected. Remember when we saw Rees-Mogg there in disguise, looting Woolworths? If only people knew the real him.

Blanche, I never explained to you why I did what I did. Do you remember we were standing next to the scaffolding on the corner of the square with the miners who'd coached down from Sunderland? They were really going for it. Some of them had your beehive printed on the back of their t-shirts with Bollocks to the Poll Tax on the front. Everywhere you looked there were police with batons hitting out at anyone and everyone. I can understand now, looking back, they must have been scared. Completely overwhelmed and outnumbered. I admit I disproportionately lost control of my senses. I looked to my left and saw a group of officers man-handling a man in a wheelchair, hitting him when he couldn't defend himself. I asked them to stop but they couldn't hear me over the chants. I pleaded to them, but they just carried on. I watched as they attempted to clamp his wheels. The next thing I knew I'd picked up a brick the miners had thrown from the scaffolding and I was hammering it into a policeman's helmet. I could see the determination on your face when you saw them trying to cuff me. I never knew you were so strong. You were like a gladiator the way you picked up that scaffold pole and charged at the Met. When you commanded me to run, I did. I couldn't go far because of the crowd. By the time I looked back, they already had you cuffed and halfway into the police van.

I waited at the side of Trafalgar Square for the riots to cease. I was in complete shock at what I'd done. When the African Embassy had been set on fire and the smoke crossed to the protestors, I used it as my cover to get away. I walked all the way back to Hackney. Your picture was on the front cover of every newspaper the next day, beehive flattened, skin dirty from the debris. The face of the riots. I'm incredibly sorry Blanche. It should have been me.

I couldn't face you all those years later when Tony asked you to run his election campaign. I was still too afraid to face you. It was fortunate that no one recognised you with your reconstructed beehive. I know I've got a nerve writing to you, but we NEED you again Blanche. The party needs you. Corbyn is in his last days as a leader, and we were decimated in the election last November. We need someone to come and lead us to success again. You delivered a miracle in '97 and we need another one.

Respectfully yours,

Diane

Blanche
Boadicea Manor
Salford 6

Diane,

It's all looting under the bridge as far as I'm concerned. Plus, the period of incarceration resulted in a great love affair for me — it's over now but I'm a better person for it. I'm fine thanks for asking, I'm great in fact, like I've got a whole new lease of life.

I got seven years: two for assaulting a police officer and five for inciting a riot – I was out after twelve months. Cilla paid the judge to shred my conviction, she couldn't cope without me. All the filming at LWT had got too much for her without me by her side. She sent a weekly bribe to the governor which allowed me some privileges: a bottle of gin every week, an extra 10 minutes in the shower on my own with my favourite bath lotion by *Mary,* and a packet of custard creams every other day which I shared with Jacqueline, my common cell partner.

It was all worth it to see the front page of the *Daily Mirror* on the 29th November 1990. The governor who was normally a hard screw had bought a copy for every cell. There was a celebration that swept across our wing when we woke to see The Iron Lady reduced to a skriking tin can. Kicked down the road and well and truly out of Downing Street. We all got extra Spam that evening.

I remember you weren't so fond of Tony, I liked him, apart from that nasty business with the weapons of mass destruction. We had fun on his campaign trail, we even had a brief encounter during a publicity call at the Walkers' crisp factory, he got very excited over a packet of prawn cocktail. Afterwards, he delivered a marvellous speech to the workers and the press. I think that's what clinched him a few extra votes in Scotland. Cherie never knew, she wasn't interested anyway, it was a marriage of convenience for her. She was convinced Tony was going to be Prime Minister since the day they met, and she'd always wanted an SW1 postcode.

We were confident Tony was going to win but we didn't quite expect the landslide victory he had. I put it down to the naked photoshoot he did for *Gay Times*. It won him the pink vote. Tony wasn't keen on the idea at first but soon stripped off on the promise it would give him the image of a very modern man. He was bare arsed in seconds. Nothing but a red rose to cover his modesty. When David Dimbleby announced the exit polls it was me that Tony turned to and thanked first, Cherie was furious. She forgave him the next day when she was able to send notification of her new postcode to her family in Merseyside.

Can I take down the Tories? Blindfolded with one hand behind my beehive.

Blanche

From: Alex Huntington
To: Blanche
Subject Single and lonely

10th January 2020

Dear Blanche,

What do you reckon to this? I'm a thirty-nine-year-old single woman from Peterborough. I work in a doctor's surgery as a receptionist. I enjoy my job, but I dread turning on the phone lines in the morning. For the first half an hour all I get is abuse from patients who I don't have appointments for. To be honest I don't really care about the job. The truth is, when I finish work, I want someone to go home to other than my cat. I've made it my New Year's resolution to meet someone. Meeting someone at work, like lots of my friends have done, just isn't an option for me. The only men I see have prostate problems who are knocking on heaven's door. It's like God's waiting room. Mr Robinson asked me out once, he was seventy-five and had just had a hip replacement. I would have gone for some company, but he was dead the following week.

I've started watching Gay Date TV for company. I throw myself into my work to keep busy, I can make the organising of the waiting room magazines last for hours. *Bella* is the most popular. I like to put that at the bottom of the pile to make the patients look at the other magazines first. I feel the *Angler's Times* doesn't get the recognition it deserves.

I get on with my colleagues, but they all have their own lives. Occasionally we will go for a drink after work. Dr Altman is my favourite. Every summer she throws a BBQ. She starts organising it the second the clock strikes midnight to bring in the New Year. She's got it all: a six-figure salary, a handsome husband who's very high up in pharmaceuticals, Land Rover and a four-bedroom house, it's *really* nice. It's always a lovely event, but I dread being set up with one of her single friends. Last year it was Edward, a taxidermist who after four Snowballs said he wanted to stuff me. I didn't take it any further after the fifth date. Do you think I can find someone before I'm completely over the hill? As much as I like my colleagues, I'm sick to the back teeth of them calling me *Bridget*.

What do you reckon Blanche, have I got time to find someone before the Summer BBQ?

Eternally Single,

Alex

From: Blanche
To: Alex Huntington
Subject Re: Single and lonely

Dear Alex,

I reckon it's very sad. You're the superior bitch who won't give me an appointment. I've been calling every morning since 2013 and the first available slot isn't until next year. I'm desperate to get my roommate Fergie in for a check-up after a recent breakdown she had whilst watching *Homes Under the Hammer*. She said it reminded her of being evicted from the palace. I call her my flatmate but we're much closer than that. Interwoven you could say.

It must be very lonely in your studio flat. Though I would love some peace and quiet right now. I've been none stop all week. I've become quite the celebrity since sending these letters. Mr Patel pushed a note under my door asking me if I'd like to cut the ribbon on his new washing machine at his launderette, *Wishy Washy*. I couldn't make it as I was busy counselling Judy Finnigan, her divorce from Richard come through. She's been on the gin for two weeks solid, celebrating. Me and Judy go way back. I met her when I did a brief stint as the resident aerobics' instructor on *Good Morning Britain* in '88. She joined in my workout one day as she wanted to shift a bit of timber. She wore a gold leotard over her trouser suit ready to start filming.

Do you have halitosis? It was the first thing that sprang to mind when you described the absence of a partner and friends. It can be quite a debilitating condition. Me mam used to say me dad suffered with it because he always spoke shite.

Have you tried speed dating? They do one evening a week at Broadmoor. Perhaps not the perfect location to find a suitor but it will get you out the house. Mind you, it's a bit far from Peterborough and I don't recommend public transport. Last time I went on a train I was on my way to see Princess Di, we had a big night planned at the Bingo. A tall man in an anorak came and pushed himself against me on the 15:20 into Euston. I rode that same train back and forth all week and never saw him again. Di got a full house that night and won a cement mixer. She was over the moon. She put it on the middle deck of Dodi's yacht to use as a TV stand. It was set it up so that every time Camilla came on the screen it would switch itself on and put Camilla on an aggressive spin.

Have you tried downloading a dating app? You'll have an army of men at your fingertips to choose from. I believe it's how Meghan met Harry. Select a good photo to upload if you have one. Keep your description brief too, you don't want to bore anyone. You really do need to learn the art of seduction, but for now, focus on the basics, straightening your hair and brushing your teeth.

Blanche

From: Jessica Watkiss
To: Blanche
Subject Labour pains

13th January 2020

Dear Blanche,

I saw your advert and had to write. I've enclosed a bottle of Jaffa Cake Gin Liquor. I was going to drink it myself, but I can't take the risk of getting pissed and then wetting myself. I've just had a very traumatic labour. I was trying to squeeze a human out of me for forty-eight hours. Then they hoisted me out of the birthing pool like a beached whale and flopped me onto the operating table for a C-section. My husband, the bastard, was by my side for all of it apart from when he popped out for a cheeky Nando's. He brought me back some Peri-Peri chicken. It was bloody gorgeous, though the midwife frowned at me when I dribbled some coleslaw in the shallow end.

The baby screams night and day and is only happy when it's got a teat in its mouth, just like its dad. No one tells you you're going to poo yourself when you're trying to squeeze a tiny human out your tuppence. The midwives were trying to fish the floaters out with a crabbing net. That was the last good poo I had for days.

After theatre I woke up desperate for a wee. I could feel a tidal wave ready to gush out. The midwife told me to just go there and then on the bed. I told her I didn't want to piss the bed before she explained I had a catheter in. I was mortified that someone had seen parts of me where previously only shadows had lurked. I had that many bags around me collecting fluid it looked like I'd done the Friday night big shop. I had a tube out of every orifice.

I kept pressing the button for assistance as I was in agony. I thought my bladder was going to explode. The midwife shouted, 'Just go will you'. She had one eye on my empty wee bag and one eye on her Pot Noodle she was halfway through at her workstation. After ten more calls, she finally checked my catheter and told me it was put in wrong. She whisked me away to the bathroom where she yanked it out. I filled up five cowboy hats of piss.

Why did no one tell me about the contractions you have after birth as your stretched body tries to return to the shape it once was? Only it ends up looking like a leotard on a clothes peg. The surgeon came back in to tell me I must have an MRI. He wanted to make sure they hadn't cut anything vital whilst they were in there as 'we were in a bit of a hurry'.

The worst was the constipation after the C-section. That's the sort of info you need on a leaflet before you give birth. I had a suppository so big that I feared passing wind in case it shot out like a torpedo and gave the midwife a nasty bullet wound to her chest. Two days went by before I got the rumble in my stomach. I thought the traumatic bit was done, what was to come was far worse. I needed to go there and then but the sodding nurses and doctors kept coming in. One shouted encouragement, 'Bear down on it'. I thought they'd seen enough of me over the last week that I couldn't face any more humiliation. My husband, the bastard who got me into this mess, held me over the toilet as I tried to go, but I couldn't push in case I popped a stitch. He told me to try and push out one bit at a time. I told him that I was going to have to go in and dig. He said, 'You've got to do what you've got to do.' I chiselled away at my bum like a prisoner from the great escape.

I think I ended up with four fingers up there trying to scrape out what I could. The bastard wiped my arse as I washed my hands, three times. I had the smell of hospital food on my fingers for seven days. The first week home he was following me around with cupped hands in case I sneezed and shat on the laminate.

Blanche, what am I going to do? How can we ever look each other in the eye again? I'd like to say the birth was worth it, but to be honest, the child is the Devil's spawn.

Mortifyingly yours,

Jess,

From: Blanche
To: Jessica Watkiss
Subject Re: Labour pains

Jess,

You must have bigger flaps than an Airbus. I hope you remembered to collect your dignity from the reception as you left the ward. This is the reason Madonna adopted. I suggest next time you fancy having kids you send off for a brochure. I can ask Madonna where she got hers from, I think it was Littlewoods. In the meantime, I suggest putting in a coil. Although, by the sounds of it you might need something a bit bigger, how about a rotating washing line?

The gin you sent is absolutely delicious. Only it's a bit dangerous as you can't taste the alcohol. My flatmate Fergie was drinking it with her breakfast, she thought it was a new vitamin loaded juice drink. She's very maudlin with gin. Luckily after a few swigs of *Jaffa*, she was asleep by the end of the breakfast news.

You may wish to invest in some heavy-duty underwear. Possibly some scaffolding. You could consider having some reconstructive surgery. Have you thought about going on one of those makeover shows? Just last week a woman went on one with a vagina the size of the Channel Tunnel. She'd slipped and fallen on a bollard outside the NatWest. All she had to do was show it to the nation and she got it nipped and tucked for free. A small price to pay when you're trapping your labia every time you close the car door.

You'll have to give it time before your fella can look you in the eye, especially if he's been using the dog's pooper scoop on your faecal matter. He'll soon come round when he wants to copulate. Now, have you thought about surrogacy for future kids? Princess Di was my surrogate. It was a bloody surprise when we found out she was having twins. By the time she gave birth my circumstances had changed, my husband had died suddenly and I didn't fancy being a single mother at the age of forty-one. I couldn't face the stigma. I could hear the whispers of the women of Langworthy Road, 'I told you she'd amount to nothing that one, all fur coat and no knickers.' Di kept one and called him Harry and gave the other one to a family who couldn't have kids. She'd met them whilst she was doing a ward visit on the gynaecology unit. Apparently, they were thrilled when they opened the gift box.

Poor Di was huffing and puffing for England at the delivery when the surgeon brought in a group of medical students to gawp at her royal passage. She was very calm, she just carried on smoking. There's no shame in paying someone else to cook your bun in their oven, especially when yours is in need of an overhaul. I've heard of a new procedure that can do that: they take the womb out, put it on a spin cycle and a quick dry before popping it back in, good as new. You just have to be careful you get your own one back.

Blanche

Blanche
Boadicea Manor
Salford 6

14ᵗʰ January 2020

Hello Boris,

Remember me, your little Maid Marian? It's been a long time. How's the guttering in Downing Street? I bet it's FILTHY.

I'm sure you remember you once said to me, 'If you ever needed anything Marian, then take up your arrow and shoot from the hip.' Well, I'm shooting now, Boris. Before you discard this letter, let me refresh your memory.

November of '91 and a glamorous blonde with a perfect beehive in orange overalls paid you a visit. I was sent from community service to do your guttering the weekend you were sent home early from Brussels. You'd been suspended from work for letting a stink bomb off in the communal kitchen. I was up a ladder with a gutter trowel in my hand when you pulled up in a black cab from Gatwick.

Your eyes undressed me the second you saw me removing autumn leaves from your outlet pipe, you filthy little boy. You stood on the driveway using your *Thomas the Tank Engine* lunch box to cover your excitement. You offered to hold the ladder to keep me stable in case of any freak gusts of wind on what was a still day. Thinking about it now, if someone was the sort of dirty beggar to look up, they could you see right up into my overalls from down there. Did you notice? You left to make a cup of tea but returned with a Vodka and Tonic. You kept a steady stream of them coming until I knocked off at five. Is it coming back to you yet? How you invited me inside *to slip into something more comfortable*. Your tongue was hanging out your mouth and tiny beads of sweat had collected on your brow, like a deviant in a Soho cinema.

You spent the next two hours telling me how unhappy you were in your marriage. How you weren't satisfied emotionally or physically. How you longed to be understood. You turned on the charm, it was bloody awful. I saw you use your finger to dab fairy liquid behind each ear and gave your nether regions a quick once over with the dishcloth. You told me all about your fantasy and begged me to act it out. I told you I didn't do anything for nothing. You gave me a blank cheque to buy my silence. The easiest money I ever made. You handed me a bag and told me to dress up in the toilet. I returned to find you stood in the kitchen, drooling, a bundle of nervous excitement. You looked a chubby vision standing there in your homemade Robin Hood costume. The light green jumper was too short to cover your stomach and showed off your outie. I was dressed in a crumpled green tennis dress, so small it barely covered my knickers. My face dirtied like a peasant, as instructed.

For the next thirty minutes you made me run around the house pretending to be Maid Marian, fearful of capture from King John. Whilst you, Robin Hood, tried to save me from peril. By the time we'd finished, you were panting like a dog and begging for more. You'd shot your little arrow in every room in the house. Imagine the headlines if the story ever got out; *Bojo chases a con.* Your career would be over.

Your secret is still very much safe with me. For now! You see, I've just started a new venture. Consider me a public service to replace all the ones you've cut. I'm an agony aunt now Boris, and I'd like to be your agony aunt too. I can rescue you this time. You can write to me and I will sit here in my tight green tennis dress and wait for your correspondence. I'll fulfil all your needs and your cabinets too. Slip them my address and allow them to share me, Boris. Share your Marian with your Merry Men. Would you like that Boris, someone to share every dark secret with? I do hope so because you've no sodding choice.

Blanche

P.S I'll expect a cheque for £700 with every letter. No need to make them out to anyone, leave them blank.

From:Randy Mottershed
To: Blanche
Subject Just an ordinary man
18th January 2020

Dear Blanche,

I saw your advert in the local press offering your services of advice to improve marriages. As I'm going through somewhat of a celibate period with my wife, sixteen years, I thought you may be able to help. I consider myself a fairly ordinary man. I collect used luggage labels from airlines. I'm a member of the National Trust and I have a moderate wardrobe consisting of the same polo neck jumper in four shades of brown: mustard, chestnut, beaver and chocolate. They all have matching cord trousers. I'm also a very keen dogger.

Nothing gets me more enthused than a willing couple in a parked-up Ford Cortina. I've been proudly dogging for twenty years. It started on a trip to Chester Zoo. My wife, Mangled Mel, as she's proudly known in the dogging circle, suggested we pull over in a lay-by and copulate. I'd never heard her moan with that much pleasure. She was throwing her head back in complete ecstasy and her eyes rolling into the back of her head, she'd lowered herself onto the gear stick. A woman knocked on the car window whilst I was mid-rhythm, I thought bloomin-eck, it's bloody Jane McDonald from that cruising show. She asked if she could watch. My wife told her she was a huge fan once we'd finished off. Jane then gave us a lovely rendition of *Time to Say Goodbye*. I bought her a Mr Whippy as a thank you. The experience gave us such a whopping release of adrenaline that we've continued dogging three nights a week since. Jane meets up with us whenever she can. She doesn't join in, she just provides the soundtrack.

We did try swinging in the colder months at a couples' retreat as Mel had frozen her intimate parts to the bonnet of a Morris Minor, that's how she got the nickname Mangled Mel, but we missed the flashing headlights and the smell of petrol. I'm a telephone mast inspector by day. It's my job to inspect the wood and cables to ensure the people of Preston don't face any interruption to their telecommunications. I take great pride in my work and consider myself to be a member of the emergency services come the harsh winter weather. Unfortunately, I'm averse to being high up on a mast due to suffering from acrophobia. I find dogging helps to cope with the rush of adrenaline.

I very much enjoy the voyeuristic side of dogging and like to watch Mangled Mel with other men. Dogging has really changed her, she was very quiet and timid when we met, now she's a right little goer. I am naturally very proud. We do put a lot of effort into dogging and consider hygiene to be of the utmost importance. I splash my face with Joop and have a spray of Lynx Africa and Mel covers herself in Charlie. Mel doesn't get as much action as she once did. I like to think she's still desirable, but most of the time she's left out in the cold wrapped in the dog's blanket with her nipples in the wind. Mel takes a thermos now and a couple of jam sandwiches to pass the time. Actually, she takes the whole loaf and a couple of pork pies. She's put on a few pounds over the years, I love her as much today as when we first met. I think it's the weight gain that has put her off being intimate with me. I think she does try to please me as she still makes an attempt with the other men. We've recently had to trade in the Fiat Panda for an HGV due to Mel's weakness for a Cream Horn.

You meet all kinds of people dogging. We met an undertaker and his wife, we did it in the back of their hearse; a bank manager who gave us a fantastic deal on our mortgage; and a fireman. It's a real community. Although the internet is killing it slowly. There are too many apps to bring people together for uncomplicated intimacy. It takes the excitement and apprehension out of it. It's very sad to see the car parks laying empty after 9 pm. Blanche, how can I entice new doggers to join our community?

I have enclosed a bottle of gin. I'm afraid it's only a supermarket brand but it is their premium range. I've enclosed a *Go Faster* sticker for your car windscreen too.

Yours sincerely,

Randy

From:Blanche
To: Randy Mottershed
Subject Re: Just an ordinary man

Randy,

Poor Mel, it sounds like she's left like a piffy on a rock. Try taking away her Greggs' loyalty card. Thank you for the gin. There's nothing wrong with a good supermarket's own brand, me mum was partial to a drop herself. She'd take a bottle with her to the bingo to top her glass up, she never paid for more than one drink. I've put the gin aside to offer visitors, not that we get many. My flatmate Fergie is socially inept, she spends all her time repeatedly watching her wedding video. I've been encouraging her recently to channel her heartache into a creative outlet. She's taken up creative writing. She's shite at it mind. I rewrite it for her in the afternoons after she's knocked herself unconscious with a morning gin. I'm halfway to finishing a Mills and Boon.

I think I'm familiar with that Ford Cortina you mentioned. Princess Anne used to have one. She was a wayward child. Liz was always having to drag her home from Hyde Park after she'd drank a bottle of absinthe on the park bench. That's why she was sent to boarding school. Liz was at the end of her tether. It was her last hope to straighten Anne out. It didn't work though, she left with two A-levels, woodwork and ironing. She only got them because she'd seduced the home economics mistress in a lesbian affair. They're a very incestuous family. Charles met Camilla whilst on a dogging trip with Anne and Andrew Parker-Bowles. They'd gone in that very Ford Cortina you mentioned to a lay-by near Balmoral.

I suggest you write to Princess Anne, I'm sure she'd have some great ideas to pull people into your community. Have you thought about having a celebrity guest or a loyalty scheme? You could give away a commemorative Princess Anne mug or a Beef Hula Hoop flavoured condom on every visit if they sign up to your mailing list. Keep them away from Mel though, I fear she'd suck the flavour of them.

I'm a little concerned about Mangled Mel's incident. I bet she looked a vision frozen to the Moris Miner in the morning mist, like a fat Aphrodite. Are you sure it isn't rising damp, and she wasn't sitting in a puddle of her own piss? You might want to ask that fireman you mentioned if you can use his hose to shower Mel down afterwards in the back of the HGV. Squirt some fairy liquid over and dry her properly, there's nothing worse than the smell of a damp dog.

Blanche

Boris Johnson MP
10 Downing St
Westminster

19th January 2020

Dear Blanche,

Of course, I remember you. One quite often recalls the memory of you when I'm in those endless meetings. It's my happy place. They would be so laborious if I didn't think of you tripping up the stairs and flashing an inquisitive ankle. I'm sure you'll be happy to know I've invested in a professional costume. I realise I must have looked a little amateur. One has since raised the bar, not the tone.

I appreciate your furtiveness on the subject. I would love nothing more than to be looked after by you Blanche. It's an absolute blessing we've reacquainted after all this time. One does have many questions. However, I always find it better to ask none. Remain silent and you'll find no nasty surprises.

I've already briefed the cabinet on your new service via a send to all email. I've codenamed you AA. You must have already built up a great friendship with Gove as he's been telling me he's been in AA meetings every night this week. We must use this relationship to bring out the very best in our government. No U-turns on the arrangement. It's been a shaky start to my premiership. All help is needed to keep the party on the straight and narrow. I've just got over my seven consecutive defeats in the Commons. It was a ghastly affair which took me back to when I lost all my marbles to a bully. The feeling of embarrassment and shame came flooding back to me as I was cornered by an absolute brute, she's the Secretary of State now.

I took a holiday shortly after my Common's defeat, spending Christmas and New Year trekking the Australian Outback. I was looking for one of my offspring. I had a Christmas card from an Aborigine I once had a dalliance with whilst out hunting for Kangaroos on a quick visit in '94. It was a brief affair. We were both standing next to each other in the queue for ketchup at a campsite bomb fire when I sneezed and impregnated her as she reached for the coleslaw. Being so fertile can be a curse.

It was smashing to get away. I didn't find the little chap I was after. Nevertheless, wonderful to escape the English winter and the Brexit drama. It's such a kerfuffle. I flew to Brussels just before I broke up for the Christmas break, in September. I offered Barnier five of my best WWE cards in exchange for control of all fish in the waters from Brighton to Corfu. He was totally unreasonable and said he wouldn't accept any number of cards. He even turned down a night out with me and the boys at our favourite Eton club, The Soggy Biscuit. Absurd.

Fortunately, The Royals have been up to their old tricks; Philip made a pass at Meghan and now she's leaving the country and taking Harry with her. It's on the front page of all the nationals. The royal mafia is fearing another Martin Bashir interview. I don't think I've ever had a child with a royal. Although it's possible, I did meet Princess Ann one night in a Morrisons' car park.

The question now is, who will pay for the security of Meghan and Harry? I would offer but the UK's money is tied up in shares in Rees-Mogg's pyramid schemes. We're bound to make millions. What you do is invest in a large number of egg timers, then sell them on to more people, who like eggs, to sell onto even more people who like eggs, and then they sell onto people who like eggs even more than they like eggs. Each person pays a little bit more than the last, everyone gets rich and has eggs for breakfast. Fantastic. We will not fail. We will get, the eggs, done!

Do let me know your thoughts on how to pay for the security of the actress and the ex-prince. Do you think we could perhaps exchange emails, it would come in quite useful for attachments.

Kind regards,

Boris

P.S Please find enclosed a cheque for £700 — left blank as requested.
P.P.S I don't suppose you could send me a picture of you in that tennis dress.

Blanche
Boadicea Manor
Salford 6

Boris,

Thank heavens that there is at least one bloodline you haven't infected. The visions of a mini-Boris with a crown sitting upon the throne has left me feeling rather bilious. Although nothing would surprise me of Princess Anne. And no Boris, we cannot exchange emails. It's too easy to accuse emails of being fraudulent, plus I find letters are far more intimate, don't you?

It just so happens I know a man in security. I must warn you though, he can be a nasty piece of work if you get on the wrong side of him, Sir Trevor McDonald. He travels the world in the guise of a journalist but in reality, he has drug runners and weapons of war on every continent. I met him when I was kidnapped by an obsessive fan back when I was a Tiller Girl in the mid-60s at the London Palladium. I'd just come off the stage when I was asked for my autograph. As I was pulling a pen out of my corset, I was hit over the head with a fire extinguisher, hooded and bundled into a boot of a VW Beetle. I spent a week tied up in a bedsit in Halifax. The police were useless, they launched a manhunt but clocked off every day at lunchtime. They never looked further north than Leamington Spa.

It was Cilla who got in touch with Sir Trevor and asked him to find me. He didn't charge her a penny. He just asked if he could place a couple of AK47s in the shipment of her latest album to the States. If you look very closely there's a tribute to him on the sleeve cover of Cilla's album, *Cilla Sings A Rainbow.* In fact, the leading single, *No Place to Hide,* was a tribute to the whole saga. It was a very difficult time for Cilla.

Sir Trevor tracked me down using a sniffer dog. I was the only woman in the UK who wore a scent by Mary called *Mary*. Mary was a stall keeper on Salford precinct and would give me a bottle of perfume for free if I slipped her some fabric from the stall I worked on in my teens. You wouldn't cross Mary. She kept a baseball bat under her cash box. She'd lost two fingers in a game of Rummy at the Legion after a standoff with a bingo caller, he died. I ended up with enough *Mary* to last me a lifetime. It was the only perfume I ever wore, a sweet and sensual smell that clouded me wherever I went. Sir Trevor took the dog, a handsome Beagle called Socks, into my dressing room at the Palladium. Sir Trevor gave Socks a pair of my nipple tassels to sniff, let him off the lead and stood back as Socks shot up the M1. They found me bound to a radiator with a washing line and blindfolded with a pair of stockings. A demented Julie Andrews stood over me. Later, in the police interview, Julie said she'd been hypnotised by the way I could spin my nipple tassels at 90MPH and do the Can-Can at the same time. A shrine to me was found in her Winnebago on the set of her latest film. Locks of my hair were pinned to the wooden frame of her mirror. She told the press she could never sing again after a botch operation on her throat, it was all a lie. Cilla had gone for Julie's neck with a broken bottle of *Mary* and damaged her vocal cords in a chokehold.

I highly recommend Sir Trevor, but don't cross him. Make sure you pay up on time and be prepared to return the favour whenever he asks.

Blanche

P.S No, I won't send you a picture you dirty bastard, what would Carrie say?

From: Alex Huntington
To: Blanche
Subject Dating begins

21st January 2020

Dear Blanche,

What do you reckon of this? I couldn't wait to write back and let you know I've taken your advice. I set up an account on one of the dating apps, Tinder. I also set one up on Bumble, Hinge, Plenty of Fish and Match. I put an advert in the local classified section too:

Mature blonde seeks life partner. Likes; short, tall and average-height men; dark, fair or ginger; black, white or any ethnicity; Muscular, skinny or dadbod. Can make cinder toffee.

It goes in the *Peterborough Telegraph* this Friday. I upgraded to a full-size advert. It cost £500 but I'm hoping it will pay for itself in dates at Nando's.

It's just five months now until Dr Altman's party. She's been a nightmare to be around this week. Walking on eggshells is putting it lightly. She lashed out at one of the patients calling her a gluttonous fat cow who'd go blind with diabetes if she didn't stop shovelling Curly Wurlys into her mouth. Dr Altman later apologised for the outburst. She explained it was the stress of having to choose a caterer for the BBQ and whether to have traditional charcoal or an eco-friendly electric stove. She sent a triple pack of Toffee Crisp to the patient to say sorry. Dr Altman's husband has been working away recently with Jesus, his new assistant from Saville. They're currently in the south of France flogging expensive pharmaceuticals. Dr Altman is dealing with the organisation of the condiments all by herself. In a panic, she bought five gallons of Hellmann's Mayonnaise.

I do hope Edward the taxidermist isn't there. I didn't tell you the full story of how our fifth date ended. I was keen to hurry things along. I thought we were getting on *really* well. We'd shared a tiramisu at Mama's Italian in town. I asked him back to mine for a coffee which he accepted. I'd poured us both a glass of Chablis and we settled down in front of David Attenborough's Blue Planet. I thought it would put him in the mood as I noticed he had a stuffed puffer fish in his office. I popped upstairs to get changed into something I thought would really turn him on. When I came back into the lounge dressed as Big Bird and invited him to pluck my feathers, he shot out of the door like an emu. I'd very much misjudged the situation.

Love, Alex

From: Blanche
To: Alex Huntington
Subject Re: Dating begins

Alex,

Dates at Nando's? You'd be lucky with a date at Gregg's. It's great to see you being so picky with the type of man you want, one with a pulse. Though I doubt a flatline would put you off. Do you know lots of men pay for women to dress up in a whole range of things? I've been asked to dress up on several occasions. I was once Maid Marian for a red-faced sweaty man who was obsessed with power. I do admire a girl who tries and puts themselves out there, perhaps don't be too available. No man finds a bunny boiler attractive. Treat them mean and keep them keen. My friend Cilla was a right bitch to her Bobby. She had him well and truly under her gusset. She kept tabs on every move he made. If he ever dared to answer her back, she'd make him sleep in the chicken coop. He loved every saggy inch of her.

If you're meeting random men online, you should consider protection. Pop a rape alarm and a brick in your bag. You're probably better off with the taxidermist. At least if he kills you, he won't get rid of your body. Never give up. You're sure to find love when you least expect it, I was shoplifting a bottle of peroxide when I found my first love.

Take care,

Blanche

From: Sophie McBride
To:Blanche
Subject Cheating bastard

29th January 2020

Dear Blanche,

I've just found out my husband Marcus is gay. It's killed me. At our fifteenth wedding anniversary party, his, I can't bring myself to write it... his boyfriend left a gift for me on the doorstep. He's ten years younger than Marcus, an ex-student of his at the university. All our family and friends were here at the house when he knocked on the door. He didn't wait for me to answer. He left a gift bag with a photo album inside. It was filled with pictures of them together. Arms around each other on various days out on the beach, on city breaks, at theme parks, a shrine to their relationship. I'm so stupid. Every late night, every field trip, and every working weekend, I didn't question any of them. All that time he was with him. Being gay.

People think they know what it's like to be humiliated, but they don't. I took one look at Marcus with the album in my hand and he knew that I knew. He said he was sorry. I screamed at him, 'Get Out, Get Out, Get Out.' I picked up the anniversary cake and threw it at him. It splattered all over the wall like blood from a crime scene murder. My brother had the pleasure of knocking Marcus into the middle of next week with a smack across the jaw.

The party atmosphere that surged throughout the house just twenty minutes before had sunk into a depression, and everyone scurried out. I was grateful, to be honest, I couldn't face anyone. I was doing OK for an hour. I must have been on automatic or in shock. Then I poured a glass of wine and sat on the high stool at the breakfast bar and glanced over at the fridge. I cried and sobbed and howled. There was a picture stuck to it by a magnet that we'd got from Corfu last year. It was of the four of us: me, Marcus and the two kids, (John 15 and Tilly 7), on a trip out to the Old Town whilst on holiday there. We all looked so happy. I sobbed for the children, I cried for the holidays we'll never have together again as a family, and I howled for me — for the twenty wasted years.

I was filled with questions, Blanche: how didn't I know? Did I turn him gay? Did my body repulse him when he saw me walking out of the shower? How could he? Who else knows? How will I get over it? That's why I'm writing to you, I need to know the answers. I looked at myself in the mirror this morning and I just see an old, weathered woman staring back at me, vacant. I'm only thirty-seven. Marcus has been paying for a flat in town for him. I couldn't afford a new dress for that party. I sewed up an old one that had a rip in it. Meanwhile, he's been paying for a second mortgage for his double life for years. What a bleeding mug. I bet they were laughing their heads off at me.

I'll never forgive him. I can't bring myself to speak to him, or to look at him. He calls every day, every hour in fact — I never answer. What would I say? The kids are OK. They think it's cool to have a gay dad. I just think it's bloody cruel. They've asked to meet him, over my dead body.

Twenty years Blanche. Twenty sodding years!

Kind regards,

Sophie

From: Blanche
To:Sophie McBride
Subject Re: Cheating bastard

Sophie,

Well, that was a bit maudlin. The gin you sent was lovely — Rose and Liquorice —but I think a quarter bottle is a bit on the tight side. It was finished by the time I read your letter. It's not the end of the world Sophie, having a gay husband was all the rage in my day. All the stars were at it. Lavender Marriages they were called. Judy Garland married a queer, her daughter Liza did the same, all the greats of Hollywood. Are you a movie star? This could very much work in your favour. Divorce him and take every penny, let him keep the kids.

Gay men have great genes, you're very lucky to have had kids with one. I'm sure Marcus will look after you. Freddie Mercury treated Mary like a princess long after they split up. Mind you, it's important to remember that for every Elton John there are a thousand Michael Barrymores. You don't have a swimming pool, do you?

Women drive themselves insane with torment when they find their partners have been cheating, wanting to know every last little detail of the sordid affair. There's really no need for such questions when you understand that all men are dirty bastards. They really don't care who they sleep with when they get the urge. Ann Widecombe used to be down the Liverpool docks five nights a week. She'd take full advantage of returning sailors after they've been at sea for eight weeks. Ann was the first woman they'd clapped eyes on when they stumbled out of the pubs at the end of the pier. She had marriage proposals from the most handsome men, she ate the morning after pill like coco pops.

Starting a new life is hard but it's not without its benefits. You can be more than just a housewife now. Some women would kill for that. I met a few that did when I was residing at Her Majesty's pleasure. There was one woman, Sonia, who'd been locked up for murdering her husband. She'd come from a life of drugs on the Wirral. She smuggled 10kg of cocaine internally from the Isle of Man on a Jet Ski across the Irish Sea. She broke the record for the fastest time it took for a sea crossing from Douglas to the Albert Docks. She got arrested five days later when she hit the munchies and got caught stealing a variety pack of Walker's crisps. The police raided her flat expecting to find stolen goods but instead found the half-mutilated body of her husband. She was caught on CCTV cutting him up into domino size pieces and feeding him to the seagulls. She didn't remember a thing but said she didn't regret it. He'd been a right bastard to her. He'd run up a huge bill in late fees at Blockbusters.

Her fiery red hair once matched her temperament, but she was a lot calmer when she left the cells. She'd cleaned herself up, come off the drugs and signed a record deal. She represented the UK at Eurovision in the nineties. She was robbed of victory on the last vote.

For now, take each day as it comes. Try and remember the woman you were before you met your husband. You've got this Sophie. You can rise like a phoenix, or at the least, a pigeon.

Blanche.

Boris Johnson MP
10 Downing St
Westminster

31st January 2020

Dear Blanche,

I am afraid I'm in somewhat of a pickle! The pyramid scheme that I invested all the UK funds in has, well, scrambled. It turned out that the eggs were from chlorinated chickens. Blanche, I can already see the headlines, *Boris put all eggs in one basket*. I'm praying for another Royal meltdown to take the heat off me.

I had to fire Sajid Javid to make it look like he was to blame. I felt awful for a few minutes as he did try to stop me investing. But then, he hasn't been very nice to my best friend Dominic recently. Dom asked for some extra cash from the Treasury so we could buy Giant Jenga to play between meetings but Sajid refused, it serves him right. I have allowed him to remain on the backbenches as long as he doesn't reveal to the press the egg situation. Rees-Mogg feels terrible, well I think he did, he was laughing when he said it.

The calamity of the situation has resulted in me heeding your advice. I have contracted Sir Trevor McDonald to guarantee the security of Meghan and Harry. However, due to the above, I have no means to pay. Sir Trevor sent a heavy-handed cameraman round to see me yesterday. He threatened me to cough up or else my child will get it. I'm left rather perplexed as he didn't instruct which child. He then snatched my packet of strawberry bon-bons and tipped them over my head. Thug. I'm ashamed to say I had a little accident.

I called an emergency meeting with Dom. I took advantage to talk to him whilst it was quiet; there was a COBRA meeting regarding a virus in China going on next door. I didn't bother to attend — it will be something or nothing. Dom and I brainstormed how we could re-claw some of the money I lost. Dom had a genius idea to brew our own wine. We've already converted the Parliament cellar into a vineyard, Theresa and Priti are crushing the grapes. We're going to call the wine *Larry's*, after the Downing Street Cat. With some good fortune, it will be stocked in every supermarket in the UK and I'll be able to pay Sir Trevor.

I am concerned regarding the threat to the child. What child does he mean? If only there was a way to track and trace them all.

Kind regards,

Boris

Blanche
Boadicea Manor
Salford 6

Dear Boris,

I hate to say *I told you so*, but you need to be careful of Sir Trevor. It would be awful to open the morning papers to see your body had been found on the banks of the Thames...Second thoughts, I'm sure you can talk your way out of it. After all, you're known for your competent speeches.

You could send Raab down to Hackney market to set up a stall to sell your wine. I'm sure it will go down a treat. Make sure Theresa has had her corns removed before she crushes any more grapes, you don't want someone finding a verruca in their Merlot. You can get some rough people going to these markets, I should know, I used to work on one. Although I'm sure Raab can handle himself but send Gove as backup. Make sure Raab practices his sales pitch before you unleash him on the public, he's got all the charm of a U-bend.

I've compiled a list of possible offspring, forty names so far. There was a baby-boom at the end of last year along the old Labour wall. I've posted DNA tests to their mothers. Well, not a DNA test exactly, it's a lie detector. The babies are asked ten questions, if they answer just one of them truthfully, I rule them out as an heir. The problem is it now appears you've fathered 365 middle-aged MPs.

I feel you should pay close attention to this virus. When Priti had gonorrhoea last year it spread like wildfire during the Tory weekend at Chequers. You can't afford to have half your cabinet on sick leave again, and I certainly don't want to see any more selfies of Hancock rubbing cream into Priti's warts, health secretary or not.

Thank you for the cheque. Keep them coming.

Blanche

FEBRUARY

Diane Abbott MP
House of Commons
London

1ˢᵗ February 2020

Dear Blanche,

Your forgiveness sets me free from the guilt I've carried these last 30 years.

Blanche, we must act quickly. There is a new Labour adviser by the name of Cilla. Corbyn is intent on following all her advice which has thus far proven destructive to the party. She insisted he sat on the Brexit fence during the last election campaign. Despite our disastrous result, he is still insisting to his shadow cabinet that we act on all her instructions. Fortunately, most of the MPs have ignored her advice, it's hard to listen to faceless correspondence.

We need to stop her before the party is doomed forever, only no one has any idea of who or where she is.

Cordially yours,

Diane

Blanche
Boadicea Manor
Salford 6

Diane,

I know exactly who Cilla is, I knew that bitch couldn't rest in peace. A menace to Labour if ever I knew one. You don't have to worry about who she is. I've taken down bigger and uglier in my time. Get me the address, I don't care how you do it, she needs to be paid a visit.

Don't you worry, I will have a small loyal following soon enough. It takes time to win people over, even if they are drenched in desperation. Though I do feel some compassion towards them, just not as much as I feel for myself.

Blanche

Victoria Townsend
29 Hellbourne Close
Salford

2nd February 2020

Dear Blanche,

To answer your question from your last, yes, I have thought about killing him. I think about it at least twenty times a day. I sometimes fantasise about his funeral and how I'd have to hide my smile behind a black veil. Sadly, I think he will outlive us all. He's monstrous to live with, it's like a dark cloud of misery hangs over the house. Time stands still when he's in residence. Every tick, every tock, every tick, every tock. Each sound marks a second I didn't leave. The passing of my life. If I met myself back then I would have told myself, *Run. Run girl. You've no idea how much strength you've got. Don't waste it on fighting to stay. For goodness sake, live.* I'd drag that girl away from that pub in Manchester, away from his motorbike, away from that registry office and I'd push her straight back to nursing school. I'd push her anywhere but Hellbourne Close. Then I'd warm her up and I'd tell her, *never wait in the bloody car for anyone.*

Sorry, Blanche, I had to put the pen down then and gather myself. I made a coffee. I've been making it for forty years. Dave was prescribed antidepressants to combat his mood swings caused by the steroids he takes for his colostomy. They don't work. He went through a bad spell late last year, took to his bed and refused to take any medication. He said his life was over and he didn't want to live. I didn't even feel guilty that I agreed with him. I would have happily helped him speed up the process if he wasn't my children's father.

It was intolerable. He walked around the house hunched, a grunt with every step. An *oh* and an *aww* to let me know how much imaginary pain he was in. He's not happy unless everyone else is miserable. After three weeks of him refusing a doctor and piling up his filled colostomy bags at the side of his bed, I'd had enough. I crushed his antidepressants and put them in the Lurpak. He'd have you believe he didn't eat despite his diabetes and beer belly evidencing otherwise. One of his favourite sayings is, "*I don't eat me.*" I think, *who the hell are you trying to kid?* He gets through a loaf of Warburton's thick slice a day, he uses toast as a vessel for butter. That's how I knew he'd eat the contaminated butter.

He doesn't see his faults and I've long since learnt there's no point in arguing with a man like that. I curse him under my breath instead. I wonder if he thinks this life we live is normal? That this is married life. My parents never spent a night apart in fifty years. My dad died first, Alzheimer's, my mum passed three weeks later of a broken heart. Fit as a fiddle until her last day. They were always exploring together, away on a coach trip or in Ibiza. They went there three times a year to the same hotel. Everyone knew them. They'd sit in silence some evenings, still very much together within it. Our silence is different.

I don't think I could join a social club. What would I do Blanche? I can't do anything. I'm too old for sport and I don't have a conversation in me.

Kind regards,

Victoria

Blanche
Boadicea Manor
Salford 6

Dear Victoria,

You've got to get out the house. You owe it to yourself to be happy in your wilderness years. Life is there to be enjoyed. Judy Finnigan hasn't looked back since leaving Richard. She's signed up for all the classes she's been meaning to do for years: burlesque, wrestling, dry stone walling. It's never too late to start living.

You can meet some very open-minded people in evening classes. I taught one myself in '74. It was a quiet time for me between my careers as a Tiller Girl and one in politics. I used to teach *Electric for Beginners* at Brighton college. I'd taught meself everything I needed to know by rewiring the alarm tags on the clothes in Salford precinct in me teens. I once rewired Cilla's conservatory and installed a Bucking Bronco. One night she was on it for hours with a cider in one hand and a lasso in the other. She launched it and caught nothing but Syphilis.

Me first husband really got under me skin. It was the small things he did like leaving the teabags in the sink, toenail clippings left on the sofa, empty toilet roll left in the holder, wet towels hung over the door to dry, bottle caps left on the side, leaving the bed unmade, his shavings in the bathroom sink, breathing. Eventually, everything he did would drive me to the brink of insanity, and I've always been a very calm level-headed woman. I felt trapped living in his house. If I had my name on the deeds, I would have sold it beneath him. Sadly, I wasn't that clever. I was innocent back then and he was a gob-shite. He thought he was head and shoulders above everyone else because he had one stripe on his store detective uniform. He'd take that stripe off his shirt, iron it and rub black shoe polish on it to make it stand out. He was forever trying to cross-examine me. I was grateful when he filed for divorce. I loved moving back in with me mam, custards creams on tap.

Could you have an affair do you think? I know a lovely man named Randy who travels quite a distance to meet women. He's not fussy, works hard and strives to please. You could do a lot worse. You are doing a lot worse. I could see if he could pop along and see you. Do you have a big enough driveway for an HGV? If you don't fancy meeting a man in the flesh you can start up one of those sex lines. My flatmate Fergie used to do it. She was strapped for cash and thought it would be an easy way to get rich. It all unravelled when The Queen called Directory Enquiries wanting the number of Crown Jewel Pizzas, fed up with being in the holding pool for his new job for 57 years, Charles had established a pizzeria as a distraction. Liz, ravenous after a day of excitement opening the new exhibition at the Pencil Museum in Keswick, was furious when instead of being able to order a large thin crust Abdication Special (baked beans and anchovies sat on a spicy plum sauce), she was put through to Fergie's Fondling Fun phone line. Liz heard Fergie exaggerate a slurp as she performed her own toe-sucking special. Liz was repulsed, although a little envious of Fergie's body confidence. Not being allowed to sever Fergie's head, Liz severed her allowance instead. You could give the number for your phone line to your husband, it might encourage him to talk to you.

Victoria, I don't like the sound of you waiting in the car for your husband. Can you not use it to run him over? You could have the whole house to yourself then.

Look after yourself, my love. No man is worth being unhappy.

Blanche

Boris Johnson MP
10 Downing Street
Westminster

9th February 2020

Dear Blanche,

I'm in somewhat of a conundrum. After a successful week in parliament in which I didn't face any defeats, we were on leave, I decided to throw a party in my chambers. It was congenial. Splendid. Carrie did us a buffet of crab paste sandwiches and put out a few bowls of Twiglets. I made a cheese and pickle hedgehog under the supervision of Dominic. Gove made a Chocolate Brownie Space Cake and Rees-Mogg bought us some Jerk-Chicken from Bury Market. He was up there admiring the Victoria Wood statue, he's weighing it in for scrap. We were all in high spirits and didn't want the shindig to end, so we popped open the barrels of *Larry's* we'd planned to sell. Within two hours we'd drank another sixteen barrels between the 365 MPs, plus Dominic. We got awfully carried away. Theresa led us in a routine of *Gangnam Style* and Priti belted out a duet with her reflection of *Don't Go Breaking My Heart.* She's got a set of lungs on her, like a ship's foghorn on a stormy night. Unfortunately, Priti got very aggressive when Emily Thornberry came to ask us to lower the music. Priti jumped down from her makeshift stage and shouted, 'Kick her in the tits.'

It was two days later when it dawned that I would have no way to pay Sir Trevor now all the wine has been consumed. I'm thinking of going into hiding.

Worst of all Blanche, Valentine's Day is on the horizon and I'm in a complete kerfuffle about what to do. I'd like to spend the day with Dom, but Carrie is rather insistent that I spend the day with her. Why would anyone want to spend the day with a crazed, pregnant, redhead when they could spend it with a gladiator of a man that is Dominic?

I'll never forget the day we met. We were teenagers, excitable and enthusiastic. He was the drummer in a rock band, *The Iron Lady*. They were headlining at a gig in the student bar at Eton. His greasy hair was grown halfway down his leather jacket. When he flipped it back it was as if it was waving at me, a signal of a great friendship to come. The atmosphere was electrifying, if not a little moist from the sweat of the lead singer. Every time he turned his head droplets sprayed into the audience. I caught one on my tongue and savoured it, salty yet sweet. How I wished it was Dom's.

After the gig, I bought him a pint of Babycham and he invited me backstage to jam with the band. I'm afraid I wasn't terribly good. The other band members, two guitarists and a man on a triangle, sniggered at me as I attempted to jive to their version of Easton's *9 to 5 (morning train)*. Dom looked right into my eyes as the singer rocked out the verse,

'All day I think of him, dreamin' of him constantly
I'm crazy mad for him, and he's crazy mad for me
When he steps off that train, I'm makin' a fool, a fight
Work all day to earn his pay, so we can play all night'

I've lived by those lyrics ever since — except the bit about working all day. Dom has them tattooed on his chest above his heart. Whenever I have a bad day in the office, which is on a Wednesday, as it's the only day I go in — Dom whispers those lyrics into my ear. I simply must spend Valentine's Day with him.

I've got him the perfect gift; I've arranged for us to spend the day at Go Ape. It will be boisterous. Get the testosterone pumping. I've bought Carrie a steam mop. I thought it would make it easier for her to do the bathroom floor now she's several months pregnant. Hygiene is of the utmost importance with this virus going around which one hears others drowning on endlessly about.

Blanche, just how do I get Carrie out the way? I simply must spend the day with Dom.

Kind regards,

Boris

Blanche
Boadicea Manor
Salford 6

Dear Boris,

Not since Deirdre and Samir has there been a more tragic love story than you and Dom. What you need to do is come up with a plausible alibi, it's no use saying you're working late or putting extra hours in at the office. What is it you normally do in the evenings, tiddlywinks with Hancock? Just tell Carrie you're very sorry but you have been selected to be the referee at a boxing match for Priti.

Valentine's is such a wonderful time of year. Me and my first husband had a whirlwind romance. We met in Boots off the Precinct in 1960, we were married by '61 and divorced by '62. He was a store detective, handsome, strong jawline and a Roman nose. He'd caught me slipping a bottle of peroxide into the rim of sparkling white go-go boots. He stood over me like a headmaster, he could tell I was getting ready to bolt out the door when he grabbed my wrist, looked me solidly in the eye and said, 'The Royal Oak, Liverpool St, Friday at nine.' He let go, gave me a wink and put a hairbrush in my other boot. It was only Wednesday, I spent the next two days with butterflies in my stomach.

On the Friday I arrived in my go-go boots, a yellow A-line dress, fashioned with my beehive and roots touched up courtesy of the pilfered bottle. We had a lovely evening. He retold tales of how he'd captured some of the biggest store thieves this side of the Manchester Ship Canal. Once he captured a woman trying to shoplift a washing machine by taking it out in a double pram, she was singing a nursery rhyme to it as she walked out the door.

We finished off the evening sharing a bag of chips before he walked me to my front door. He was the perfect gentleman that night. Me mam was delighted that I'd met such an outstanding pillar of the community. Things turned sour when he had one of me mam's friends arrested for lifting some heated rollers and a packet of Fisherman's Friends. Me mam was shunned by Barbara who gave out the dabbers at the bingo for being associated with the store detective who'd arrested her daughter. The humiliation tormented me mam until she got a full house on the national game. Barbara soon came running back with her bingo wings flapping.

That drama pretty much spelt the end of our whirlwind romance. Me mam always comes first, plus I hated him. The final nail in the coffin was when we were given a selection box of biscuits for Christmas and he turned his nose up to a custard cream. I packed my bags and left him there and then. Never trust a man who doesn't double-dip in his brew.

Boris, remember a woman never forgets. She might tell you she does, but there will always come a time she'll throw it back in your face when you're least expecting it. Make sure she hasn't got any intimate photos of you or knows any bizarre sexual desires that she can sell on to the national press. I'm assuming she might have quite a few judging by the photo you seem to have mistakenly enclosed with this letter. It came in quite useful; I've pinned it to the wall to hide a stain. My flatmate Fergie threw a glass of red wine after she saw a positive story on the news about Prince Charles and Camilla's day out to Thorpe Park.

Yours truly,

Blanche

From:Randy Mottershed
To: Blanche
Subject Dogging night

10th February 2020

Dear Blanche,

Despite taking your advice of trying to get a celebrity guest we have not achieved an increase in numbers to our local dogging site. Karaoke Kev, our local celebrity who hosts weekly events at The Nag's Head did attend sadly, no newcomers could be enticed. Kev can't walk into the doctor's surgery without knowing someone and he's provided the music at every wedding, 18th, and 21st celebration for miles around these parts. He remains grounded and will often greet me with a raised eyebrow on a Thursday as I sit quietly with my stout and pork scratchings. We advertised his attendance on his Facebook page and sent several messages to our WhatsApp dogging group. Three men did descend upon the gathering, however, they all made their excuses and left once Mangled Mel had gone to greet them. I think they were discouraged by the evening's precipitation.

We called Jane McDonald, as you know she's become a good friend. She was off the coast of Argentina on a swingers' cruise, she's filming it for Channel 5. She's the star turn at the Barbara Star bar in the evening — the bar is named after Barbara Moore, patron saint of swingers. She died in a flash flood at a caravan site in Pwllheli in the Burns Day Storm of 1990.

My anxiety is increasing as I'm concerned Mel might call an end to our marriage. She craves excitement. I told her I'll try anything to ignite our sex life and fulfil her needs. She had me dress up as a maid and stood me in the upstairs bay window with a mound of ironing. Mel sat and watched with a tub of popcorn. It must have done the trick as every few minutes she let out a few groans. She said, 'if you really want to finish me off then you can scrub the grouting in the bathroom.' I was at the tiles for two hours. Mel stayed downstairs, insisting the mere thought of me with a rubber glove was driving her wild. It must have worked as she was soon in the back of the HGV navigating me to another dogging site. That was abandoned too. Mel sent me into the woods whilst she stayed in the back reading her Jackie Collins. She's gone through her whole back catalogue now. I fear the consequences if I don't satisfy her sexual needs soon. I've heeded your other suggestion and have written to Princess Ann for advice and to invite her to become the ambassador for our little community.

With sincerest best wishes,

Randy Mottershed

From:Blanche
To: Randy Mottershed
Subject Re: Dogging night

Randy,

Have you thought of enticing Mel into bed with a buffet? Sounds like food is her thing, maybe she's into sploshing. I saw that on a Channel 5 documentary. It's dirty bastards who get off on covering themselves in custard and trifles for sexual gratification. What a waste of good food. You could cover yourself in a three-course meal and put profiteroles around your rude bits. Just be careful the gluttonous bitch doesn't bite them off. Don't put anything on your toes. You don't want pictures of her sucking them leaking to the *Daily Mirror*, the psychological impact can be immense. It happened to my flatmate Fergie, she's been unable to wear an open-toe sandal ever since.

It sounds to me like you need to make these dogging evenings into more of an event. Get Kevin to bring down his karaoke and Mangled Mel to rustle up a few sandwiches. Sell tickets and give it a theme. Pop down a few deck chairs, throw up a few fairy lights, clear an area for a dance floor (you could park the cars around it), and Bob's your uncle, Fanny's your aunt, you've got a venue. Make sure Mel has a shower, no one wants to accept a prawn ring from a woman who smells like she's got one.

Princess Ann would be sure to attend if you send her an invite, she loves an opportunity for fancy dress. She once attended a party of Princess Di's as a Moomin. Rumour has it she turned up to Harry and Meghan's wedding reception as Michael Jackson. Liz sent her to change into a spare black skirt and white blouse from the caterers. Ann was furious, she stayed in the corner all night sipping her WKD Blue and giving Camilla dirty looks. Make sure you have some WKDs in for Ann and some Desperados for her husband Timmy. The two of them are the life and soul of the party when they're together. They met each other at a swingers' convention on the grounds of Balmoral. It was love at first thrust. That's why she divorced her first husband Mark.

You could set up the back of your HGV as a VIP area for Ann. Set a little stage up in the corner ready for a cameo from Jane McDonald, put mirrors on the ceiling, flavoured condoms in a crown and a circular bed that spins around. Ann would love it. You could use the bed later to put Mangled Mel's on a spin-dry after you've hosed her down.

It could be a very lucrative venture for you both. I wish you every success.

Blanche

From: Jessica Watkiss
To: Blanche
Subject Fido

16th February 2020

Dear Blanche,

I gave serious thought to your suggestion of a designer vagina, fortunately, everything seems to be shrinking back into place. Though I doubt it will ever be the fanny it once was. I needn't have worried about my husband looking me in the eye, he got frisky as soon as I had my stitches out. I'm thinking about putting up an electric fence in the middle of the bed so he can never get his leg over again. I'm not interested in sex at all. I'm too bloody exhausted. I told him, 'You try pushing a tiny human out of your fanny and see if you still want sex.' He said, 'I don't have a fanny.' I just stormed out and slammed the kitchen door, waking the bastard baby up again.

I thought the birth was bad, but nobody told me about the absolute nervous wreck I'd become once the baby comes home. I'm paranoid I'm going to kill it, and everyone will find out what a terrible mother I am. I didn't plan to have a kid, I got caught out. I forgot to take my pill after a bottle of Pinot Grigio. I'm constantly checking if it's still breathing. I'm so exhausted, all I want to do is sleep. The second it goes down I'm trying to check if it's still alive. In the evening I'm telling my husband to shut up every thirty seconds so I can listen to the baby monitor. I can't breastfeed either. I tried but the bugger chews down on my nipple and it hurts like a bastard, it's more like its dad than it knows. I feel bad for using the formula. I'm thinking is it the right one, will he grow up disadvantaged because I didn't let him suckle on my breast, will he have mother issues for life?

Night feeds are the worst. I look down at it and I think, 'I used to just be crawling out of clubs at this time.' What happened to my life? How did I swap bottles of Malibu for bottles of SMA instant formula? That bastard promised me he'd help with the night feeds when I was pregnant, he's done two. Both times he's woken me up to test the milk. I hate him. Other mums I speak to say they wouldn't change their baby for the world. I smile and agree but inside I'm thinking, I'd gladly swap him for a full night's sleep, the ability to go for a wee without thinking a tiny person is dying in the next room, and a packet of Walker's Sensations.

I'm neurotic from the lack of sleep.

We've finally chosen a baby name after everyone had their say. His mum wanted us to call the baby Harold after her father, I said no bastard way. She wasn't too pleased but as she'd seen me in the birthing pool any formalities we once had are out of the window. My Mum suggested Donald. I said she must be off her bleeding rocker if she thinks I'm naming my son after a racist American President who looks like an inflated Cheesy Wotsit. She was offended and told me Donald was actually the name of her birth father who saved her life by pulling her out of a burning building, I just thought he was called Grandad. I can't say anything right at the minute.

I still hadn't chosen a name by the time me and that bastard went to register the birth. I was panicking when a man walked past and shouted at his dog Fido to sit. It was the only name I could think of when I went in to complete the forms. I've named my baby after a bastard Golden Retriever. It doesn't look like a Fido. It's going to grow up to be one of the kids in class who doesn't get picked to be on any of the teams or invited round for tea because he's got a stupid bleeding name. I've ruined its life with a name. I'd go into town to change it, only I can't be arsed. I'm too tired to even put pants on never mind get dressed and going into town. I live in my dressing gown. I caught a glimpse of my reflection in the hallway mirror and thought we had an intruder. I quickly turned away and decided I'd try and make more of an effort. That was two weeks ago, and I've still not managed to brush my hair or shave my legs. I'm hoping my gorilla look will put that bastard off any attempt at funny business for at least a month.

We attempted to go out last week for a walk but the amount of luggage I have to take wasn't worth it. The nappy bag looked like it had been packed for a fortnight in Spain. I decided it was easier to just hold the baby up in the window to see the outside world. The pram itself is the size of a small tank that you need a bastard degree to operate. I tried to fold it up and put it in the boot of the car to go and do a weekly shop, but I just ended up sobbing on the side of the road with the left wheel in my hand. Suzie, who lives next door, has three kids under the age of five. She's a size zero and her youngest who's 18 months can already count to fifty in five languages. She came out and looked me up and down with pity in her eyes, I punched her in the left one. I didn't really, I visualised it though. Suzie swiftly unfolded the pram making it look easy to press the buttons in the right combination. She patted me on the shoulder and said, 'it's not easy it is the first few weeks?' I died a little inside. When we got to the supermarket, I realised I'd left my purse at home and I was still wearing my slippers. I sobbed a little in the mother and baby parking before turning around and going home. I've decided to not leave the house until it's three years old. I keep calling him it, I just can't call him Fido.

I'll do the shopping online. Blanche, does it get easier?

Please forgive the stain on the envelope, my boobs leaked as I bent down to get it out of the bottom drawer. It took me 20 minutes to get back up.

Jess x x

From: Blanche
To: Jessica Watkiss
Subject Re: Fido

Dear Jess,

No need for an electric fence, keep a rounders bat under your pillow and play Whack-a-Mole if he tries anything before you're ready.

You're very lucky you have the milk formula, don't feel guilty for using it. Me mam would have given her right *and* left arm for a box of it when I was a toddler, we were as poor as could be. The damp in the house seeped across the ceiling like a spilt drink on a table. Me dad would spend all his wages down the working men's club and more often than not, take what little me mam earned from the theatre with him. On several occasions, she'd go to Salford precinct with an empty bottle and get the new mothers to donate a few drops of their own breast milk. She'd hobble her way there in white stilettos, postbox-red lipstick and her beehive done to perfection. She carried poverty well. The mothers would all happily oblige. Everyone knew the daily battle to make ends meet. The woman who lived five doors down was still lactating even though her kids were 16 and 17. She had gigantic breasts, like hot air balloons desperate to break free of their moorings. She'd fill a pint glass up for us every Wednesday and me mam would sneak her into one of the new releases at the cinema in return. I sent her a Christmas card every year until she died in the early 80s. She tripped over her left breast and fell down the stairs. I felt terrible guilt. She was a true martyr to the women of Chimney Pot Park. I was furious when Thatcher tried to get rid of free milk for schools, she had no idea of its importance to families like mine.

Babies are tough little things, you really don't need to watch over them every minute of the day. When Di was bringing up little William, she smothered him with love. Drove herself mad in panic with his every sneeze. No matter what time of night or day she would summon the palace doctor to take William's temperature. He had a thermometer permanently up his backside for the first two years of his life. By the time Harry and his twin came along she'd worked herself into such exhaustion that she couldn't be bothered. She ragged Harry about from pillar to palace, luckily, he was ginger so he could pass as a Spencer. Harry's twin was a natural blonde, that's how she made the decision of which one to keep and which one to gift to the couple in the ward. She used to leave Harry in a sock draw all day whilst she'd go out and perform ceremonies. Not uncaring, she understood the resilience of a baby.

So, Jess, no need to worry at all, babies are strong little things. You've absolutely no need to fret about them when they're that old: it's when they hit puberty and start talking to strange men online, going to all-night raves and experimenting with class A drugs that you need to be worried about. The second you see them trying to sneak out of an evening you ground them until they're twenty-one and chain them up to the bunk beds. My advice would be to keep them away from the TV. These modern programmes are enough to corrupt any young mind. One true story boxset on Netflix and he'll be practising *How to Get Away with Murder* and have his face splashed over the front cover of every national paper.

Mind how you go,

Blanche

Boris Johnson MP
10 Downing St
Westminster

20th February 2020

Dear Blanche,

I thought long and hard about your last letter and I concluded that you were indeed correct about women. I decided to postpone my evening with Dom and attend to Carrie on Valentine's Day instead. Besides, she warned me that if I went out that night, she would release pictures of me in my adult nappy to the press. It's nothing sexual, I just adore a costume, as you well know.

Dom bought me an amazing gift, he's had the drawing-room made into a drawing room. He filled it with dot-to-dot books, crayons and pastels. I spent the whole day on the 15th colouring in my favourite pictures of our warships. There is one named after me, HMS Unthinkable.

I've taken a mighty beating in the press again this week, an absolute pounding. Storm Dennis has battered the UK and Wales like it's a Labour candidate in the last general election. There is damage right across the UK. Theresa's underwear got blown off the line into Farage's backyard. He refuses to give them back. The papers are asking, Where's Boris? Due to my absence from the worst flood-hit areas. I can hardly tell them I'm staying at home because I can't swim. I've been having secret lessons in case of an eventuality like this, and thus far have not managed to get out of my High School Musical armbands. I have a panic attack as soon as I let go of the sides. It's debilitating.

I've bedded down in Dominic's basement for the week until it all blows over. I'm safe down here, away from the press and from Sir Trevor McDonald. It's allowed me to spend time with Dom and make up for our lost Valentine's date. He brings me down my Ready Brek every morning and then a couple of rusks for elevenses. If he's in a good mood I get a bottle of ale with my lunch. Man stuff, none of the piffle the tank-topped bum boys drink. I like it down here, there's a train set I can play with. I can't wait until I get my very own set, HS2. It's expensive but worth every penny to please my friends with shares.

There is talk in the papers about where the money for the flood defences has been spent. It's another reason I'm down here. Dom thought it best that I don't answer any questions as I get so very nervous when I have to lie. You see Blanche, the flood defences money was invested into the Downing Street Garden. It's a lovely little paradise in the heart of Westminster. It has a little water feature which Gove stares at to soothe him when he is coming down from the weekend. In the far corner is a little sandpit, that was my idea. Dom lets me play in at lunchtime with Hancock if we've both done our sums, it's not very often. I'm considering taking money from another department to pay Sir Trevor. Perhaps libraries or youth clubs, neither provide any return on investment.

Why are the press such pigs? They are cruel. Without mercy. One cannot see how any human can put such lies in print.

Kind regards,

Boris

Blanche
Boadicea Manor
Salford 6

Boris,

Weren't you once a journalist? I think the best thing for you to do is to remove all floatation aides and throw yourself in at the deep end. I'm sure you'll soon swim, if not, it won't be long until you float to the top. I would suggest going down the well-travelled road of blaming others for the lack of flood defences. I'm sure you can find a way to pin it on the NHS.

I don't want to worry you now, however, Sir Trevor McDonald has been in touch to ask about your whereabouts. I've made excuses for you so far, he isn't stupid though Boris, he'll soon be hot on your tail. Now is the time to speak to Sir Trevor before he gets nasty. I've seen Sir Trevor take on a whole team of terrorists and win. A group of foreign tourists were taken hostage in a hotel-casino in Kabul. There had been anger that the casino was allowed to be built. The only gambling taking place was on 2p machines which had been shipped over from Barry Island. For three weeks the terrorists stood their ground. They refused to surrender after one of them got addicted to the toy-grabber and wouldn't leave until he'd won a stuffed Pokémon. The SAS didn't want to get involved.

Armed with only a plastic spoon from the hotel buffet, Sir Trevor prised himself into the casino through the fire exit, broke the arms of 5 terrorists, left three of them blinded and executed two that were carrying machine guns. It was all over in the blink of an eye. He moved so fast that the security camera picked up nothing but a breeze.

Be very careful Boris, Sir Trevor will find you. I suspect Dominic's is one of the first places he will look. You could always see if he's got any use for one of your children? Perhaps give him a couple you've not bonded with? You could probably supply him with a small army.

Don't worry about the press, tell them you're out shopping for a new fridge.

Blanche

P.S Boris, you forgot the cheques. I will expect double next time.

From: Sophie McBride
To:Blanche
Subject Fridays

25th February 2020

Dear Blanche,

I thought hard about your last letter especially when you wrote, *you can be anything you want to be.* The trouble is all I ever wanted was to be a wife and a Mum. I can't remember what life was like before Marcus. We met when we were seventeen, he was so cool. I'd gone down to the pier with some of my friends, there were five of us in our clique. We all wore matching denim like we'd been vomited on by Levi. Marcus and his group of friends came down in their checked shirts and jeans, walking like they'd had an accident in their pants. Hair cut past their ears like a cheap imitation of Oasis. We thought they were so cool. Us girls would all put together and buy a packet of cigarettes to smoke, trying to impress the boys on the other side of the pier. All we cared about back then was having enough money to buy cheap fags, a bottle of cider and making sure we knew all the words to the songs in the top ten.

We'd be so loud desperately trying to get their attention. We'd never look directly at them, they had to come to us. We always ended up snogging them at the end of the night. We were a mess of hormones, hairspray and spots. We'd all gone our separate ways since school, we'd meet up at the weekend to carry on our playground antics. I wasn't clever enough for university, so I settled on a hairdressing apprenticeship. I've done it ever since. I like it. I love talking to all the women who come in and tell me their problems and what's going on in their lives. I feel like I've been through life with some of them: marriages, divorces, deaths, kids, promotions, redundancies. They tell you everything when they're in the chair having a cut and colour.

It was freezing this one night on the pier. The group had started leaving one by one until only me and Marcus were left. I stank of cigarettes and him of Carling. We took shelter at a bus stop, I sat on his knee, my arms draped around him, and we chewed each other's faces off. Oh God Blanche, he made me laugh. He made me laugh for years.

Friday nights were always our night. It didn't matter what sort of week we'd both had, we always got together with a takeaway and it would just be us. Those Fridays became more important than ever when I gave birth to John.

I can't remember exactly when the laughter stopped. Looking back, it was about the same time we stopped our Fridays, shortly after Tilly was born. I just put it down to life. Not for one second did I think he was out with a male student or even a female one.

When you say you can be anything you want to be, I'd settle for being happy. I just feel ashamed. I drop Tilly off at school and I can see the other mums go quiet when I approach. I'm sure I can hear them say, 'See that one, she used to be a size eight. No wonder her husband turned gay.' I never got back down to my pre-baby weight after Tilly. I've hovered between a size twelve and fourteen ever since. And they're right, I keep thinking did I turn him gay? And then I think why now? After twenty years together, why now?

I've spoken to Marcus since and he's stayed over in the box room. I allowed it because Tilly begged me to let her dad stay over and read a bedtime story. I couldn't bear the confusion on her face. I don't know why but I offered him a glass of wine when he came back downstairs. He accepted. A glass turned into two and then a bottle and then two bottles. I asked him why, he just apologised, said he'd always known. I asked him how many men he'd been with whilst we've been married. He changed the subject. That itself was an answer. It didn't matter if it was one or one hundred, he'd done it and it was clear it was more than once. I asked him if I'd turn him gay. He muttered some rubbish about how I should never blame myself, I can't really remember what, the Merlot had taken hold. The next morning, I couldn't look at him, the anger was back. I wanted him out of the house. He's going to sign it over to me. It's the least he can do he says. At least I don't have to worry about selling up. I'm not sure I want to stay here but the kids have had too much change already.

Embarrassment. Every bit of me is embarrassed. *How the hell did she not know*, that's what everyone will be saying. I'm saying it myself. I'm dreading telling my friends. Thanks for listening Blanche. It's nice to sit down and write, to put the feelings down on paper.

Thanks again,

Sophie

From: Blanche
To:Sophie McBride
Subject Re: Fridays

Dear Sophie,

I once had a lesbian affair in 1990 with Jacqueline the mute Lion Tamer from the Birkenhead circus. We shared a cell at HM Prison Holloway. I was inside for taking the rap for a friend. Jacqueline had been incarcerated after one of her lions escaped and ran amok at the pick-n-mix counter in Woolworths. It was incredibly unfair considering it was her first offence. The judge mistook her silence for arrogance and sentenced her to three years. A muscular woman, her posture made up for her silence. Her eyes could tell you a thousand words. We shared stories of our childhood. I told her all about Langworthy Road, the struggle for milk and me absent dad, and she painted a scene of a nomadic youth surrounded by circus animals. She leaned over and kissed me one evening as we were playing chess, Cilla had sent me the board in with one of the corrupt screws. We were feeling brave after half a bottle of gin which had been smuggled in with it. Getting gin inside wasn't a problem, but you couldn't get tonic for love nor drugs. When Jaqueline's soft lips kissed mine, a fever swept over me. I was instantly besotted. We were side by side until she got an early release for good behaviour. She wrote to me every week, each letter had a different postmark documenting where she and her lions had travelled to entertain folk.

We'd planned to spend our days together and when I was released, I followed her North to Grimsby. The top of the circus tent was my northern star as I made my way up the M1. When I arrived, Jaqueline showed me her caravan where we were to live in sinful bliss. It had no running water, no toilet, and a leak in the roof, I instantly felt at home. We didn't even make it through the first night for I spotted a photo of

Margaret Thatcher above the bed that had been cut out from the Daily Mail. I spun around on my heels, slammed the metal door shut and that was that.

You're right Sophie, writing things down is cathartic. I hope you found some comfort in my story. I'm not sure how, but light often shines from the darkest places. Me dad used to say that when the meter ran out.

It's time to find a new hobby for a Friday evening. How about dogging? I know a man who could take you under his wing and show you a lovely time. You'd have to travel but at least it would get you out of the house. If that's not your thing how about joining a local amateur dramatics group, you'd be brilliant in a tragedy.

The man has left you and signed over the house, get out and celebrate. Women are crying out for this all over the country. Perhaps lay off on the wine for a while, clear your head and focus on what you want to be. Maybe expand that salon of yours, you could open a brothel upstairs? Or start doing liposuction? You've got a captive audience of mothers at the school gate. Talking of which, next time you hear them discussing you, go over there and tell them about your new youthful lover. That will set the cat amongst the pigeons. Then go out and find yourself a toy boy — lock him away when your husband comes round.

Blanche

MARCH

From: Alex Huntington
To: Blanche
Subject Dating dreams
3rd March 2020

Dear Blanche,

What do you reckon to this? The dating apps aren't paying off so well. I've upgraded to the premium version of them all. There are some right weirdos! There should be a law against them. I wish they knew I'm trying to find the one. I was asked to send pictures of my feet to a bald man in Leamington Spa. I sent him twenty pictures in landscape, portrait, close-up, sepia, black and white and colour, it didn't lead to any dates though. I was texting a man from Henley for a while too, he said he was originally born in New York. He was quite portly, short and blonde but ever so confident. He said he was the Prime Minister. I cancelled the date as I could never date a fantasist.

It's been hard going Blanche, I've been on seventeen dates in the last month. It's *really* having an impact on my finances. I've paid for fourteen of them. I don't know what I'm doing wrong, they don't tend to call me back for a second date. At least I got out of the house. There was a lovely gentleman who worked as a fireman who took me to the local curry house. When he went to the bathroom the waiter came over and told me I was the third person this week he'd taken in there. When he came back from the toilet, I told him I didn't mind being in an open relationship or in a quartet. He texted me the next day to say I seemed a little too eager. I was gutted as he was drop-dead gorgeous and he said he'd show me his hose. It amazes me how they can conceal something that length in such a compact space. I really wanted to see him again. The next night I set fire to my chip pan and called 999. I made sure I looked my best and wore a tiny skirt to show my legs off, my best feature. Only when the fire brigade came it was a different station that had been called out, there wasn't a good looking one between them. I still gave them all my number and told them to pop by if they were ever in the area.

Another man invited me round to his house for a coffee but when he saw me walking up the drive, he turned the lights off and pretended he wasn't in. I'd made such a huge effort. I'd crimped my hair and put on my 80s rah-rah skirt and leg warmers. I wanted him to see my *crazy* side. I wasn't going to let a man be so shallow. His downstairs window was open, so I went over to it and shouted, 'I know you're in there! You owe me a date.' I tried climbing through it, but his dog was barking at me. I got my Tinder profile suspended after that.

On top of it all, Dr Altman is now full steam ahead with her Summer BBQ plans and has started asking me if I would like to be set up with one of her friends. She's given me a brief description of some men that I might like:

Brian - 33, a primary school teacher who has five children with six different women. When I asked how this was possible, she told me it was best I didn't know

Daniel - 43, a bisexual social worker who likes walking holidays and Fleetwood Mac

Nigel - 38, once a soap star in his teenage years and is currently a bin-man whilst still auditioning for bit parts. His last role was in a Viagra commercial

Patrick - 35, a prison warden who was once on trial himself for war crimes in Northern Ireland

I think they all sound *really* lovely, don't you? I might see if it's possible to have a hotdog with all of them, like a speed dating BBQ. Hopefully, I'll find someone before the summer so we can plan a romantic holiday together. I've never been away with a boyfriend before. There was a man I use to date that took me to Western-Super-Mare for the weekend.

I found out later that he'd gone to visit his wife and kids whilst I was having a nap in the caravan.

Dr Altman said she's going to hire an adult bouncy castle for the day and some butlers in the buff to serve the arrival drinks to guests. She's still doing all the organising as her husband continues to sell pharmaceuticals with Jesus. They've moved onto Italy now. Dr Altman said there are a lot of cosmetic surgeons there who might place a big order. I hope he comes back soon to help her out as she's making some very rash decisions: she's hired Roy Chubby Brown for the entertainment. When I asked her if she thought that was wise, she screamed, 'who else can I fucking get with three months' notice?' Then stormed into her surgery and slammed the door. I could hear her sobbing for the rest of the afternoon. I didn't dare tell her that I thought tripe isn't a very good canapé.

Blanche, what am I doing wrong? Will you help me trap a man before I'm a mad old cat woman who has afternoon tea with Tibbles the tabby?

With love,

Alex

From: Blanche
To: Alex Huntington
Subject Re: Dating begins

Dear Alex,

It is quite unusual that you haven't been able to get a second date. Maybe turning up in a wedding dress is a little off-putting. Now I know I asked before, are you sure you don't have halitosis? When you're offering it to a man on a plate like you are, it's very unusual to find one who won't take advantage, a trip to the dentist can't hurt just to be sure.

I had quite the opposite problem when I was a Tiller Girl at the London Palladium. There'd be a queue at the stage door of men trying to get a glimpse of me to ask me out on a date. Every night I was wined and dined by the most handsome men. I found the Hollywood stars were always the least confident, Clint Eastwood was a nervous wreck. He became obsessed with me after watching the show. I once caught him collecting my armpit shavings from my dressing room sink. I didn't say anything, I don't judge. Cartier watches, pearls, an Aston Martin, he bought me everything I could ever wish for. I felt like Marilyn Monroe. She was right, gentlemen really do prefer blondes. I know that for a fact as Cilla was very jealous of my gifts. In all the years she was on stage she only received one letter from a fan, and he was in an asylum.

Cilla was consumed by jealousy. One night she broke into my dressing room whilst I was on stage spinning my tassels, she went through my handbag and stole the keys to my Aston Martin. It was a beautiful V8, a shimmering silver beast. It was a reflection of how fast I can spin a tassel, 0 to 100 mph in fourteen seconds. The steering wheel and leather seats were as red as Cilla's hair.

I'd only had the car for a month before its ill-fated drive with Cilla. She'd drank a bottle of cider before climbing into the driver's seat and zooming off into the night. She managed to get as far as Brentwood before she lost control whilst reaching for her hip flask on the passenger seat. She wrapped the car around a pussy willow. Fortunately, Princess Ann was out at one of her *"evening events"* and had seen the car come speeding around the corner. Ann ran straight over to it, climbed into the mangled wreckage and dragged Cilla out before it burst into flames, cremating itself in a lay-by on the A1023. Ann's friend, Rusty Rick, performed mouth to mouth on Cilla who came round singing, 'W*hat's it all about, Alfie.*'

Ann bundled Cilla into the back of her Scimitar GTE and brought her back to the Palladium for my care. I forgave Cilla instantly. You can't hold a grudge when someone is gripped by jealousy. That incident was a turning point for Cilla, she never mixed Strongbow with Lucozade again. Ann and I sat Cilla down in that humble dressing room (I'd tried to brighten the place up with colourful feather boas, but you can't polish a turd), and counselled Cilla till she felt better. It all came out in her 1964 hit, *It's for You.* She wrote it with Paul McCartney. It was all about her experiences that led up to that crash. She was very good at expressing her feelings through song, but she couldn't sing. All her songs were dubbed. They were actually sung by a scouse midwife who didn't want the fame. She passed away in the summer of '93 after taking a suppository to the chest from a patient who'd just had a C-section. That was the end of Cilla's new music.

Keep an open mind about Dr Altman's blind dates. I'd stay away from the soap star though. Actors are very self-indulgent and there isn't a more repulsive quality in a human. Did you happen to see any of my shows yourself? I was quite the leading lady.

I am slightly concerned about your fire-starting. You don't want to go down that road. Princess Ann did the same thing at Windsor Castle in '92 after a brief affair with a station officer. Ann had met him on the forecourt of a petrol station on the B3022. Ann was good at emotional detachment, however, this particular officer had insisted that Ann paid for their coffee after their late-night meeting. She was instantly smitten. No one had ever tried not to impress her before. Liz was furious when it all came out in the wash and rushed through Ann's wedding arrangements to Commander Tim Lawrence that December. That's why the wedding was held in Balmoral, they didn't have enough time to allow for RSVPs to fill Westminster Abbey. Could you imagine getting married? Maybe one day Love.

Take care,

Blanche

Victoria Townsend
29 Hellbourne Close
Salford

9ᵗʰ March 2020

Dear Blanche,

If I got rid of Dave, I can assure you, I wouldn't want another man in my life ever again. I would be happy spending the rest of my days with my grandchildren. They're my purpose now. They're my daughter's children, Emily is seven and Peter is three. They're at the age when everything is new to them and each new object raises a thousand questions. I'm exhausted after I spend the day with them, it's equally nice to hand them back as it is to receive them.

I love taking them out to the zoo or the park. They give me such life. Emily is cautious, she'll look at something and weigh up the pros and cons of the activity before joining in. When she goes near the swings, I think she carries out a risk assessment first. She'll work for the council when she's older. Peter is the opposite, he rushes in and doesn't care if he tumbles over and gets a few bruises. He'll have a life of adventure, a modern Michael Palin. On the few occasions Dave has come with us, he sucks the life out of the day. He's so worried they will get hurt that he doesn't allow them to live. From the minute we arrive he stares at his watch wondering how soon we can leave to go back home and sit in that house. That prison.

He's ruined every holiday we've ever been on as a family. I once booked a holiday to Wales for William and his friend for the Easter break. It was only a caravan getaway, they counted down the days until they could play in the pool. We were packed and ready to go and Dave said, 'I'm not coming.' No reason, no argument, just didn't want to come and that was that. I was delighted. Relieved to have three whole nights peace and quiet. The kids were too excited to care. I think that annoyed him. The first night we played Monopoly and I took the kids to the campsite bar where they stood mesmerised at the Tiger Club mascot, Rory. Their eyes were popping out their heads at this six-foot tiger, oblivious to the fact it was a spotty teenager inside. They both had a blue Slush Puppie which stained their tongues and William's t-shirt. The cup had slipped out of tiny hands and the coloured ice hailed onto his chest. They were the most adorable picture of carefree kids. I treated them to a chip cone each on the walk back to the caravan, they didn't come up for air. I'm glad they had one nice night.

The next day it rained none stop. The kids had just put their wellingtons on when I heard a car pull up outside. My heart sank. I just knew. He didn't knock on the door, he just thundered in. The holiday was over the second the door closed, *he* stood there on the *Welcome* mat. 'It's too wet to go outside,' he said. We didn't leave that caravan for two days. That night we had a blazing row. William come out of his room in his blue Thomas the Tank Engine pyjamas and asked us to stop. He wasn't upset, he was used to the raised voices by then. They all told me to leave him, family and friends. This would be another round of ammunition to add to their *I told you so's*. I don't look at it like that now. I think they told me to leave him because they could see what a genuine bastard he was. Is.

Yours sincerely,

Victoria

Blanche
Boadicea Manor
Salford 6

Dear Victoria,

Don't worry about the kids, they should be bloody grateful you took them on holiday at all. I used to go on such beautiful holidays with Cilla, the Bahamas and the Greek Islands. We never booked accommodation, we'd just get our flights and get a taxi to drive us around until we found a place where we wanted to stay. Cilla would then get out the car and go to the hotel reception and say, '*Surprise, Surprise*, it's Cilla here.' She was always met with confusion, but she very much believed in her own celebrity.

Have you thought of taking yourself off on a luxurious holiday? Be sure to leave Dave and the colostomy bags at home. How about Turkey? I've seen many a single white female travel to Marmaris on an all-inclusive holiday, believing a toy boy comes free with the premium spirits. The women end up falling in love and drag a very willing Tarquin back to the UK. He counts the left-over travellers' cheques whilst she sits there oblivious and besotted. The women end up heartbroken and bankrupt after signing over their life savings before he's pissed off back home. The women then sell their stories to *Take A Break*. They've no shame in airing their shitty laundry in public. The mothers of Langworthy Road had more class. When Audry from number 232 came back from Scarborough with a suspicious looking bump, she was sent away for 9 months to her "auntie's". When she returned, she was shunned by the mothers. I hugged her. We all slip up. We've all been overpromised to by a man only for them to underdeliver or piss off into the night to be never seen again whilst they slide their wedding ring back onto their finger.

I can't help but feel like you're missing an opportunity on these days out, Victoria. Can you not take Dave to the zoo and accidentally push him into the lion enclosure or drown him in the penguin pool? Next time you take the grandkids to Blackpool you could push him off the end of the pier. What're sixteen years inside when you've served several life sentences staying with him?

We need to toughen you up. Get some Langworthy grit in you. You wouldn't believe it but Judy Finnigan was quiet as a mouse when I first met her. She wouldn't say boo to an overbearing bastard. After a few nights out in the West End with me and Cilla, she soon toughed up. She was loved by the queens in Old Compton Street. Her self-worth came flooding back after a drag queen mimicked her on stage. You should get yourself down Canal Street and meet one. I used to know a drag queen called Miss Kitty Lashes who worked the door on several of the bars. She was always dressed as Marilyn, naturally, I found myself drawn to her. She was that tiny I could put my hand around her waist. She must have had a couple of ribs removed. You don't have to go to those extremes, thigh high boots could work for you. You could stomp around the house in them and scratch the flooring just to really piss Dave off.

Keep your pecker up,

Blanche

Rishi Sunak MP
House of Commons
Westminster

15th March 2020

Dear Blanche,

Good morning to you. I assume it is the morning when you collect your post. I am Rishi, Chancellor of the Exchequer. It's a very important job. I've recently been promoted after my boss, Boris, fell out with my predecessor for not allowing money to be spent on an emotional support animal for Downing Street. Boris wanted a lion. He left me instructions to write to you if I get in a pickle, and I'm afraid, I rather am.

Boris has been overspending on his personal expenses, he's chartered a private jet to take him and his children to Majorca for a weekend. Actually, it's sixteen private jets. His offspring are flying in from all over the world. The heirs are appearing quicker than Boris can deny them. We've decided in the cabinet to launch a Test and Trace app for any child who thinks they may be a descendant of Boris. It's money I could do without spending. Such is his fertility that any woman who comes within a one-mile radius of Boris is alerted to order a pregnancy test.

I do worry about the Prime Minister, he has become very nervous of late. He's been asking me for blank cheques and to make them out to a Mr T McDonald. Do you know who this beneficiary is? When I refused to issue the cheques, Boris started sweating profusely and told me that if I didn't grant the cheque, I'd be paying for a state funeral. I sent him to his drawing room to calm him down. He mumbled something about the ten o'clock news as he left.

Blanche, do you know what is causing him to be so bombastic? It's not like him at all, he very rarely clings on to any single thought this long.

With due diligence,

Rishi.

Blanche
Boadicea Manor
Salford 6

Dear Rishi,

I'm delighted to hear from you. I've been expecting your correspondence since Boris made me chief agony aunt to the cabinet some months back. What awful times you find yourself in. Fortunately, you've come to the right woman. Me mam used to have a very sympathetic ear, her ticket booth at the Ambassador Theatre would double as a confessional on matinee performances. The women of Chimney Pot Park would be queuing past the pick 'n' mix to offload what sins they'd committed that week. Even when the police come knocking asking questions about the body of a man that had turned up in a ginnel with his mouth sewed up, she didn't give anything away. She knew all about it of course. Mary from number 23 was forever shouting at her husband, 'you talk to me like that one more fucking time and I'll sew your bastard mouth up.' Rumour has it me mam hid the needle and thread at the bottom of the popcorn concession. So, Rishi, your secrets are very safe with me. I've inherited the inability to ever be a babble-merchant.

This app you talk about sounds very expensive, he can't possibly have any more children. Wouldn't the money be better spent on coffee mornings at the Bingo Callers' Union? You should keep them onside. They can be barbaric if ignored.

Should it come to organising a state funeral I know some fabulous women who can cater on a budget. I do love a good funeral, don't you? You can always tell how liked a person was by the spread at their wake. If it's a few stale triangular egg sandwiches and a packet of ready salted supermarket crisps poured in a bowl, you know they must have been a bleeder. Me mam's funeral was quite the do. Princess Di brought vol-au-vents from Waitrose, Cilla brought a beautiful Black-forest gateau from Netto and Cliff Richard brought his portable disco. He did a wonderful job filling the dancefloor. Di and Cilla called a cease-fire for the day and even sat legs akimbo one in front of the other for *Oops Upside Your Head*. We danced all night long and only stopped when Cilla put her back out after she slipped on a cheese and pineapple stick. The funeral was voted Function of the Year 1980 by the Bridge Club of the British Legion, Langworthy Road. There's a commemorative plaque in the ladies' loos.

I think you'd be wise not to leave your chequebook lying around. You don't want Boris gaining access to the country's purse strings and don't worry about funds for a state funeral, the Legion does a cracking rate for function rooms.

Blanche

From: Jessica Watkiss
To: Blanche
Subject Daisy the cow

20th March 2020

Dear Blanche,

I decided not to put any electric fencing in the bed to keep *him* away. Instead, I calmly told that bastard that if he dares to bring his erection near me again, I'll cut it off with the fish knife and feed it to the dog. He might be able to forget the labour, but I'm still living in the panic that the birth has been lived streamed by one of the student doctors. I have nightmares that my contractions are doing the rounds on the university TV. I wish I had your mother's problem of not being able to express milk, I'm hooked up to an electric milk pump like Daisy the bastard cow. Mind you, it has its uses. We'd run out of semi-skimmed for his morning brew, so I used some tit liquid to stop him moaning. If I'm not mopping up breast milk, I'm wiping away baby vomit whilst covered in shit from the eco reusable nappies. It's enough to make me think, sod the bastard environment and hand me over a nappy made of concrete. They need to be a solid material to withstand the tiny explosions Fido, (god I hate that name) has every hour. It's nappies smell that much it's like the shits have been cursed.

I can't stop Blanche. Knob-head will be home in 30 minutes wanting his tea. I'm going to pop a Rusk in the toaster and serve it with a side of gammon.

Kind regards,

Jess x

From: Jessica Watkiss
To: Blanche
Subject Re: Daisy

Dear Jess,
You need a holiday. I've attached an e-brochure for Tuppence Tours.
There's a lovely all-inclusive to Malaga.

Blanche

Boris Johnson MP
10 Downing St
Westminster

25th March 2020

Dear Blanche,

I, at last, seized my opportunity to show the country what a strong man I am, and what a competent leader they elected. It seems this virus is sweeping across the nation, but it can't get me for I am strong, like The Hulk. I've been warned by our scientific advisors to not shake anybody's hand and to advise the nation not to do so either. What drivel. I prefer instead to listen to my Magic 8 Ball which assured me it was perfectly safe to shake the hands of all I meet.

Today I told the British public to sing *Happy Birthday* to themselves whilst they wash their hands, I just think it will cheer them up. I'd been playing pass the parcel earlier that morning at one of my friend's parties and the tune was still stuck in my head. I didn't win the main prize in the game, I imagine it was a fix. I was made to stand in the corner after getting too excited and blowing out the candles on the cake. Dominic wasn't impressed, he said I should have been in a briefing. He can be such a bore. I won't invite him to my next party.

This evening I've been at a hospital doing a press call. I shook the hands of everyone in the Covid ward. I purposefully held onto their hands a little longer than necessary to show the country my virus defeating strength. It felt so good. I treated myself to a McFlurry on the way home to celebrate. No virus nor man called Sir Trevor is going to bring me down. I feel so full of life after my short stay in Dom's basement. Blanche, I feel so alive. Things are finally going right and I haven't heard from Sir Trevor MacDonald all month.

Kind regards,

Boris

Dominic Cummings MP
House of Commons
Westminster

27th March 2020

Dear Blanche,

Boris has asked me to write. He's currently in bed after contracting Coronavirus. He's too weak to write. I have enclosed a picture he drew for you which he insisted I sent. I think he's going delirious as he's drawn himself as the King of England, the Spice Girls are his ladies in waiting.

My heart breaks for him. I've been sitting vigil at his bedside, mopping away the sweat from his brow, he's filled two buckets this afternoon. I've bought him some new Super Ted pyjamas as his Buzz Lightyear set was threadbare. If I could take his pain away and suffer instead then I would. He was crying out in his sleep, *Trump, TRUMP*, I woke him up. He's clearly delirious, I'm his best friend after all.

We spent the morning watching cartoons, *Tom and Jerry* is his favourite. He likes to pretend Tom is Corbyn. When we announced the news to the nation last night, we thought we would receive bundles of cards through the letterbox from well-wishers. None so far, but he did receive a new colouring book from Trump which rallied him somewhat. There was a rather threatening correspondence from a T McDonald. I've burnt it as I don't want Boris to shed any more tears.

He took a turn for the worse this afternoon, it was clear he was slipping in and out of consciousness as he was spluttering, *free school dinners for all*, and *fund the NHS*. I've had him sedated.

Blanche, how I long for his recovery. I don't want you to worry though. I'll be here by his side looking after him.

Kind regards,

Dominic

Blanche
Boadicea Manor
Salford 6

Dear Dominic,

Not worried.

Blanche.

From: Sophie McBride
To:Blanche
Subject Fridays

29th March 2020

Dear Blanche,

I'm absolutely mortified. I went to the sex clinic to get tested just in case my cheating husband had passed anything onto me. I didn't mind the examination, once you've given birth and had doctors staring at your private bits it takes a lot to get embarrassed, but the questions I was asked left me feeling dirty. 'How many sexual partners have you had?' the nurse asked. When I told her only one, she raised an eyebrow to insinuate I was lying before continuing, 'Anal?' I don't know what came over me, but I replied, 'Yes. My husband was gay.' She gave me a knowing look, then pressed on with the interrogation: 'Have you had unprotected sex,' 'Anything unusual,' 'Any stinging or discharge.' I had to get on the table and remove my knickers whilst she took a swab. That bit was over in a flash, but the questions ran through my head all day. It's another reason to hate Marcus. I prepared for that health test like I was going on a date, I shaved my legs and trimmed down below to make myself look presentable. I had to google the latest trends in pubic hair, I didn't realise there were so many styles. I don't take much notice of the beauty side of things at the salon. I almost cried when Amanda, the therapist, said, 'I'll just give you the once over with these first,' as she took a pair of clippers out of her top drawer. I must remember to give her a pay rise. Anyway, all the tests came back clear.

It's been a tough couple of months, Blanche. Crying is no longer the first thing I do when I open my eyes in the morning. I'm not ready to start celebrating yet as you suggested. I did manage to clear the house out of all his belongings, a small win. I can have a fresh start now without constantly being reminded of him every time I look up. I've even had the front room repainted in a nice eggshell blue. It's covered up the stain on the wall from where I threw the cake.

As for getting a toy boy, I could think of nothing worse than getting another man just yet. I'm going to spend some time getting to know myself.

Sophie x x

P.S I've sent you a case of his poncy red wine I found in the shed. Enjoy.

From: Blanche
To:Sophie McBride
Subject Re: Fridays

Dear Sophie,

Thanks for the red wine, I'm not normally a fan of but it does taste so much better when it's free.

Visits to a clinic are no fun. I once went to get checked out after a busy week on the beat. I got to the clinic and the nurse told me to get ready whilst she popped out, I dropped my knickers and climbed on the couch. You should have seen the look of horror on her face when she came back into the room to find me naked from the waist down. She was an Optometrist; the receptionist had misheard my request for an STI test. Turns out I had perfect vision.

Absolutely right to get rid of all the reminders of the husband. I had a terrible time with my roommate Fergie and her maudlin over her ex. Anyone would think he was the next king of England the way she carried on. Plates and pot towels with their wedding picture on them were everywhere when I moved in. She'd sit there all day in her wedding dress watching the video of her nuptials and would invite the neighbours round for a reception. They only came to see what they could nick. On seeing the state of furniture that she had in the front room, they took pity on her and had a whip-round. Terry from two doors down brought his steamer and removed the wallpaper. He replaced it with a beautiful autumn floral scene which looked magnificent despite the air bubbles. The money wasn't much but it paid for a new cinema screen TV, half price off the back of Terry's truck.

What have your in-laws been like? Fergie's have been horrid on all accounts. I won't discuss it in case they are having the mail infiltrated, I wouldn't put anything past them.

Kind regards,

Blanche

APRIL

From:Randy Mottershed
To: Blanche
Subject Online dogging

2nd April 2020

Dear Blanche,

Success. Princess Ann has replied — she'd be delighted to be the patron of the Doggers Trust. She said she approves of any activity that gets people outside and away from the TV. She wrote:

the characteristic I despise most in others is a slovenly existence. I once had a sister-in-law who was the very definition. I would be delighted to encourage the masses to get away from their sofas and into the thrill of the night.

It's very unfortunate that due to the Covid restrictions we've had to cancel the VIP Dogging Weekend we'd planned. Both Princess Ann and Jane McDonald were going to make an appearance. We put numerous hours into the preparation. Mel was making sandwiches and marinating chicken drumsticks for the best part of two weeks. Nothing got wasted though, she ate them all for elevenses after she had a strenuous walk to the shop. She goes once a week for her favourite magazines, *Scaffolding for Women* and *Kittens of World War One*. I was going to put the food over my body to entice Mel into bed as you suggested, however, by the time I got home from work there was only lettuce remaining.

Mel proposed we take the event online. I didn't think people would sign up for virtual dogging, I was proven incorrect. Mel set up a Twitter account — @MangledMel — to advertise our intentions. After a few retweets from @TheJaneMcDonald, we had forty couples signed up plus one single lady. We don't normally admit singletons but an intelligent young woman who is a doctor's receptionist from Peterborough requested to join in, she was rather eager.

Mel had been filming little videos to put online to entice people to join the event. One of them went viral of her pleasuring herself with her vibrator. The bedroom was dimly lit and mistakenly picked up a tube of Deep Heat instead of the KY jelly from the bedside table. It got forty-eight thousand likes and was shown on a late-night blooper show on Channel 5. Mel ended up with over forty thousand Twitter followers. At their suggestion she has created an OnlyFans account. It's where you upload videos to your followers in exchange for a monthly subscription. Mel charges her fans £7.99 a month to watch her gorge herself on cream cakes. I'm very proud of her entrepreneurial skills, although she won't let me in any of the videos. Apparently, I'm best suited behind the camera. Mel acquired some home studio equipment with the subscription money. The rest she put to one side to replan our VIP Dogging Weekend for when the lockdown is lifted.

The online event was a huge success. Jane McDonald hosted the proceedings introducing the couples to one another. She'd then randomly select two couples to enter a private meeting room where they could fulfil their voyeuristic fantasies. As an interval act, Jane hosted a brief Question and Answer session followed by a medley of Cilla's greatest hits.

We'll continue with the online events every second Friday until physical meets are allowed once more. I've asked Princess Ann if she knows of a suitable location for fifty cars, we're hopeful Mel's new fame will attract participants.

Thank you for all your advice, Blanche. If there's anything I can ever do for you, please do inform me.

Fond regards,

Randy

From:Blanche
To: Randy Mottershed
Subject Re: Online dogging

Randy,

I'm very pleased things are going well. Perhaps you could use some of that money to have Mel's jaw wired shut for a few months. I knew Princess Ann would come good for you. She's always been an exhibitionist. You can't be a Royal and have inhibitions. Ann has always revelled in being nude. She loved to shock people as a teenager by wandering around the palace naked. The Queen's ladies in waiting used to rugby tackle her if she went anywhere near the famous balcony.

I'm thrilled one of my ideas has paid off for you. I think you should go big Randy. Imagine having the biggest dogging group in the world. You'd be famous. You could quit climbing those telephone masts for a living.

It's funny you should mention a studio as I'm no stranger to a TV set myself. I was always with Cilla when she was doing her recordings. She had terrible stage fright and always found it a comfort to have me backstage. I used to love it, meeting all those families on *Surprise, Surprise.* They'd been flown halfway around the world to meet a long-lost relative they'd not seen for half a century. They'd walk on set and fall into each other's arms as Cilla stood over them looking smug. The second the cameras stopped rolling you could see the family members suddenly remember the reason they hadn't spoken to each other for decades. Old grudges would ignite the second the director shouted *cut.*

There was a window cleaner from Sunderland who hadn't seen his twin brother since the funeral of their parents. They'd died twenty years earlier after capsizing in a narrowboat on the Norfolk Broads. He sobbed into his shammy leather as Cilla, tipsy from the contents of her hipflasks, screeched, '*Surprise, Surprise* Ted. You've not seen him for twenty years.

We've tracked him down all the way in Canada where he fucked off to get as far away from you as possible. It's the twin you couldn't stand. Come in Stan.' The editors earned their keep on that show making sure Cilla's frequent outbursts were left on the cutting room floor. The second the twins left the set the window cleaner punched his twin square on the nose. He shouted, 'That's for being a grave-digging bastard, where's my inheritance.' They both left via different exits.

You'll have fun behind the camera, Randy. You can get yourself one of those director's chairs and figure out Mel's good side, if she has one. Let me know how your relaunch plans go. I'm sure the lockdown won't last long, you'll be back flashing your headlights before you know it.

I am glad you offered to do me a favour for me as there is a little something I need doing. I won't burden you with details now, it may involve getting your hands dirty.

Take care and stay safe,

Blanche

From: Alex Huntington
To: Blanche
Subject Wedding plans

5ᵗʰ April 2020

Dear Blanche,

Do I ever dream of getting married? Ever since I was a little girl. I've got it all planned out. He'll propose to me in a *really* romantic setting, like under a waterfall or on the edge of a cliff. Somewhere *really* Instagramable. It will be filmed, not obviously so. It'll look like someone was just passing by and happened to catch the moment on camera. Authentic. The ring will be perfect, a beautiful diamond that sparkles when it catches the light. Understated and classy. We'll send the invitations out in a really funky way, probably carrier pigeon. The wedding will take place somewhere people will be *really* envious, Cape Town is my number one choice. It's expensive to get there but dead cheap once you arrive. We'll hire out a vineyard for five nights and pay for everyone's accommodation. Dr Altman will be jealous as she got married whilst she was still at medical school and could only afford a registry office. I'll be walked down the aisle to Elbow's *On A Day Like This.* I'll be following my three nieces who will be wearing matching coffee-coloured gowns as they scatter red and white rose petals. Table Mountain will provide a backdrop as I say, 'I do.' The guests will have a choice of steak or fish and then we'll all dance the night away. Instead of a traditional cake, we'll have a giant pork pie that people can eat when they're pissed and going off to bed. I've not planned it all though, I want my groom to have some input. He can choose his own tie.

God only knows if I'll ever get a proposal, I seem to be destined to stay single forever. Because of lockdown, I can't leave the house so last

Friday I signed up for an online speed dating session. It was full of lovely people. It took me a while to realise that they were all couples, which I thought was strange. It was hosted by Jane McDonald. I got a chance to ask her where her favourite place is to go cruising. I don't think she understood though as she said, 'Clapham Common.' It was a lovely night. I got talking to a man called Randy and his wife Mel. She was very aloof. Randy did all the talking, he seemed genuinely interested and asked me lots of questions. Mel just stared at the screen whilst shoving Wagon Wheels in her mouth. I felt quite sorry for Randy, I could tell he was craving attention. He asked me if I'd like to have a *private chat* with him. Jane McDonald started to sing when I was in the middle of telling Randy about my brief love affair with the fireman. She's very loud, I couldn't tell what Randy was saying. I made my excuses and left but agreed to chat again soon.

Dr Altman hasn't been very well recently. She's been banging the doors in the surgery and quietly crying between patients. I think it will do her good when her husband comes home. I did ask when he was due back. Him and Jesus have moved on to Croatia selling their pharmaceuticals. I can't help but think this lockdown might be the best thing to happen if it means Dr Altman has to cancel her BBQ. It's a lot of pressure for me to take the right date. I can always meet the men she wants to set me up with down the Wacky Warehouse when it reopens, they do two curries for a tenner on a Tuesday.

I must dash as I'm at work and Ted Leggett is due in for his obesity check-up. It takes four of us forty minutes to squeeze him through the front door then three minutes for Dr Altman to check his blood pressure, tell him he's still fat and give him a lollipop for being a good boy. It's no life for a nine-year-old.

All the best,

Alex

From: Blanche
To: Alex Huntington
Subject Re: Wedding plans

Dear Alex,

I'm not known as someone to put a dampener on things, but don't you think your wedding plans are a little too optimistic? I'd hate for you to be disappointed on your big day. Maybe be more realistic and see if Greggs has a function room.

My second wedding was top-notch. Lord Woolworth Mountbatten had been introduced to me by Prince Philip after I spun my tassels on stage at the Royal Variety Performance in '69. Unbeknown to me, Prince Philip was mesmerised by my nipple tassel spinning. His clammy face and eyes of filth were broadcast live to the nation, putting me on the front cover of every national newspaper the next day. He didn't help matters when at the meet and greet after the show a live microphone picked up him saying, 'One could be hypnotised all the way to paradise by your bazookas.' I made the news at ten in thirty-seven countries. The BBC ran with the headline *Boobs, Beehive and a Prince. Has this Northern temptress got it all?* Liz was furious when she saw the picture of Philip taking a sideways glance at my chest. He never looked at Liz like that. She calmed down the next day once Philip explained he was simply expressing boyish banter with Lord Woolworth Mountbatten, his friend from boarding school. Their surnames were a fortunate coincidence which fooled many to believe they were real brothers. Plus, both their mothers were mad old cows. Philip had a soft spot for me for many years but that turned to stone when Di and I became friends. He was grieved by our friendship. The final straw came when Di asked me to be a bridesmaid. The morning of the wedding he had me locked up in the palace wine cellar, I missed the whole damn thing. That's why

Di looks bloody miserable in all the photos. I managed to get a bit of revenge, I drank four bottles of priceless rum Philip had received as a gift in the Caribbean in '66.

Woolworth was a handsome man. Heir not to the high-street shop, as some assumed, but the inventor of the first super noodle to be eaten in space. His boil-in-a-bag noodle patent earned him millions when Neil Armstrong took his historic steps for the convenience food industry. Tall, dark, handsome and always wore a cheeky smile from ear to ear. He was a complete lover of life. He was extremely thoughtful and a true romantic. He proposed to me outside the McVities biscuit factory in Manchester, placing the ring upon a custard cream. Although the wedding itself was an intimate affair with just Cilla and me mam as witnesses, we followed in the footsteps of Philip and Liz and had our wedding cake made by McVitie. Unlike them, we didn't give pieces of cake to local schools, we gave ours to the mothers of Salford Precinct. We married a year after we met at the Royal Variety Show. I wore my hair in a blonde wave, like Marilyn in *How to Marry a Millionaire,* and chose to wear a red dress in homage to her for the ceremony. Plus, I thought a virginal white gown would have been a tad distasteful. It was a beautiful but all too brief marriage. Cut short by an incident with a petrol lawnmower in '84.

Do keep in touch with Randy, he sounds like he's salt of the earth. Maybe you can invite him to Dr Altman's BBQ?

Mind how you go.

Blanche

Boris Johnson MP
St Thames Hospital
London

7ᵗʰ April

Dear Blanche,

I'm currently in intensive care after catching this blasted Covid virus. It's highly inconvenient, I had planned to cook Dom a romantic dinner which I've had to postpone. He's been with me night and day and has let me choose which funding to cut next to cheer me up. It appears Blanche, I wasn't as untouchable by this retched virus as I first thought. The scientist was correct, I shouldn't have been shaking hands. I've decided to let Gove tell that to the nation. I'm going to try and capitalise on the public's sympathy whilst I'm on the ward. I may see if I can book in for an extra week, the food is marvellous. Plus, they have security on the door. I feel safe knowing Sir Trevor McDonald can't get me in here. Did you watch Her Majesty the Queen's address to the nation yesterday? Awfully good. I wonder if she would be willing to write my speeches. Thank heavens the papers have filled their headlines with her yesterday and given me a day respite.

Dom says he's going to tell the press I'm at death's door so we can spend a little more time together in this isolation unit. The nurses have brought another bed into my private room for him, we've decided to top and tail.

Must dash Blanche, they've just brought round the jam sandwiches and juice.

All jolly good,

Boris

P.S I've not sent a cheque as I'm not really seeking advice, I just thought you'd like to know how I'm doing after the friendship we've forged.

Blanche
Boadicea Manor
Salford 6

Dear Boris,

Never mistake service for friendship. Didn't an American lady already tell you that? Unfortunately, I didn't get the opportunity to watch the Queen's address. The very sight of her sends my flatmate Fergie into palpitations, she can only be calmed with a tranquiliser. We watched a documentary on the other channel, *Truthful Politicians,* it was very short. You wouldn't have liked it.

Don't be so confident that Sir Trevor can't get passed the hospital security. He's probably halfway up the ventilation shaft right now.

Stay calm,

Blanche.

From: Jessica Watkiss
To: Blanche
Subject Hen party
10th April 2020

Dear Blanche,

God, I need a break. From both the baby and that bastard, he's like a man possessed. Possessed with the bastard horn. I've told him to lock himself in the bathroom for half an hour with his iPad and his favourite Joanna Lumley documentary.

I've connected with him now, the baby, and I can just about manage to put the pram up without reading from the instructions. I've not put any pictures of Fido on social media yet, but I have allowed family and friends to visit. They swoon over him and say, 'Isn't he beautiful.' They must be taking the piss. He looks like a cross between a gremlin and Quasimodo. You can't say that though can you, *excuse me but your baby looks like a leper*. He does have that new baby smell though. Him upstairs has already asked to have another one. I told him there's no pissing chance whilst my nipples are still chewed to bastard buggery from this one.

Every time I put Fido down for a sleep, I sit there with a brew and a tub of Miniature Heroes. I've hidden them at the back of the cleaning cupboard as I know it's the one place knobhead won't look. I've been gazing slowly and longingly through the brochure you sent. I look at all the sun loungers around the pool and I try and imagine myself on each one. I've folded the corner of the pages for all the hotels that have a kids club and a swim-up bar.

To be honest I'm dreaming of a holiday with the girls. It seems a lifetime ago since I went away on a girlie trip. It was two years since we went to Benidorm for Mandy's hen weekend, she works on the service desk at work. I've not told you what I do for work have I, Blanche? I'm the receptionist for a shit car dealership. One that advises on TV. You can come to us when no one else will give you credit and we'll give you a car you can drive away with on the same day, as long as you bring your passport and two utility bills. By the time you've paid the car off at £50 a month at five thousand percent APR, we've charged you £100k for a shit 2k banger. You get a free car freshener to hang off your rear-view mirror. It smells of bubble gum and shite, which is exactly how our house smells, Fido is still delivering nuclear nappies at the rate of one an hour.

Thirteen girls let loose on the Benidorm strip on our last all-girls trip away, plus Johnny, the token gay friend of Mandy. Mandy's sister Meryl organised it. Shit me, she's rough. She wore the same bra for the whole weekend and pulled an entire rugby team. She blamed her funny walk the next day on a ride on a Bucking Bronco, I said, 'That's no way to talk about the Wigan Warriors.'

It was lethal Blanche; we went to this bar where they were doing drinking games. We were playing *shag, marry or kill*. You get given three names and you have to say which one you'd shag, marry or kill. I shagged Ashley Banjo, married Dermot O'Leary and killed Piers Morgan; Mandy shagged Daniel Craig, married Paul Hollywood and killed David Walliams. Meryl shagged all three of hers.

We spent the day by the pool drinking followed by getting ready drinking and then going out drinking. Meryl fell asleep on a sun lounger without suntan lotion and woke up four hours later, blistered and furious that no one had woke her up for a vodka. That night she wore a flame-red PVC mini skirt and boob tube to match her tan, with a white bra underneath. You couldn't tell where her outfit finished and her sunburn started. It's a good job the skirt is wipe clean, she couldn't get to the toilet so just squatted on the dancefloor and shook herself dry to *Night Fever*.

You should have seen us on the plane home, we were hanging out our arses. Meryl insisted we finish off the weekend with a bottle of overpriced mini-Prosecco each. I don't know what she does for a living but the amount she spent on the duty-free cart would stock Santa's workhouse. She bought four airline-exclusive gift sets of *Northern* by Jane McDonald, each containing an eau de toilette, body spray and hand cream.

When I got home, I spent the next week stinking of vodka, trying not to be sick, and swearing I'd never touch alcohol again. I'd do anything to go back. Instead, that bastard wants us to take the baby to Majorca. I said, 'Who's going to pack?' He said, 'You are.' I just looked at him with hate. We compromised in the end, we're off to Cyprus and his mum is doing the packing.

How can I get out of it? The last thing I want to do is take an infant on holiday. I want to spend the money on a girls' weekend in Ibiza.

Luv ya Blanche,

Jess.

From: Blanche
To: Jessica Watkiss
Subject Re: Hen party

Dear Jess,

What you need is a pamper session. I realise all the beauty salons are shut because of Covid but surely you know a beautician who can come round to your house and do your nails on the sly? It might freshen you up a bit. You can send the baby to its grandmother for the afternoon and send your fella to Coventry. All the women around here are having illegal facials. "Cleaners" are coming around at an alarming rate. All armed with moisturiser in their bleach bottles and nail files in their cleaning kits. Wendy at number forty-three had a nasty accident last week when her "cleaner" forgot to put moisturiser in her bottle of bleach and gave Wendy a Toilet Duck facial. She was in the burns unit for a fortnight, her skin looked bloody amazing when she came out.

You're very lucky that your in-laws are so helpful. My flatmate Fergie has been up the walls all week. Literally climbed onto the top shelf and stayed there shaking like a shitting leaf after her ex-in-laws made contact. She received a letter to say they were withdrawing her paid protection. By Wednesday afternoon a burly bloke had come round and confiscated the corgi and swan which stood guard outside the flat. She's convinced herself that every noise is a hitman out to get her. She's even started barking at the door to scare people away. Luckily, thirst forced her from the shelf and after a couple of gin and tonics later she calmed right down. She's much easier to control when lubricated.

I know it's not the same as a girlie holiday, but you might be able to rekindle the romance with him upstairs. Failing that, you can latch on to another group of girls on the first night and leave him to deal with Fido. Try and relax. Stop putting too much pressure on yourself. You'll soon be back from maternity and behind that desk at the dealership.

Blanche

Michael Gove MP
House of Commons
Westminster

14th April 2020

Dear Blanche,

Boris is in hospital and it's left me plotting, purely for the good of the country you understand, if the worst was to happen, who should replace him? I'm charismatic, educated, well-rounded and come across tremendously well on all televisual engagements. I can't help feeling that I am a natural choice for succession. What do you think? I'm hoping the position might help Widdecombe to notice me. She's power-mad and loves a leader of a political party. She makes my loins wobble in a way that I haven't experienced since I saw my picture in the paper for the first time. She's currently all over Farage like a rash. I ask myself, what's he got that I haven't? The only plausible answer is he has his own party.

It drives me to despair when I see her visiting the Parliament bar, I'm completely unnoticeable to her. It crushes me when I see her and Farage sitting cosily in the corner. They play footsie whilst she downs a pint of stout and he sips a Cinzano and lemonade. I have to have a few lines of Columbian marching powder to perk me up. I want to declare myself to her. To cha-cha over and take her by her saggy jowls and kiss her.

I'm going to carry on making entries into my little book of blackmail. Should Boris succumb to this virus and the opportunity arises for a new leader, I want to make sure I have the best shot possible of getting the nominations needed for the leadership. When I visited Boris yesterday, I put a DNR sign above his bed. I felt a twinge of guilt, but it only lasted until I reached the door. Sometimes we must create our own destiny.

Please find enclosed the blank cheque as required.

Kind regards,

Michael Gove MP

Blanche
Boadicea Manor
Salford 6

Gove,

I could think of no one more superior than yourself to run this country. I often think, who has all the talent on the front benches, despite having a face only a mother could love, I can think of no one other than your egocentric self.

It's healthy to have a passion in life. Most people enjoy sport, literature or music, if Widdecombe is your thing, who am I to judge? I will obviously. I'm sure she's a fine tractor of a woman for you to focus your attention. You could be like the Posh and Becks of politics but without the talent or the looks.

Yes, being Prime Minister would suit you very well. I think perhaps, the only way you're going to get your lady Widdecombe, is to stop at nothing to become the leader. You have my vote, Gove. There will come a day in the future when you know I am going to make it all happen for you. Have trust and faith, and you will lead.

Blanche

Victoria Townsend
29 Hellbourne Close
Salford

15ᵗʰ April 2020

Dear Blanche,

I'd love to go out down Canal Street, I'd love to just go out, who would I go with? I don't have friends to call up and talk to, never mind going out into town. We couldn't now anyway with the lockdown. I'll keep it in mind when we get to the other side of this pandemic. I could ask my sister if she'd like to accompany me. What would we look like Blanche, a couple of women nearly seventy going out into town? They probably wouldn't let us in the pubs. I hope they come up with a vaccination soon so we can all get back on with our lives. I realise that sounds ironic coming from the lady who doesn't really have one.

The days feel a whole lot longer now we're stuck in the house together. I used to look forward to the respite I'd get from him whilst he was at work, a break from his smell, now there's no escape. I think I'm glad to be honest, it's really made me look at him. There is nothing but venom between us. I'm already old Blanche, but I certainly don't want to be bitter. I thought to myself how much happier I'd be if I was enduring this lockdown on my own. Maybe it's time to sell up and get a little one-bedroom flat or a caravan somewhere nice. I've always liked South Wales. The kids could come and visit me during the school holidays. It would be nice to spend some quality time with them. I see them now, they just rush in and out, they've always got somewhere to go. I could get myself a little job on the caravan site, perhaps in the launderette. I could see myself as a modern-day Dot Cotton. I'd have a chance to meet people and have a conversation whilst I folded up their smalls. I might even make some new friends. It would be nice to watch *Emmerdale* with someone I liked.

I'll keep this letter short, there seems to be even less to talk about whilst in lockdown than usual.

Kind regards,

Victoria.

Blanche
Boadicea Manor
Salford 6

Dear Victoria,

Now you're cooking with gas. Get planning your great escape. Get that house sold and disappear into the sunset, or wherever it is you want to go.

I planned an escape once, I was in Holloway at the time. A couple of the girls on the wing had planned it all out and invited me to go with them after I'd shared my contraband custard creams. We were to chisel our way out onto the landing and then shimmy up the ventilation shaft onto the roof. Once there, we'd zip wire ourselves over the perimeter fence and over the guards' heads to freedom. One of the girls who was inside for an unpaid parking fine had got a bent screw to install it for her. This prison officer had once received a parking ticket for stopping on double yellows. He'd pulled up outside the vets in a rush to be with his Dutch Hound whilst she took her last breaths. He's hated traffic wardens ever since and was fully sympathetic to my fellow inmate. The escape was planned for a night this warden was on duty, it had been timed for him to take a bathroom break at the stroke of midnight.

I didn't go in the end. I had a lover on the inside. That's not the reason I stayed, I'd drank a bottle of contraband gin and slept through the whole thing. Three of them got away and live a wonderful life in Scarborough by all accounts. Last I heard they were running a crazy golf by the prom.

Let that be a lesson to you Victoria, even in a maximum-security prison, there's always hope for escape.

Take care cock,

Blanche

From: Sophie McBride
To:Blanche
Subject Home Schooling

17th April 2020

Dear Blanche,

The in-laws are a waste of time. I asked them if they would look after the kids to give me a break, they said they couldn't as we're not in their Covid bubble. I can't believe Boris has shut the schools. I understand there is a virus on the rampage but how is any single mother supposed to entertain a child and a teenager? It was bad enough having to close the salon. I don't know how I'm going to pay for everything over the next few months. I miss the gossip from my old dears. Now I'm stuck in with two kids who are rebelling because their dad has buggered off. I'm going out of my mind. Marcus hasn't sent a penny despite promising he'd always be there. Where is now eh? With his toy boy. I sent him a text and said *your a pissing teacher, you teach the kids*. He texted back, *it's you're, not your*. I'm worried I'm going to send them back thick as pig shit.

   I'm really trying but I have no idea what I'm doing. I've tried to teach them about Ancient Egypt. I think they understood the importance of the Nile, but then Tilly, the youngest asked me, 'Mummy, how did they make the Pyramids?' I didn't have a clue, so I just wrapped her head to toe in bog roll and let her run about the house like an Egyptian mummy.

   Maths isn't going much better either, trigonometry may as well be a foreign language. I've never used it since I left school so it can't be that important. I've shown John adding and subtraction by using Tangfastics as counters. If he gets a question right he can have one. He said now he's fifteen it's a bit immature and he'd rather do it with cans of beer. They're both on a sugar rush all afternoon.

I can't wait to drop them off again at the school gates. Virus or no virus, the second those school bells ring they'll be in uniform. I'm considering camping out to form a queue the night before it reopens like they do when there's a sale on at Next.

Tallulah, my best friend, has been posting videos on Instagram of her teaching her kids Latin and the clarinet. I can't even teach mine to brush their own teeth. Tilley decided to do some handprints last week, I thought she'd got the paint out, but she'd done it by using her own poo. They're both possessed. Surely they can't be mine.

I've put them both in front of Finding Nemo and told them it's a lesson on global warming. They've watched it 3,984 times. I mixed it up by putting Toy Story on but John said it was childish. I told him to shut up and watch it or I'd put the child lock back on the wifi. I'm one teenage hormone-induced tantrum away from locking him in a cupboard. This year his teacher, Miss Tickle, can have whatever she wants for Christmas. I don't know she copes with thirty of the pubescent horrors on a daily basis. By the time it's their afternoon lesson I'm normally on my second glass of Chardonnay, Tilly has stuck something up her nose and John has tried sneaking away five times to leave a teenage gift in one of his socks.

Blanche, help me before I've gone completely insane. At least having the kids at home has taken my mind off Marcus and his fella during the daytime. As soon as the house goes quiet, I'm back to torturing myself with *what-ifs* and *buts*.

Demented regards,

Sophie

From: Blanche
To:Sophie McBride
Subject Re: Home Schooling

Dear Sophie,

With friends with pretentious names like Tallulah, you're asking for trouble. She's probably bribed her child with the promise of a new pony to make that video. You're being far too soft, I've enclosed two muzzles and a cattle prod. Now chain the snotty-nosed little shits down to the table and tell them they are not leaving until they can recite Moby Dick off by heart. If they dare to look up from the book, lunge at them with the prod and punish them by making them watch a Boris Johnson press conference. Their homework can be to de-babble it for the nation.

Afternoon lessons should be home economics, give them a scrubbing brush and bleach and tell them to get going. Make sure you give them rubber gloves, you don't want to burn their hands and arouse suspicion of neglect. Your primary mistake is thinking of them as children, they are slaves.

I speak from my own teaching experience. When Princess Di asked me to home school the princes I was very strict. I had to be. Di had let them run amok in the palace. They came to me with no boundaries and left two months later with a few broken bones but as fully rounded humans. When she passed, Charles phoned me up and asked if I would like to adopt them. He had no idea Harry was biologically mine. I would have helped him out, only I wasn't maternal and had my hands full as Tony Blair's advisor. Camilla didn't want anything to do with them, she made the boys sleep in the Corgis' beds for the first few years. When I schooled them, I taught them everything they needed to know to grow up to be modern men. I replaced English Literature with Victoria Wood studies and replaced geography with day trips to HMP Holloway, it's what Diana would have wanted.

Don't worry too much about formal education. Even if they are as dense as a brick, which they sound, they can always get a job as a politician. Talking of which, you're absolutely right to be annoyed that they've closed the schools. If I was you, I'd be marching at Number 10.

On a serious note, have you considered going to group therapy to discuss Marcus? You might bump into Philip Schofield's wife. That really was the worst kept secret in showbiz. But still, shows you you're not alone in turning your old man into a screaming queen.

I'll love you and leave you,

Blanche

Diane Abbott MP
House of Commons
London

24th April 2020

Dear Blanche,

Sorry it's taken me a long time to write back with the details of Cilla. It's been an emotional month: Jeremy left the office as our leader for the last time on the 4th April, I've been sitting in my office clutching his picture ever since. I've been playing Celine Dion on loop. I only snapped out of it when the cleaner came in to mop up the tears which had seeped underneath the door.

I managed to find Cilla's address for you. She is relentless in her communications with Jonathan Ashworth MP. They've been in direct correspondence on an almost weekly basis. She's been offering him ludicrous suggestions which will doom the party should he act upon them.

I infiltrated Jonathan's office in the dead of night at the end of March. I'd gone during the daytime when it was open and signed myself in under a false name, Enaid Ttobba, then hid in the toilets until eight o'clock. When I crept out into the lobby it was pitch black apart from the light from the vending machine. As I was a little peckish, I stopped by for a Star Bar. I didn't have any coins on me, luckily it had chip and pin. I can never have chocolate on its own because of my diabetes. I made a cup of tea in the little kitchen to accompany my confectionary. I was far too eager to drink it, I scolded my tongue. I'm afraid I spat it out and spilt the rest on the floor in shock. I rinsed the mug and then filled it with cold water to submerge my tongue in. Remembering my first aid training I kept it in there for ten minutes. I may have left a red lipstick mark on the mug as I didn't have time to clean it, but I knew the cleaners would be in first thing and I was determined to act with stealth-like speed and precision whilst not leaving any evidence.

I woke up at one am on the kitchenette floor. I only shut my eyes to adjust them to the light in the hallway. I must have been exhausted on the account of my diabetes. I found my way to Ashworth's office by feeling my way along the corridor. His door was locked. I used my hairpin to fiddle the flimsy lock. I left it in there to make sure I didn't get trapped if the door shut behind me. It was pitch black but thinking on my feet I put my password into his computer to get light from the screen.

It didn't take long to find what we wanted. There was letters from Cilla going back to August 2015. He kept them unlocked in a cabinet filled under *manifesto*. It was next to his copy of *How to Win Friends and Influence People*, it was still in its protective cover. I took all the letters and left. I'm certain I didn't leave a single trace of myself anywhere. I've shredded all the letters but photocopied the one below to give you Cilla's address.

Kind regards,

The Midnight Spy

P.S I didn't sign it from myself in case the letter was found — Diane x

Dressing Room 3
ITV London Studios

7ᵗʰ December 2019

Surprise, Surprise Jonathan,

Cilla here. What's it all about Jonny? You've been on that campaign trail for weeks now, you must be shattered. Jeremy looks like he's gorra cob on. I've had a think about your last letter. I bet if the public can see how funny you are, you'll win the elections in a landslide. Let the electorate know you've got a sense of humour, that you don't mind a bit of joshing. Follow my advice and you'll be entering parliament as the Government in office and not a member of the opposition. Imagine that feeling when you step inside love.

You're my world, you know that don't you Jonny, but you're just not connecting with the voters. Reach out to a member of the Tories and give them some filth on Corbyn. People admire those who can communicate on both sides of the benches. It can be your moment of truth. If I were you, I'd do it in a very public way to ensure election glory.

Will you write back soon and tell me all about it?
Ta'ra for now,

Cilla

Blanche
Boadicea Manor
Salford 6

26ᵗʰ April 2020

Randy,

That thing I needed you to do. Get down to the ITV studios in London. I need you to stake out dressing room 3, I want full descriptions of all who go in and out.

If anyone stops and asks you why you're out and about in lockdown, tell them you're a Tory MP.

Give my love to Mangled Mel.

Blanche.

MAY

From: Jessica Watkiss
To: Blanche
Subject Lockdown

5th May 2020

Dear Blanche,

Boris has only gone and extended the fucking lockdown. Our holiday has been bastarding cancelled. I got an email from the tour operator saying I could either have my money back in twenty-eight days or I can have the amount in vouchers immediately. I chose vouchers as I'm determined to get away, infant or no infant. I went online ready to rebook only to find the cost of all the holidays had doubled and my vouchers are worth sod all. They're taking the absolute piss. I was looking forward to getting to the hotel, handing over Fido to the kids' club, putting my all-inclusive wristband on and then picking Fido up two weeks later when I checked out.

That bastard isn't arsed. He's a key worker so still gets out of the house, since when did being a mechanic have the same social status as being a doctor? All he does is change the oil filters. We've been going to the front door and clapping every Thursday for the NHS and keyworkers like everyone else on the street. Suzi next door has made clapping into a competition, she's illuminated her brickwork with the rainbow flag and put a huge *THANK YOU NHS* sign on a professionally printed banner which hangs out of her bedroom window. There's a little picture of a vehicle from each one of the rescue services underneath.

When we came out to clap last Thursday she was done up like a dog's dinner: she had stilettos on that looked like tiny scaffolding poles on the underneath of each heel, skin-tight leather pants and a white blouse without any sort of debris collected on it from a day battling with the kids. I stood there in my Eeyore onesie, I'd not taken it off for the last five days. God, I hate her. She shouted over to the bastard, 'Course, we're all clapping for you too you know, we appreciate all key workers.' I turned to him and said, 'I ain't bastarding clapping for you'. Then I looked over at that practically perfect bitch, looked at her rainbow-coloured brickwork and said, 'I didn't know you were a dyke, Suzie.' I turned in my giraffe slippers and marched straight back inside. I'm not proud of it but it gave me momentary satisfaction. It must have struck a chord as the next day she'd replaced the rainbow colours with projected images of the NHS logo.

I couldn't get a supermarket delivery slot this week, I had no choice but to venture out to do a big shop. We got there and they had no special prams to put Fido in, I had to put him in the baby carrier and strap him to my back. The trouble was, he'd fallen asleep and I forget he was there. I only remembered when I leaned against the wall. The check-out assistant looked at me in disgust, especially when she bleeped through three bottles of wine for £12.

I'm usually a very calm person when out shopping but during the lockdown, I've found myself wanting to murder people for getting so close that I can feel their breath on the back of my neck. I've taken the lockdown rules seriously. I haven't socialised with anyone at all. I'd have to get dressed for a start and I haven't got the energy. Why are people so desperate to snatch a bag of wonky onions that they can't wait until I've passed the hazard markers on the floor?

Do you know anyone who wants to buy £900 of holiday vouchers? I could do with the money for more wine. What I really want is to get back to work to be my own person again. I must be the only mother who can't stand being on maternity leave. I tell you, if Boris dares to put us back on lockdown when I'm due to go back I'll kill him.

Wish I was there,

Jess x

From: Blanche
To: Jessica Watkiss
Subject Re: Lockdown

Dear Jess,

I would suggest throwing yourself on the floor in a dramatic coughing fit the next time an eager shopper comes into your personal space, they'll soon back off. Other techniques I recommend include a good old-fashioned slap across the face or barge into them as they pass a very fancy shop display. There is something rather satisfying about seeing a woman lying spread-eagled in a fallen display of Canesten Duo. Give them a firm push as they're reaching into a deep freeze for a prawn ring and swiftly close the lid. Princess Di used to do that when the photographers got too close to her in Kwik-Save.

I'll take those holiday vouchers off your hands. I know a woman who is desperate to get away from her husband a little more than yourself. I've enclosed a blank cheque, make it out to yourself and sign it B. Johnson. All perfectly legal and preapproved. If you could send the vouchers direct to her that would be grand: Victoria Townsend, 29 Hellbourne Close, Salford. Just put a little note in to say, *Love from Blanche.*

Don't be too hard on him upstairs. I know you're exhausted, but have you considered making a bit of an effort for yourself as well as for him? You might find it'll do you good. Have a wash and peel yourself out of that onesie. Bring the holiday to you. Send Fido to his grandparents and have a nice night eating pizza and drinking wine. Remember what life was like before having the baby. Princess Di loved a date night. She'd get a video from Blockbusters with Dodi and pack the boys off to their dad for the evening. She'd be a new woman the next day after having an evening out of the media circus. They say a change is as good as rest don't they, what a load of old shite. Wear your spandex pants and squeeze into your little black dress. Before you know it, you'll be back at work and won't have time for each other, especially with a baby thrown in the mix. You're absolutely right to be furious at Boris, can you imagine the number of holidays he's ruined? I'd be very tempted to protest at Downing St if I was you.

Keep safe.

Blanche.

From:Randy Mottershed
To: Blanche
Subject Amanda Holden

8th May 2020

Dear Blanche,

I drove down to London as soon as I received your letter. I collected Alex
on the way as Mel was too busy taking selfies for her OnlyFans account.
She's doubled her subscribers since I last wrote to you. She's spent some
of her new money on a vending machine she keeps next to her bed. She
asks her Twitter followers to vote for which chocolate bar she should
consume next. I'm worried she won't fit out of the house soon. It's not
healthy eating twenty-eight chocolate bars a day. I said that to her and
she just replied, 'It's my body my choice Randy, have you not heard of
#MeToo?' I thought that was against sexual harassment, not diabetes.

It took forever to get to London due to my detour to Peterborough
to collect Alex. It's such a small world isn't Blanche? I couldn't believe
it when she said she knew all about you and how nice you'd been
helping her find a man. There was no funny business between Alex and
me. I told her all about mine and Mel's lifestyle choices. She was very
understanding but said it wasn't for her. She was splendid Blanche.
She didn't mind waiting in the car when I pulled up in a layby on the
outskirts of Luton. Mel had tweeted to her followers that I'd be stopping
there which resulted in a queue of cars filled with men trying to get
their hands on a signed photo of Mel.

London was a bugger to park. No one asked us what we were doing
out and about during lockdown. We walked around the studios and Alex
had an idea that we should just be bold and go in the main entrance to
try and find the dressing room. A very pleasant receptionist with a red

bob and the teeth of Janet Street-Porter asked us to sign in. She was talking to people on her headset at the same time, 'I don't know Brad, I'm not a pissing psychic I don't know why they haven't turned up.' Then she turned to me and Alex and said, 'Do you know about extramarital sex?' Alex replied to her, 'He's a dogger with a wife who flashes her unmentionables on Twitter, and I don't have sex in marriage never mind out of it.' The receptionist beamed, pressed and held the button on her headset and talked into the mouthpiece, 'Brad, I've got an idea.'

We were both marched upstairs, shoved through a door and sat down on a sofa in front of Ruth Langsford and Eamonn Holmes. Lights shone in our faces and separate cameras focused on each of us as Eamonn talked directly into another camera, 'Welcome back to *This Morning*. We're joined by a man that knows a thing or two about dogging and an open-minded single woman who's looking for the perfect partner.'

We were both a bit stunned but answered questions as we were grilled for ten minutes on the most intimate parts of our sex lives. I told them all about Mangled Mel and her OnlyFans site and how I work the camera when she's performing. Alex said how she couldn't take part in dogging even if she wanted to as she couldn't find a partner to go with. Mel text me afterwards to say one of her videos had gone viral because of our appearance. By the end of the show, Mel had gained another 100,000 followers.

When the cameras stopped rolling Ruth asked us if we'd like a tour of the building as we'd saved the day by standing in at such short notice. Said she wouldn't mind giving dogging a go herself but Eamonn wouldn't share a packet of crisps never mind his wife. It was an education seeing the workings of a professional studio. Alex had a genius idea to ask to see the dressing rooms. Dressing room number one was shared by the *Loose Women,* number two was Ant & Dec and number three was Amanda Holden. I gave a knock on the door and Amanda answered. She was there recording a new series, *Britain's Pets Have Talent.* She sounded like a pissed scouser when she spoke. She cracked the door open enough that I could see the room was filled with fan mail. Alex walked right past her inviting herself into Amanda's room and asked for a selfie. Whilst Alex distracted Amanda, I had a quick look at the letters. They were all addressed to Labour MPs. One name had multiple correspondences, Jonathan Ashworth MP.

I hope that's of some use to you. I didn't realise it would be so much fun in London. I felt Alex brought me out of my shell. Despite the dogging, I'm quite the introvert. Alex insisted we stayed in London for the day before heading back up north. We had a lovely walk down the Thames. I enjoyed a two-way conversation, though Alex's phone was constantly interrupting. Honestly Blanche, I rather relished being the centre of attention, just once. If you ever need anything else, just say the word.

All the very best,

Randy

From:Blanche
To: Randy Mottershed
Subject Re: Amanda Holden

Dear Randy,

You're like a Hercule Poirot, I had no idea you'd make such a good detective. I hope Mangled Mel knows what a lucky lady she is to have such a talented man to keep her warm at night. I'm sorry I didn't see your TV debut. My flatmate Fergie gets upset if she doesn't get her daily dose of *Homes Under the Hammer*. She's waiting for the day they show a suitable castle she can pay for with her supermarket loyalty points. Anyway, the information you got for me was priceless Randy and I'm forever grateful. You may just have saved the future of our country.

I'll let you get back to planning your dogging event. With all the publicity you and Mel have had, you'll have to look for a bigger venue.

Kind regards,

Blanche

Boris Johnson MP
10 Downing St
Westminster

10th May 2020

Blanche,

How wondrous to be writing to you again after my brush with the virus. I've been back at work for three weeks now. I've begged Dom to put me on furlough. I've been busy making decision after decision and addressing the nation daily. I'm getting rather a lot of stick for my conferences. If only the people of the nation were as easy to have beaten up as journalists. I may stutter and stammer my way through the conferences but so would you if there was a chance that lurking behind all those press cameras was Sir Trevor McDonald. I'm terrified the next press question could be from him. I've been getting some nasty things posted through the letterbox and I'm sure it's him. Last week an unsolicited parcel arrived containing an iron and a hairbrush, I'm treating it as a hate crime.

It was awfully mean-spirited of you to jest that Sir Trevor could get into the hospital. The fear kept me from my slumber, I had to discharge myself for sanity. It was a disappointment as I enjoyed the daily jam sandwiches for elevenses.

I've become very strict on the expenditure in Downing Street to make up this damned money to pay Sir Trevor. I put a stop to the purchase of a new clicker for the presentations at the daily conference. I've briefed the team to say, 'next slide please,' and Theresa will press the button in the next room. Every penny helps. I'm looking forward to being finished with the whole sorry saga.

I do wish you'd never mentioned Sir Trevor McDonald. A couple of

Eton bullies would have been much cheaper for the protection of the ex-Royals. I told Dominic the whole story. He said he'd keep me safe and take full control of my office to give me some R & R. He's given me a tiny earpiece to wear. Now he can tell me exactly what to say when I'm questioned. It's marvellous. I said to him, 'Dom, it's like I'm your puppet and you're my master.' He told me to shut up and eat my beans on toast.

Things have been a little strained between me and him recently. He's moved into the spare room in number ten in case there are any emergencies during the night. Carrie isn't pleased, but as I said to her, it's only for a short time and at least he's not at the foot of the bed, which is a shame as I find his closeness a comfort.

It's a true delight to have someone like-minded to talk to Blanche. I don't understand the big words Carrie uses, Dom explains them to me in pictures. Between you and I Blanche, I'm desperate to get away on a little break. I've been thinking of visiting Trump. He sent me some pictures of his bunker on Snapchat, it's like a man cave. If I didn't have to find the money for the protection of Meghan and Harry, I could build my own. Somewhere to escape from my subordinates in Parliament. It's become a playground I can't control.

Do you have any money to pay Sir Trevor, a couple of million as a down payment should keep him at bay. Yesterday I found the brakes on my bike had been cut. It's a good job I tested them before I set off to the office or I could have gone a cropper. He will stop at nothing to terrorise me.

With great worry and affection,

Boris

P.S I've enclosed another blank cheque for your service. The only true value for money service this Government has got right so far. Whoever is in charge needs a bloody good kick in the old gluteus maximus.

Blanche
Boadicea Manor
Salford 6

Boris,

You can't run from Trevor forever. Have you tried negotiating a payment plan? You can call a debt management company to do it on your behalf. Me mam had to do that when she ran up a huge debt with the catalogue, they're bleeding awful things. You can have a new set of pans for £3.49 a week for thirty weeks. You think, *that's cheap and manageable*, and before you know it you've kitted out your whole house and bought a snooker table for the kitchen. You pray on a bingo win to pay it all off. She was a proud woman me mam, she'd never take a handout. She was paying off her all-weather lilac pashmina until the day she died.

Blanche

Blanche
Boadicea Manor
Salford 6

12th May 2020

Cilla
Dressing Room 3
ITV Studios
London

Well, well, well. Look who's trying to make a return from the dead. Couldn't be happy to bow out with your posthumous ITV special, you've had to resort to inhabiting the body of a *Britain's Got Talent* judge. Always desperate for the limelight wasn't you Cilla?

What are you playing at handing out shite advice to Labour MPs? You swore you had no idea you'd been booked to sing at the Tory party conference all those years ago. Blamed it on Bobby and said you'd turn up anywhere if there was a microphone. I recall a time when you'd turn up anywhere and do anything for five bob and a packet of Woodbine. I know the real you Priscilla White and don't you forget it.

The spring of '63 when you come trotting down the Blackpool seafront in your red knee-high cowboy boots and mini skirt. You had your thighs on display and shown even more to the highest bidder. Don't ever forget we're cut from the same cloth me and you Cilla. I was working the promenade because I had no choice after I walked out on that sap of a first husband. I had to bring home money to pay me mam some lodgings after dad had pissed off. You did it for attention. Hemming up your mini skirt so it was nothing but a belt. You had no regard for the rules of the street. You thought you owned the promenade from Tower to South Pier. You took the punters from all the working girls every night for two weeks solid. Taking the food out of their little ones' mouths.

You know, we all talked, all wanted you gone. You went a step too far the night you let a stag party take you up the tower. There was enough of them for every working girl to earn enough to keep themselves for a week, but you kept them all for yourself. You broke every unwritten rule in the working girls' book. That's why I pushed you in front of the Blackpool tram. It was no accident. I saw the heel of your left boot stuck in the tram track and took the opportunity for all the girls on the beat that night. You should have seen your face when that tram was coming towards you, screaming like a common tart.

I've never seen such a good performance as the one you gave that evening. The tram didn't even touch you. The brakes had been pulled so hard it stopped at least two feet away from you. You gave the performance of a lifetime to those crowds and emergency services. If it wasn't for the sympathy you got from the national press because of that incident, you would never have got your first number one. *Anyone Who Had a Heart*, ironic coming from the bitch who voted for Thatcher. You turned your back on Liverpool quicker than you used to drop your knickers when your first royalties came through.

We might have become best pals Cilla, but it suited your narrative to be seen in the public's eyes as the girl so kind she could forgive anything. After all, they were the ones buying your records, if only they knew they were dubbed.

I'll get to the point, back off sending letters to Labour or you can be sure the actress whose body you're in will find herself beneath a bus, and this time I'll make sure it hits.

Blanche

P.S Shag, marry, avoid - Les Dennis, Neil Morrisey, Simon Cowell.

P.P.S Remember that last holiday in Jamaica, what a bloody blast.

Cilla
Dressing Room 3
ITV Studios
London

14th May 2020

Blanche,

What can I say, you found me. Walking into these studios again was like coming home. I might be in Amanda's body but I'm still Queen of Saturday night TV. She got her big break as a contestant on *Blind Date*, she owes everything she's got to me.

You're forgetting I got you your big break too. If I hadn't introduced you to that producer, you'd be less Tiller Girl and more backroom girl, which is what you were when I met you. It was good though wasn't it Blanche, the day I got me first number one. We went back to Scotty Road, put my record on repeat and sang it all night.

Let's not fall out Blanche, we had too many quarrels when we were alive. Well, you were forever swanning about with that Lady Di, you were like the cat that got the cream when you hung around with her, Lady Muck. We were a killer team you and me. You with your tassels and me on the small screen, no one could match us. You know, I didn't say it enough, but I didn't half love you, Blanche. There was nothing we couldn't do when we put our minds to it.

I was in pieces when you were kidnapped. I was down the police station morning, noon and night putting pressure on the bizzies to find you. I took it to the press when you were still gone two days later. It didn't help though did it, they were still bleeding useless. That's when I called Trevor.

Of course I knew it was the Tory party conference I was singing at, you are soft at times. Bobby didn't book anything without checking it through me first. Apart from you, Thatcher was the only person I looked up to. She was hard, she had to be. I understood her. In a man's world, a woman has got to have the biggest balls. I never let your support of Labour get in the way of our friendship and I hope to God you don't let it now.

I won't stop writing to Labour, I'll be making sure the Tories are in power for a long time yet. You're forgetting who you're threatening Blanche, I know your bark's worse than your bite.

Oh Blanche, I'm dead sorry about leaving your body on the plane. I'd taken two Valium with a bottle of cider, I didn't have a clue what was going on when we landed back in London. Still, I gave you a lovely send-off at your funeral. I kept your ashes in an urn in the downstairs toilet so I could talk to you every time I went to spend a penny. Like we use to do in the clubs. It's a shame no one came to your wake. I felt guilty about forgetting to put an announcement in the press. The papers didn't cover your passing at all, they were too busy printing about the millennium bug and the trial of a doctor turned serial killer. No one knew you were gone, you just faded away into insignificance.

Love you old girl,

Cilla

P.S I shagged all three

Victoria Townsend
29 Hellbourne Close
Salford

15th May 2020

Dear Blanche,

Thank you so much for the vouchers, I don't know what to say. I was stunned when I opened the envelope. Thank you doesn't quite seem enough. We're all brainwashed by the news to believe there's only bad in this world and there's not, there are kind people like you. I've booked myself a week in Santorini next month. I'm just hoping the travel restrictions are lifted by then. I'm not going with anybody, just me. I've not even told anyone Blanche, I feel like Shirley Valentine, only I'll definitely be coming back. I can't wait to be me, to reinvent myself for one whole week. I won't tell people I'm Victoria who's trapped in a semi-detached in Salford with a husband she hates. I think I'll tell people I'm Vicki who finished nurse training all those years ago, or perhaps I'm Vicky who is a retired primary school teacher, I would have liked that.

I invited my three kids for dinner last week on a night Dave was out. I'd planned it meticulously and rehearsed what I was going to say: *You know I love you all so very much, and I know you all love me and would want me to be happy. Well, I haven't been happy for some time with your dad. I've decided to be happy but to do that I need to leave your father and start a fresh life without him.* It didn't quite happen like that. The three of them were arguing over something stupid. I can't remember what it was now. I asked them to listen but they kept talking over me. I'd spent all day preparing this meal, a beef roast. I'd even done extra gravy for

Sharon as I know she loves it, cooked pigs in blankets for Nicholas and bought a mint Viennetta for William. I set the table with the good cutlery, I even polished it. They didn't notice. Why would they? I wanted a calm atmosphere for what I was about to tell them, sounds stupid now writing it down. I ended up slamming my knife and fork down and snapped, 'I'm leaving your father.'

You know, they didn't ask me why or if I was OK. They didn't seem to care about me at all. Sharon and Nicholas just questioned who would get the house and how would their inheritance be divided up. I feel like spending the lot. I can't believe I've raised such selfish sods. I told them not to tell their father. He'd sooner see me dead than walk out of this house and be happy.

The youngest, William, texted me later that evening, *Get out and live. Love you.* It froze me to the spot. I was completely overcome. I cried, Blanche, for the first time in years. The next day Sharon came round with a suitcase, hugged me, and offered to help me pack. She's a good girl really, my girl. Tough as old boots is Sharon, but has nothing but love in her heart. She's the sort of person you'd always want on your team. It's funny what you accept when you don't know any different. I can't wait to walk out that door a free woman. A single woman. Me.

I'm going to plan a whole new life while I'm lying on a beach drinking cocktails. You've done this Blanche, given me strength. Anything I can ever do for you, I will be humbled.

Sincerely yours,

Vicky x

Blanche
Boadicea Manor
Salford 6

Vicky,

You can repay me by making sure you get out there and live your life and give the barman a good rogering. Children can be such shits, can't they? Sell up and spend their inheritance on a round-the-world cruise. Live out your retirement disgracefully.

Don't you mention those vouchers again. I'm sure a time will come when I need your help, we've built up quite a friendship haven't we, Vicky? It's my pleasure to be able to send you away for a week and I do love Santorini. Well, I've never been to Santorini as such, but I once went to a Greek fish restaurant in London, so it's as good as. Me and Princess Di popped into *Constantino's The Hake* in between my matinée and evening performances. It was 1982 and I was starring as Marilyn in the West End transfer of *Insignificance*. I was overlooked for a Laurence Olivier award, the original cast member got nominated, not that I'm bitter. I don't remember the food from *Constantino's,* the waiters were delicious. Great big hairy Greeks, hands like shovels and with the sexual stamina of a bull in mating season, so Di tells me. She was popping back for coffee and afters three times a day until she met Dodi.

I'm quite sure I could have had any of them I wanted but I was devoted to my late husband, Lord Woolworth Mountbatten, Monty for short. He was the love of my life Victoria, not like your Dave. Monty was the full package: handsome, rich and besotted with me. If only I'd known he'd be taken from me too soon, I would have appreciated the time we had all the more. I still have flashbacks of the petrol lawnmower incident. It makes my flatmate Fergie jump out of her skin. You don't get over something like seeing your husband chased down by a Polish gardener who's forgotten to take his antipsychotic meds easily you know. By all accounts, he should have been in an institution, the gardener, not my husband. Monty was a very caring soul and had signed the gardener out of the hospital into his care for rehabilitation.

We got married in 1970 and immediately moved into a beautiful semi-detached in Brighton. It was huge, like a manor house had been split in two, it was in the perfect location for my commute to the theatre. We'd only been there two minutes when Monty moved the gardener in after he met him at a ceremony for the Duke of Edinburgh award scheme. He was with us the whole time we were in that house without incident until the summer of '84. The gardener, Aleksandra, not a name I'll ever forget, climbed naked from the upstairs window, down the drainpipe, and broke into the garden shed. Alarm bells should have rung then, he could have just as easily used the stairs and he had the key for the shed. He started the mower up and rode it down the driveway shouting, *I'll have two pints of Newton Ridley's finest please Annie*, in a perfect Lancashire accent. Monty tried to calm him down, but it was no use. Monty could see Aleksandra was heading straight for a seagull and being a member of the RSPB, Monty leapt to the mower to try and take control and steer them back into the shed. He lost his balance on take-off and fell underneath the front wheel. The seagull got away, took off and shat on the bonnet of the mower. The driveway was covered in shredded flannel. Aleksandra was carted off and locked up. Last I heard he'd earned himself two degrees and was a Michelin star chef. Monty would have been proud.

I said to Monty when he bought that mower, 'What do we need that for, we've only got a window box?' Still, hindsight's a bugger. You must feel like that after all these years stuck in the house with Dave. Mind you, I'd rather have loved and lost like myself than loathed and been trapped like you. I know you say you don't want another man, but I do hope there's a Monty out there waiting for you.

Not long to go, Vicky, and you'll be free as a seagull. Make sure you've got your passport sorted and your money exchanged. Be sure to buy a bottle in duty-free, you don't want to be paying over the odds for those miniatures they sell onboard. Send a postcard.

Warm wishes,

Blanche

P.S A bottle of gin wouldn't go a miss in exchange for those vouchers.

Blanche
Boadicea Manor
Salford 6

17ᵗʰ May

Diane Abbott
House of Commons
London

Diane,

No time to explain, keep your eye on Amanda Holden. If you get the chance to give her a nasty knock to the head, take it. Or lock her up.

Blanche

From: Alex Huntington
To: Blanche
Subject Naked Attraction

20th May 2020

Blanche,

What do reckon to this? I've been on twenty dates this month. I can't believe it myself. Most of them have been online due to the Covid restrictions but I've met up with a few for a walk in the park. I know it's slightly bending the rules but I'm a celebrity now Blanche. I'm absolutely shattered from all the getting ready and late nights. I'm going to have to slow down as I've put a few pounds on from all the meals in. It's been *really* nice though.

Randy called me after I got chatting to him on the online dating site, turns out it was for doggers. I must have pressed the wrong link, anyway, it doesn't matter as Randy's such a softy. He invited me down to London, he said he had to do something for you. Work was closed due to one of the doctors having Covid so I thought, why the hell not.

We only end up on *This Morning* talking about dogging. I was explaining to Ruth how I couldn't find the right man, my phone hasn't stopped buzzing since. I've had all sorts of men asking me out on dates and agents offering me deals for TV shows. I'm going to be a celebrity. I was invited to audition for *Naked Attraction*, I failed it. The casting director of *The Undateables* said they'd call me back but nothing yet. I feel like a new woman with all this attention. It's fate I wrote to you when I did, you've given me a new lease of life. If I can ever do anything for you, set you up with one of my rejections or whatever you need, just let me know.

Some of the men have been into dogging who I've dated this month. I made it very clear that I wouldn't be taking part in any activity below the waistline until I was in a committed relationship. None have progressed to a second date. I was hoping to have a man ready for Dr Altman's BBQ next month. I can't believe how quick it's come around, hasn't the year gone fast? Dr Altman has said I'm going to be the guest of honour now due to my celebrity status. She said that involves handing out the canapes. I can't wait, I really can't believe I'm the same person as I was in January.

Dr Altman's husband still hasn't come home, though he and Jesus will be at the BBQ. They've got some news to tell Dr Altman. She's looking worried but I reckon that's just the stress of finding the right balance of non-meat options for the vegans.

Dare I say it Blanche, but I think you can start searching for that hat. I can just feel that love is waiting for me around the corner. I'm so excited I could burst.

With bundles of joy,

Alex

From: Blanche
To: Alex Huntington
Subject Re: Naked Attraction

Dear Alex,

I reckon you have all the celebrity allure of Anthea Turner. I wouldn't give up the day job just yet love. You need something to fall back on should the dating show not come through and being a doctor's receptionist is very respectful. You wouldn't catch me doing it, I'd be bored shitless, but a job is a job, and you must be grateful in this climate. Anyway, who'd want to meet their other half on a dating show?

I don't know how Cilla made *Blind Date* run as long as it did. They ran out of contestants in the end and were dragging people off the street as they walked past the studios. She begged me to do it once. I said, 'Cilla, I'd rather date Boris Yeltsin.' And those bloody questions, *if I was cold how would you warm me up, and that question is to number two.* What a load of old shite, I'd put another bar on the fire.

Stick with that list of men Dr Altman gave you. I think you could be very well suited to the man with the ankle tag. At least you'd know where he was at all times, and something tells me that's very important to you.

Have a lovely time at the BBQ. Don't get pissed and make a tit out of yourself.

Blanche.

Matt Hancock MP
House of Commons
Westminster

31st May 2020

Dear Blanche,

I'm desperate for your help. Boris said you're dependable in a crisis. I've significantly messed up this time. I've been taking my facts and figures for all the government briefings from Priti Patel. I've just found out that she failed GCSE maths. I've lost the original matchbox that I had the true figures written down on, I think Rees-Mogg took it to light up one of his special cigarettes.

I fear the truth will be out soon if I don't find it. I've looked in all of Rees-Mogg's favourite places; The Shooting Room, it's where he lays back on his chaise lounge whilst he fires darts at people on benefits then WhatsApp the video to Gove; Ann Widdecombe's bedroom — fortunately that scandal hasn't made it into the nationals. Rumour has it Mogg makes Ann read the *Daily Mail* to him as they make love. She must have a revolving bedroom door, I can't keep up with the rumours of her love life.

That matchbox was perfect. Where will I ever find another one small enough to write the Tory manifest? Please help Blanche, before I'm found out and I'm turfed onto the backbenches. I'd never survive back there with the big boys.

Kind regards,

Matty

Blanche
Boadicea Manor
Salford 6

Matty,

What a terrible mess you're in. I know how you feel as I once lost Cilla Black's little black book. It had all the names of the cabin crew she'd had shot over the years for daring to look at her. She incriminated herself when she put cabin crew into *Room 101*. Luckily for Cilla, Lulu had set fire to it when she knocked over a flaming Sambuca at the BAFTAs. Cilla had asked me to look after it but I'd left it on the table after one too many glasses of Blue Nun.

Who was it that said, 'You can fool all of the people some of the time, and some of the people all the time, but you cannot fool all the people all the time'? They clearly hadn't met the front bench MPs. You all seem completely baffled 100% of the time. It's been reported that Priti thought she was off on a trip to MFI when she was invited to join the cabinet.

Back to the matchbox. Don't worry about it, get yourself a postage stamp, surely it will be big enough for the Tory facts and figures. I would suggest writing down all your fake news too so you can keep reminding yourself what you've said. Then again, you can just buy the *Daily Mail*.

When you do catch up with Rees-Mogg, please tell him to stop sending me his used underwear. I have no use for a soiled Matalan brief.

Blanche

JUNE

From: Sophie McBride
To:Blanche
Subject Dinner date

1st June 2020

Dear Blanche,

I didn't write last month as I was busy trying to get the salon ready for reopening, implementing all the social distancing and Covid regulation guidelines. I couldn't make head nor tail of them.

John and Tilly were begging me to have Marcus and his fella round, I buckled in the end and invited them for Friday night dinner. It took every bit of moral high ground I had to do it. I kept telling myself it was for the kids, it wasn't, I wanted to look the student in the eye so he could see the family he'd wrecked.

Tilly was excited to have her dad back in the house and wore her Elsa costume from *Frozen*. Even John managed to have a wash and spray deodorant without me shouting at him or making threats that I'd put him in the shower myself. I almost regretted it when I was choking on the smell of Lynx Africa all night.

I didn't know what to wear, what do you wear when your ex-husband brings his boyfriend for dinner? I don't know why but I wanted to look attractive. Why did I want recognition from them? I settled on skin-tight jeans and a new figure-hugging black vest top which had the image of the Queen's stamp portrait on it, it took a lot of effort to look casual. One thing about finding out your husband is a poof is that it does wonders for the figure. I've lost more weight on this diet than the cabbage soup, Weight Watchers and Cambridge combined. I started on the rosé at two o'clock, I couldn't face them without it. I made a lasagne, actually, I made two, one meat and one veg as I didn't know if *he*, Nathan, was a vegetarian.

They arrived at seven and it was all very polite. The kids were excited to see Nathan which pissed me off. He handed me a bottle of red which I gratefully accepted as if he wasn't the man who gifted me an album of photos with his tongue down my husband's throat. He's a blogger, whatever that is. Probably writes bollocks about bollocks and gets paid for it. We sat at the table, I purposely positioned him opposite the two kids so he could look them in the eye every time he bit into his lasagne, he chose the vegetarian one. Do you know what pissed me off the most, what drove me to the point of insanity? It was that I quite liked him. I thought he was funny and charming and intelligent. All the things I wanted to take the piss out of him for later, I couldn't. Marcus seemed happy and relaxed like this was normal. The kids were fine, Tilly sang some *Frozen* songs and John managed to have a full conversation without a single grunt or a *get off my case will you*, which he clearly reserves only for me.

By the time I served dessert we were all chatting along like we were best friends and not a totally dysfunctional unit. Nathan even made the coffees and found his way around the kitchen with ease. He didn't ask where the cups or spoons were. That's when it hit me. He'd been here before. He'd been in my house, in my kitchen, in my cupboards and no doubt, in my bed. My face must have changed as Marcus suddenly looked uncomfortable. I had visions of belting them both round the head with the cafetiere and gauging their eyes out with the teaspoon. Instead, I just said, 'Two please' when Nathan offered me sugar. I even accepted an invitation from Nathan to their flat warming party, 'Well it's not new, but now everything is out in the open I thought we'd make up for it' — I added a butter knife through the chest to my visions.

As they got their coats on to leave there was a knock at the door, the police. John had put on Instagram that he was having a dinner party with his new dad. Some bastard reported us for a breach of Covid guidelines. I was stung with a £120 fine. I didn't even think of the guidelines. What are the guidelines when your kids miss their dad who's pissed off from the marital home?

I was in a mess the next day. I needed someone to talk to who wasn't a friend or family member who could judge me so I took your advice. I googled support groups and went along to one at the LGBT Foundation's offices in the city centre. I say I went, I sat outside and watched all these women go in. I thought they'd all be masculine or dowdy women, but they weren't, they were just like me. A couple of men went in too, their wives must have run off with other women. I didn't get out of the car. I'm going to go next week though Blanche. Thank you for suggesting it, I never would have thought there'd be other people going through this too.

Take care,

Sophie.

From: Blanche
To:Sophie McBride
Subject Re: Dinner date

Dear Sophie,

Of course, you're not the only one. There are a whole gaggle of gays (is that the right word for a group of poofs), who have misled their blushing brides up the aisle and up the bum. I blame the Tories. Section 28 made it so much harder for the 90s homosexuals to be true to themselves. Imagine having the teachings of the core of who you are illegalised in schools. If you are looking for someone to blame for your lifetime of deceit, then look no further than the Conservatives. I feel it would be much healthier for you to aim your mistrust at them rather than at Marcus, who was the victim of Thatcher's law. She famously said, '*Children who need to be taught to respect traditional moral values are being taught they have an inalienable right to be gay. All of those children are being cheated of a sound start in life*'. Imagine the damage that can cause to one's self-worth. Mind you, you wouldn't have your two beautiful children if it wasn't for Marcus. You should probably still consider marching against the Tories though if the opportunity ever arose.

I'm a big believer in therapy: my mother used to invite all the mums of Chimney Pot Park round for coffee and biscuits on a Monday morning. They all drank tea, coffee was an acquired taste they couldn't afford. They'd sit there, all falling apart in their own ways. Breasts drooping down to their navel or bingo wings flapping in the breeze every time they went to dunk another custard cream in their brew. They'd discuss their good-for-nothing husbands and the dirty nets of Maureen at number 29. The highlight of the mornings was when Hillary, from number three with the nicotine-coloured door, would read the women's tea leaves. The mothers held her in high regard after she predicted her husband would be found dead if he ever cheated on her again, his body turned up three weeks later in the ship canal. The police believed he'd drunkenly stumbled in on his way home from the pub. No more questions were asked despite the canal being in the opposite direction of his way home. Hillary once predicted to me mam, *'The leaves are telling me there is a great fortune ahead for your child'*, she was over the moon. It's a pity they didn't forewarn her about my brief incarceration.

I took Princess Di to meet Hillary in the late 80s. Hillary was an old woman by then, but she still had the gift. She told Di she would have the opportunity to change the world should she choose to leave the mafia behind. Hillary had gone a bit blind so it's possible that she was mistaken. Nevertheless, Di took it very seriously and embarked on a worldwide tour visiting charities in case the tea leaves could place a curse upon her. She remembered Hillary's words on a visit to Angola in '97. I'd gone with Di to have a break from Tony Blair after agreeing to run his election campaign. Di had an idea to bring the world's attention to landmines. There was press there from every corner of the globe. She said, 'Blanche if you can run in a straight line across that sand path, I'll buy you a bottle of duty-free gin on the way home.' I was already two sheets to the wind after we'd had a champagne lunch with a local witch doctor, and I never backed away from a challenge. It wasn't till afterwards when the pictures were in the press of Di walking across a field filled with landmines that I realised she'd sent me running to clear her path. She was forever playing pranks.

Make sure you go to the therapy session. It really is a great way to meet like-minded people. You can discuss all your emotions. It would be a good idea to discuss my Section 28 theory too.

Take care, my love,

Blanche.

From: Jessica Watkiss
To: Blanche
Subject Get down on it

3rd June 2020

Hiya Blanche,

I sent the holiday vouchers as you asked. I could have cried giving them away but I cashed in the blank cheque like you said and felt immediately better. I'm going to keep the money to one side to go on another holiday when the lockdown is lifted. I've not told that *bastard* I've got the money for the holiday. He'd spend it on something practical like those things you put in the plug sockets to stop babies putting their fingers in.

I took your advice and made an effort for him. I packed Fido off to my mum's house for the night to get him out the way. I psyched myself up that this would be the night I'd put all the embarrassment of what happened at the childbirth behind us. I fully intended to replace visions in his head of me pulling out my own shite whilst he held me steady after the epidural with ones of me in a lovely fitting lace outfit. I wanted one to cover all my wobbly bits which hadn't quite deflated back into the right place. It was more for me than for him.

I spent ages looking online to choose the right one. I took advantage of Fido being silent after I'd sat him in front of CBeebies. He must be really intelligent as I didn't think a six-month-old baby would watch TV. He'll certainly be doing a lot more of it now that he does. I went on all the websites to search for the perfect outfit and finally found one which was a black sexy bra and knicker set. It wouldn't look out of place on a page three model. It had a little opaque flowing lace nightie which went over the top to camouflage my stretch marks and boost my confidence. I hate those marks. They're like little lines of my body's betrayal. As if years of shagging with the lights off to hide my cellulite wasn't bad enough, I've now had to put up blackout curtains to stop any stray light beam reflecting off my silver scars. Some of them haven't faded yet, they look like red slasher lines from a horror movie. I was really excited when this outfit which was going to transfer me from dowdy mum to sex goddess arrived. I raced upstairs to try it on. If you took it apart and stitched all the fabric together in one long line it wouldn't have been long enough to cover one fucking thigh. It was barely big enough to fit around Fido's *Paw Patrol* teddy, which is where it now lives. Skye looks like the slaggiest bitch in Adventure Bay. I stayed calm. I figured I'd just turn the lights off and hide under a twelve-tog quilt.

My mum picked Fido up in the afternoon to give me a few hours to prepare. I cleaned and scrubbed the house and washed the mountain of shitty baby grows that had built up over the last however how long. I had enough time to shampoo, condition and blow dry my hair. I even managed to shave my legs and armpits and trimmed my pubes with his beard trimmer, I figured he wouldn't mind as it was for his benefit. I wore my flowiest of pre-pregnancy dresses and even managed a bit of lippy and mascara. I felt bloody brilliant if I'm honest. I popped to Asda and bought us ingredients for fajitas and a couple of bottles of wine. When he got in at six his eyes nearly popped out of his head. He could sense he was on a promise. I told him to get showered and changed and I'd open a bottle. I poured two glasses and sat down on the sofa to wait for him. I took three huge gulps to prepare for sexy time, then woke up the next fucking morning. I asked him why he didn't wake me up, he said I was snoring louder than a ship's foghorn. He decided to just let me sleep because I was clearly 'exhausted.' Exactly what I wanted to hear, despite spending an afternoon getting ready, I still couldn't paint over that exhausted mummy look on my face. I'll try again next month.

I can't wait to get back to work. I don't understand the mothers that say, 'it's been a wonderful twelve months on maternity, I really wish I could take another two years to really bond.' I'm counting down the bastard days till I can go back to work and hand Fido over to nursery in the morning. I'll pick him up in the evening when he's completely exhausted and just wants cuddles and his bed. I've put in a request to go back to work early. I should be rightfully returned to my desk in eight weeks, talking absolutely shite with Mandy on the service desk. I love hearing about her rough sister Meryl. I like to pretend I'm disgusted by her latest antics but I'm secretly envious of the debauchery she creates on a night out. She's a filthy bitch.

I've tried to sort through my work clothes, but they are currently sit in a pile in the corner of the room. I won't go near it in case they say, *fuck off, you fat bitch*, as I approach. I'm using them as thinspiration to get me back in shape. The trouble is, I can't see them from the kitchen so as soon as I go downstairs, I'm stuffing two rounds of toast in my gob. I've got a few weeks to slim down yet. Did you ever have any problems with your weight? I need all the advice I can get.

Love from fatty-bum-bum,

Jess

From: Blanche
To: Jessica Watkiss
Subject Re: Get down on it

Dear Jess,

No, I never suffered with my weight. Not until I met my current flatmate, I ballooned overnight. Although, we're both on a prescribed diet of gin and custard creams. We seem to be responding well. I never had kids so didn't suffer the indignity of having my skin stretched beyond all recognition for absolutely no thanks. As I mentioned previously, I had twins, not that I carried them. They were separated at birth. One has done dead well for himself and the other is a member of the Royal family.

I completely understand you wanting to go back to work early. It's good to have a purpose. Some would say that trying to keep a tiny human alive is all the purpose you need, but you're like me, fickle.

Don't worry about falling asleep on your grand night back as a temptress, it was the thought that counts. I don't know why you went through all that preparation for him. He wouldn't have been bothered what state you were in so long as there was an open garage he could park his banger. A little bit of moss on the walls wouldn't have put him off. I say that from experience. Just before I moved to London to tread the boards of the West End stage, I was treading the concrete of the Blackpool prom. I met all sorts of men who had the most unusual of kinks. One punter used to ask me to wear marigolds and then slap him across his face as he lay there wearing a schoolboy costume. He made me shout at him, 'you're such a disappointment little boy,' over and over again until he finished. He went on to be Home Secretary. There were all sorts of women working there. Sharen was a forty-three-year-old typist who needed to earn some extra cash at weekends to fund her Dandelion and Burdock addiction. The sugar had rotted her teeth away until she was left with nothing but gums. The men would queue round the block to receive fellatio from her, she could charge what she wanted. Another working girl, Pamela, had boils as big as footballs all over her body. One man would pay to squeeze them for her and then masturbate into the puss. With that in mind, I really don't think him upstairs cares about a few stretch marks, cellulite or hairy bits. I'd like to say something profound like, *these are just the marks on a body which gave him a child. He's forever grateful and loves every lump and bump.* Sadly, that's not even occurred to him. Like every man, he just wants to rev his engine in any old pit stop.

Eight weeks to go and you'll have some daily freedom. That's if Boris hasn't extended the lockdown and you're stuck at home, forever on furlough.

Take care cocker,

Blanche

Diane Abbott MP
House of Commons
London

7ᵗʰ June 2020

Dear Blanche,

Tracy Brabin MP and I have been hot on Amanda Holden's heels all month. I thought it best to have someone help me follow her. As Tracy has experience with celebrity culture, I thought she'd be perfect. It was really boring, we had ten trips to the Cavern Club in Liverpool. I don't really understand Amanda's obsession with the place, she just went and sat outside and stared at the Cilla Black statue.

Tracy and I sat at a table at the opposite end of the carriage to her on the way back to London. When Amanda stood up and went to the toilet I ran down to her table and grabbed a letter addressed to Kier Starmer that was poking out of her handbag. I noticed there was a half-drunk bottle of cider in there too. I don't drink because of my diabetes. I hope she's not on the slippery path to addiction.

Here's a photocopy of the letter:

Cilla
Dressing Room 3
ITV Studios
London

Dear Kier,

I've done a lot of thinking. I believe you need to make some radical changes if you're ever going to be the leader of the ruling party. Start by promoting some of those on your hard right into your shadow cabinet. You'll soon have your *red wall* back. You should make Jonathan Ashworth your deputy. No one really cares what the party members voted in the leadership contest and Ashworth is such an engaging personality. What you need is a revolutionary manifest to win back your core voters, something bold and brave — declare your intention to nationalise women's menstrual cycle and the fast-food industry. I'm here for you Kier whenever you need pointing in the right direction.

Ta'ra for now,

Cilla x

Why would Amanda have Cilla's post? For a moment I thought it was Cilla Black till I remembered she'd sadly passed. It did seem strange to have spent the morning watching Amanda staring at Cilla's statue and then to find a letter addressed from Cilla in her bag. I didn't want to put two and two together and come up with four. I even thought for a second that Amanda could be possessed by the spirit of Cilla, but then I pulled myself together. As Tracy rightly said, there are enough conspiracy theories in government without me adding to them. Rumour after rumour at the moment. I heard Boris has hired a news broadcaster to be responsible for Meghan and Harry's protection. Apparently, he's wasted the money on landscape gardening and swimming lessons and can't afford to pay the bill. What will people come up with next?

We bumped into Amanda coming off the train. I was surprised she knew who we were. She seemed a little tipsy. I noticed the bottle in her bag was now empty. She asked us how things were going in a thick Scouse accent, she's a very good mimic. Half a day in another city and she had the accent perfected. You don't see those skills when she's sitting behind the *Britain's Got Talent* desk. I don't know what more I can do for you at the minute Blanche. Apart from incapacitating this Cilla there doesn't seem much I can do. I'm still no closer to finding out exactly who she is I'm afraid.

Yours to serve,

Diane

Cilla
Dressing Room 3
ITV Studios
London

11ᵗʰ June 2020

Blanche,

How sad you got your puppets to follow me up to Liverpool for the day. Did you think I wouldn't notice two Labour MPs jotting down my every move? Especially when one of them is so moronic she came over to me to ask me for my autograph, well Amanda's autograph, before sitting back down on a bench behind me. She didn't hide very well behind her newspaper, she had it upside down and two eye holes cut out. Next time tell her not to wear her hi-vis vest. Blanche, I don't know why you're getting your knickers in such a twist over a few of my letters to Labour MPs, it's not like you can actually do anything about it. I mean, what are you going to do, kill me?

Oh-aye Blanche, I'm in the body of a judge on one of the UK's prime-time TV shows. I'm back on Saturday night TV where I belong. There's no way ITV will let any of your ugly mugged soldiers get anywhere near me, I mean Amanda. Why would you want to anyway? We're old pals me and you Blanche. We never let politics get in the way of our friendship when we were alive, let's not let it now that we're ~~dead~~, well whatever we are. Besides, there's no way you could really stop me.

Ta'ra for now

Cilla

From: Alex Huntington
To: Blanche
Subject BBQ

12th June 2020

Dear Blanche,

You're not going to believe it, what do you reckon to this. It was Dr Altman's BBQ last weekend and I had to write and tell you all about it. It was a lot smaller than I imagined. In fact, it was just me and Dr Altman. Everyone cancelled because of the Covid restrictions. I was *really* relieved if I'm honest. I couldn't face being the *Bridget* of the BBQ and paraded around for the single men. Dr Altman got a disposable BBQ and we just sat in the corner of her garden cooking chilli sausages all afternoon. We were drinking expensive wine that tasted like bathwater on the first sip, you forget the taste after the first glass. The sausages were delicious, which is just as well as Dr Altman forgot to cancel the delivery from the farm shop. She's got one hundred of them in her freezer along with fifty beefburgers and a bucket of gourmet coleslaw in the fridge. She said she's going to cook them daily and bring them to work for all the staff.

I told Dr Altman how exhausted I am after all my dating and how fragile I'm feeling after none of them has resulted in a second date. I've even been banned from the dating apps because they believe I'm a *bot* because of the number of messages I've sent. I've decided to give the dating game a rest, for this week at least.

We were just opening another bottle of white when Mr Altman arrived home from travelling Europe selling pharmaceuticals with Jesus. They both looked like bronzed gods and were wearing matching white linen trousers and chequered shirts in different colours. Mr Altman wore red and Jesus wore blue which made his eyes pop. He's absolutely gorgeous. I was tempted to go back on my no dating rule and give him my number, only Mr Altman dropped a bombshell. As he walked into the garden, he took two glasses and filled them to the brim with wine. Dr Altman looked up at him and said, 'It's about fucking time. How long does it take to tour medical centres in Europe? You've been gone for eight months.'

Mr Altman said back to her, 'Give it up Rebecca, you know very well what we've been doing.' I was taken aback that Dr Altman's first name was Rebecca, I always thought the R stood for Ruth.

'We made business good.' Jesus said, at least I think that's what he said, his Portuguese accent was punctuating his English. The atmosphere was quite tense, I had no idea why. I'm normally *really* good at picking up on signals.

Mr Altman then told us how he'd not been selling pharmaceuticals but had been selling poppers to every gay bar in Europe. To cut a long story short, Mr Altman and Jesus have only been *at it* for the last two years. Dr Altman's been in complete denial. That's why she's been behaving like a pre-menstrual loon at work. It wasn't the stress of the summer BBQ, it was the impending divorce and having to tell everyone her husband's gay. There was an almighty row. Dr Altman said some very rude words which I was surprised she even knew. It was definitely the wine talking, she'd had three bottles by then.

After I held back Dr Altman's hair whilst she vomited up the contents of our mini-BBQ and put her to bed, I went downstairs and chatted to Mr Altman and Jesus. They told me they'd only come back to the UK to ask Dr Altman to sign divorce papers. They plan to go back to mainland Europe and carry on selling their poppers which they've named *HUNG!* There was talk of them buying a little villa in Albufeira.

It's Wednesday now and Dr Altman hasn't been at work all week. I've had to cancel all her appointments. The patients have been going mad at me and demanding I rearrange. I could hardly say to them that Dr Altman was unavailable due to drinking copious amounts of wine to deal with her imminent divorce. I texted her this morning and told her not to worry and that her secret was safe with me.

I'm still waiting for the TV dating shows to ring. Maybe I've given them the wrong number. If it wasn't for having Randy on the other end of a video chat, I think I'd go completely insane. He's got an absolute heart of gold. If you hadn't sent Randy on that mission to London, we wouldn't really know each other at all. We both owe you big time. It's so nice to have a friend to offload to at the end of the day. Speak soon.

Alex.

From: Blanche
To: Alex Huntington
Subject Re BBQ

Dear Alex,

I'm starting to think being homosexual is contagious. I don't suppose your gays know my gays, Nathan and Marcus. They live down in Brighton.

There's nothing sadder than a woman who can't let go of a man is there? You might want to remember that the next time you try climbing through someone's window. I think you're absolutely right to give the dating game a little bit of a rest. You don't want to be known as the desperate bitch who will put out for any man who looks at her once, do you? Cilla was like that. She was very jealous of the male company I had in my life. She'd make up great stories about how these men would wine and dine her at great expense. I once told her how one of my fans had surprised me at the stage door with a lovely pearl necklace and had taken me to the Ritz for supper. I wouldn't normally allow anyone who has sat in my audience to have such closeness with me. I feel it breaks the illusion. However, I made an exception for him on account of the size of his wallet, plus he had a look of Cary Grant who I loved in *Monkey Business* when he starred opposite Marilyn. When I told Cilla, she made up some cock and bull story about a crazed fan who showered her with Rolexes, flowers and weekends away. That was the trouble with Cilla, if you've got a headache, she'd died and come back to life.

In the immortal words of Diana Ross, *you can't hurry love*. Unless they've won the lottery, then you can tell him you love him till the cheque books come home. Take your time Alex, enjoy life instead of rushing through it trying to find a man. It will come when you're least expecting it. I once knew a couple who met in a bar in Vilnius, Lithuania. Whilst ordering a drink one of them was that pissed that they tripped up over their own foot and spilt a drink on the other. They were the only two people in the bar who could speak English. Come to think of it, they were gay too.

Stay safe.

Blanche

Priti Patel MP
House of Commons
Westminster

15th June 2020

Blanche,

You best sort out my mess. I've been caught happy slapping Diane Abbott with a Black Lives Matter campaign placard in the Parliament's canteen. Obviously, I didn't mean to. I thought she was one of those civil servants that have outrageously accused me of bullying. All I did was have Gove remove the brake pads on her car and turn off her airbags, hardly bullying. Just some friendly office banter. No one can take a joke anymore.

I can't face another press conference, why waste my time trying to explain myself when I know Boris will back me. He's too scared not to since I took his dinner money and flushed his head down the toilet. Men really are pathetic.

I was accused of giving a backhanded apology over the lack of personal protective equipment for the NHS: fundamentally false. I had no intention of apologising full stop. In actual fact, I'm making a nice little side-line selling face masks to surgeons on a stall in Hackney market, Hancock has fixed me up with one of his Turkish suppliers. I share the stall with Gove, he's been selling shishas and cannabis oil he's smuggled in on a Megabus.

Blanche, my only concern is that my approval rating is through the floor. I've been threatened with the compulsory attendance of a mindfulness course. I can't resign, not again.

Priti

I expect a swift response.

Blanche
Boadicea Manor
Salford 6

Dear Priti,

Why don't you pop back over to Israel to get away from it all? So, it's Gove who has been filling the post box with leaflets about cannabis oil all over the estate, I bought ten boxes. I'll be sending them back, I couldn't touch anything that's been on a Megabus. When Mick Jagger arrived at mine one summer evening on a delayed National Express from Woking, I wouldn't let him through the front gate until he'd been hosed down. Mick became obsessed with me when he caught sight of my gusset whilst I was leant over giving the kiss of life to Gary Barlow at Knebworth. He didn't need it; it was a dare from Cilla.

Your approval rating has sunk? I didn't think it could get any lower than a worm's tit. Have you considered a lobotomy? I can give it a try for you, I've got a new cheese knife I've been desperate to try out. I'll put the *Daily Mail* on the floor to soak up the blood.

Blanche

Blanche
Boadicea Manor
Salford 6

16th June 2020

Diane Abbott
House of Commons
London

Diane,

After all these years, I've finally found a suitable way for you to pay me back. I think what I'm about to ask will settle up quite nicely for the twelve months I spent incarcerated for you. I know I said it was all water under the bridge, but that bridge has just been crossed by a Saturday night TV judge.

You must take down Amanda Holden, it's the only way to stop Cilla. Isolate her, or at the very least, infiltrate her post. She should have no more written communication with any of the outside world.

Blanche.

From:Randy Mottershed
To: Blanche
Subject Doggers picnic

18th June 2020

Dear Blanche,

I'm very excited. We've been all guns ablaze this last month piecing together plans for a grand dogging event. Princess Ann has given us a permanent site on the lands of Balmoral. It's a little out in the sticks, however, as Ann pointed out, it's good for us to be out of the spotlight with Mangled Mel's new online fame. Mel's got two-million Twitter followers now. A meme of me tripping over her vagina with the caption, WHO LET THE FADGE OUT went viral. She's capitalised on the interest and opened up her own online shop. Her two best-sellers are both t-shirts: one says, 'Viagra is for Pussies,' and the other is Princess Ann's Royal Coat of Arms. Only the lion and unicorn have been replaced with two Corgis, one of them has a pair of binoculars hanging from their collar and the other has a gag in its mouth. Mel's turned into a shrewd businesswoman. I'll have to be careful she doesn't up and leave me when she makes her millions. I'd be worried she would leave me now if she could get anywhere without being loaded into the back of an HGV first.

She's gone money mad. I've been able to retire from inspecting phone masts. Mel has set about spending some of her money on decorating the house. I'm afraid she has the taste of Elton John. There's nothing but tat everywhere you look. Every wall is mirrored, including the ceilings, and there is a great big skull at least two-foot wide and three-foot tall made from Swarovski crystals in the hallway. I asked how she planned to pay for it all, she looked up from her Battenberg and said, 'Channel 5 have paid.' I don't know what that's about and I shan't be asking. She's had a hot tub installed in the yard. I don't know why, she'll never get in it unless it's filled with custard.

Mel's named our planned event, #TheDoggersPicnic. She's drawn a map of the area in Balmoral and stuck Post-It notes on it to create a layout. The cars will be parked in a semi-circle around a clearing which will be made into a small stage. On the other side of the circle, there will be a small area to park Winnebagos for our star act, Jane McDonald. We're over the moon that Jane has agreed to play at the picnic. She told us she's been working on a new song, especially for the occasion. Next to the Winnebagos are portable toilets and showers. The showers are really just five hosepipes to water people down after they've been covered in any sort of bodily fluid or ketchup, Mel's outsourced some burger vans and other refreshment concessions. We're being Covid responsible, the tickets say, '*No Mask, No Play*'. At the entrance to the grounds, there will be two assistants taking the temperature of all who attend. They will be dressed in PVC nurse costumes. Honestly, Mel's thought of everything. I'm in awe.

The centrepiece of the area is a giant throne for Princess Ann. It's been strategically placed so she can see the doggers from a bird's eye view. I did ask if her mother would mind but Ann said she could practically get away with anything after what her brother had been up to over the past year.

I'm thinking of inviting Alex to the picnic to enjoy the entertainment and educate her more about my lifestyle. We've become very close. She makes me feel included when Mel so often leaves me on the side-lines. Mel can be hard to please when I'm video editing her clips. It's hard to believe she's gone from a timid size 14 when we first met to a half-ton OnlyFans celebratory. I've not seen Alex since our trip to London, talking of which, did the information we give you help? It was a pleasure to do something for you. I was happy to be out of the house. If you need anything done again, just let me know. You're more than welcome to join us for the picnic.

All my best,

Randy

From:Blanche
To: Randy Mottershed
Subject Re: Doggers picnic

Randy,

Sounds like Mangled Mel is becoming quite the celebrity. I won't say star. Star should only be used to refer to the great Hollywood icons of yesteryear. Anyone who's caught on CCTV calls themselves a celebrity these days. You should consider popping the question now that she's made of money. Don't be shy, just come straight out with it, *will you get a gastric band?* It can't be healthy all that weight. I'm surprised your upstairs floor hasn't given way.

I won't be able to make the picnic I'm afraid. I can't leave my flatmate Fergie on her own and she's no good in crowds. She gets palpitations if she goes to Aldi. I'll be thinking of you though. I'm delighted Princess Ann and Jane McDonald are going to be there. Get used to the Z-list lifestyle, you'll soon be receiving calls for every reality tv show going. Maybe that's why Mel was referring to Channel 5. Don't let fame go to your head. My old friend Cilla was quite the diva. She didn't even wipe her own arse in the end. She had a colonic irrigation every two days, they flushed her out with cider. It's important to stay grounded when you're thrust into the limelight. Never forget your Ps and Qs and always remember to put your bins out. That's nothing to do with fame, just some very good advice handed down from my mother. She also used to say, *'Don't be daft, don't be silly, put a condom on that willy.'* You can print that on one of Mel's t-shirts.

And yes, I'm very grateful for the information you got for me. Thank you.

Keep safe,

Blanche.

Boris Johnson MP
10 Downing Street
Westminster

19ᵗʰ June

Dear Blanche,

Dom is still staying over, we binged watched the *Police Academy* movies. I've decided to splash out on a little purchase, I'm treating Dom to a new aircraft. It's a snip at just one hundred million pounds. The best part is I'm not paying. It seems Sunak has found a magic money tree and there is more than enough to go around for this purchase. I know I should really be sending the money to Sir Trevor McDonald. I just can't resist buying a little treat for Dom.

I'm spending £900,000 having the Union Jack painted on the fuselage and Dom's face on the tail. I was savaged by the tabloids once again. They can't possibly expect me to travel commercially.

Maybe you and I could meet again, come for a trip on board my little jet? Destination, paradise.

Kindest regards,
Boris

Blanche
Boadicea Manor
Salford 6

Boris,

I've had quite enough of planes to last me beyond a lifetime thank you very much. You can sod off to paradise on your own, with a one-way ticket.

Sorry for the delay in writing, I've just got back from handing out school dinners with my flatmate Fergie. She doesn't like to be seen in public so rarely ventures out, but as it was such a worthy cause I thought it was worth the risk. We've been busy delivering sandwiches made by the nuns from the convent of Saint Gina Tonic to all the needy children around the precinct. They're all starving because of the end of free school dinners. Since the cutbacks the nuns have had to resort to desperate measures, four of them lap dance on Saturdays to raise funds for the breakfast club at the local comprehensive.

I can imagine the aircraft will come in useful at weekends, you'll need something bigger than a Volkswagen to take all your kids on a day out to Barnard Castle. Priti wrote to tell me she's looking forward to being the chief cabin crew. She's been practising the safety demo all week. She had some trouble with the seat belt, lost her temper and hit Sunak over the head with the buckle. She can't wait for the naming ceremony. For the record, I think Maggie is a terrible choice.

Blanche

Victoria Townsend
29 Hellbourne Close
Salford

20th June 2020

Dear Blanche,

I'm sorry. I just couldn't do it. I couldn't go. I couldn't leave.

Victoria

Blanche
Boadicea Manor
Salford 6

Vicky,

I'm on my way.

Blanche.

JULY

Vicky Townsend
29 Hellbourne Close
Salford

2ⁿᵈ July 2020

Dear Blanche,

Thank you ever so much for sending Sarah Ferguson, Duchess of York, to see me. I didn't realise she had a strong Salford accent or that you were even acquainted. I had the shock of my life when I opened the door. Royalty in my house, what will the neighbours be thinking. It's a pity you couldn't come yourself. It would have been lovely to meet you. I'm quite astounded at how much gin Fergie was able to consume in forty-eight hours. I had to go to the corner shop twice to stock up.

I've never had such fun. Who would have thought that getting out of the house could recharge the batteries and clear the cobwebs with such force? I suspect Fergie's told you all about the weekend. She was very down-to-earth, dare I say a little common. Dave is still aghast I had someone to stay over. He's not said anything, he wouldn't. It would mean he'd have to communicate. I can see the little cogs turning inside his brain as he passes me in the hallway. I bet he was desperate to come and say hello to her. He stayed in the other room all weekend as usual. I knew it had annoyed him when he stormed out of the house and slammed the door. You should have seen Fergie, she jumped up onto the sofa, banged on the window and shouted, 'Fuck off you miserable twat! Don't come back till there's a smile on your face, make your arse jealous.' I'd wanted to do that for years. I was stunned that a Duchess knew such words. I laughed until my sides ached. I felt bloody untouchable with Fergie there. It was such a tonic.

Fergie has stopped me from doing all the chores that I normally do for him, like his washing and cooking. She was right, why the bleeding hell should I look after him when I'm lucky if he speaks to me from one month to the next? She made a point of following him around the house with the air freshener and squirting it directly at him whenever his colostomy bag stank. She didn't give him the normal sympathy he glorifies in. Every time Dave went into the kitchen she shouted, 'Eating again, fatty?' She really didn't care what he thought at all. I loved it.

In the evening we did an online pub quiz, she didn't know any of the answers. I was surprised how thick she was for Royalty. She makes up for it with her personality though. She was the life and soul of 29 Hellbourne Close, not a simple task when it flatlined years ago. Just going to the shop turned into an adventure with her. In the newsagent, she asked me what my interests are. I had to really think about it. I eventually told her history and cake. She made me choose six magazines on the subjects. I don't know why I'd never looked before. There were hundreds of glossy images across the back wall that covered all sorts of information and hobbies. I know what a newsagent looks like, but it was like I'd looked up for the first time in years. I got *BBC History* and *Good Food* magazines. I felt safe in the BBC's hands. I flicked through them with a coffee. There was an interesting feature on a manor house that's owned by the National Trust. I've decided to join them and have a cake in every one of their tea rooms in the North West. I know it sounds silly, but it's given me life and a bit of purpose. I could have got a joint membership in the hope that Dave would come with me, but like Fergie said, *fuck him.*

Fergie's got a very sweet tooth. In the newsagent, she bought four packets of custard creams. In the two days she was with me she had a packet for breakfast, one for lunch and a gin for dinner. She had a gin for elevenses too, and ten-thirties, which I didn't realise was a thing. Fergie wasn't keen to talk about the Royal family, she had lots to say about Cilla Black and Princess Diana. She had all sorts of tales about them two, she had me in stitches until the small hours. She told me how she'd been on holiday with Cilla and choked on a custard cream on the flight on the way home. Cilla didn't even help and just 'fucked off into the daylight,' to quote Fergie. That's when I knew she'd had one too many. She's got a very vivid imagination, no wonder she could write all those little helicopter books.

Fergie got a little serious just before she went home and asked me why I hadn't gone on the holiday and why I couldn't leave. I got upset if I'm honest. She made me really think. The truth is, I was scared. I've lived in this house for so long with Dave, living under this dark marital cloud that I simply don't know who I am outside of it. I thought I'd left it too late to make a change, I haven't, have I, Blanche? As Fergie said, you're only as old as the man you feel, and after her pep talk, I'm determined to find myself a nice young Greek in Santorini. Fergie wouldn't leave until I phoned up the travel agents and amended the booking. I go in two weeks. I had to pay an admin fee, but who cares? I'm feeling free, and that is priceless.

I'm walking on air for the first time in forty years. Not even the stench from his colostomy bag can burst my bubble. The kids have all been around too, although I've used Covid as an excuse to make them wait outside and talk to me through the window. I love them, of course I do, I just didn't know they were so selfish. William, the youngest, has texted me a few times though. I know as a mother I shouldn't have a favourite, but he has been mine since the minute I held him. He's been sending me links for round-the-world cruises and holidays to New Zealand. It's where I've always wanted to go but never dared. Thanks to you Blanche, and Fergie's visit, I feel like I could take on the world. I'm going to see how I get on in Santorini and then I might book another trip when I get back.

Thanks again Blanche, I feel like a completely new woman, even at my age.

All my love,

Vicky x

Blanche
Boadicea Manor
Salford 6

Dear Vicky,

There's nothing wrong with a woman who likes a drink. Fergie did tell me all about the weekend, she said you were far too tight with the gin and far too generous with the tonic.

I am glad to hear you feel like a new woman, never doubt yourself again or give a man any right to make you feel like shite. Remember, if all else fails, a pillow over his head will work just as well. Fergie said you were a right laugh once she'd dragged you out of your shell. She couldn't believe it when you showed her all the moves of every ABBA song, five times. Sounds like you're a right little party animal when you get going. The men in Santorini will have to look out with you around.

She showed me a selfie she took with you after she'd done your mini makeover. I must say, letterbox-red lipstick and a beehive does suit you.

Make sure when you go to Santorini you send me a postcard. And make sure you book that dream holiday to New Zealand the second you're back. Sod the kids' inheritance, you're here for a good time, not a long time. If they want money in the bank, they can bloody well earn it. And tell them, they aren't too old to be put up for adoption. Don't worry about having a favourite, every parent has one. Prince Harry was Princess Di's, I think that's because he didn't have Charles' genes. She would dote on him all night long when she got in from the bingo. She'd never let the poor bugger sleep whilst she was awake.

Enjoy your all-inclusive, remember just because you can drink all you want doesn't mean you should. Who am I kidding, get pissed and disgrace yourself! You can get away with anything once you reach a certain age, just ask the Queen.

Lots of love,

Blanche

Priti Patel MP
House of Commons
Westminster

6ᵗʰ July 2020

Blanche,

I'm in deep shit. I went out on Saturday and got so pissed I blacked out. I woke up on Sunday morning with blood on my hands. Me and my best mate Theresa camped outside The Moon Under the Water, our local Wetherspoon's, to be the first ones in when it opened at six am. We had a quick wash in the tent with a baby wipe then got ready in our best. Theresa wore a green sequinned boob tube with a yellow tartan mini skirt and white stilettos, I wore a leopard print catsuit with matching ears and heels.

We were excited waiting for the doors to be unlocked that we rushed in like kids running down the stairs on Christmas Day. We were sensible though, we had a big breakfast to line our stomachs, two flaming Sambucas and a Cheeky Vimto. It tasted like nectar. The only place we've been able to go in the last three months is the bar inside Parliament. You can't have a conversation in there without looking up and seeing Gove rub his thighs every time Widecombe walks past.

There was no music in the pub, luckily Theresa had thought ahead and brought her portable speaker. We played all the classics: Sonia, Sinitta, Aqua. The dance lessons have really paid off for Theresa. There was no dance floor so she pushed two tables together as a makeshift stage. When the bar started filling up, she got quite the crowd. She did the splits after slipping on her spilt Smirnoff Ice. The bar went wild. Some men even through some fivers at her. She spent the money on pork scratchings and Strongbow.

We were being bought drinks left, right and centre, Malibu, Tia Maria, Gin, Chardonnay, Merlot, Carlsberg, Stella, the lot. I was fine until someone threw a beer mat at Theresa. Nobody fucks with my sister. I jumped across the table and smashed a bottle of Bacardi Breezer against the man's head. I don't know my own strength. He went down cold. Theresa was pissing herself laughing, I grabbed her and we ran out of the bar. I thought we best sober up so we went for a kebab. The queue was massive so we didn't bother and went for another Apple Sourz instead. We were in a beer garden when a woman walked past wearing the same clothes as me, how fucking dare she. I threw my Jack Daniels over her dress and flicked my cigarette at her.

Theresa started a full-blown riot, she picked up a bar table and launched it at the woman's husband. The metal leg took his eye out and it rolled across the beer garden decking, I jumped on it. The pop of it made Theresa vomit. I blacked out after that and woke up in a police cell. Luckily, I've been able to keep it quiet by threatening the arresting police officer with deportation, he's originally from Jersey.

What am I going to do? If Boris finds out, I'll be back on another anger management course.

Priti

Blanche
Boadicea Manor
Salford 6

Dear Priti,

'Lock them up and throw away the key,' that's what many people will say, not me of course. I've always got your back. That's why I managed to get hold of the CCTV from the pub and release it to the nation to show them how it couldn't possibly be your fault. Only it backfired, it showed you smashing a man's head off the curb then shoving a quarter pounder down another man's throat. He's since released a statement that he is vegetarian, it's being treated as a hate crime.

I'm afraid that a left-wing group, Vegans Against Vandals, have been marching across London all morning to have you removed from power. Fortunately, Boris has reminded the country that Conservative MPs and their relatives do not have to comply with British rules and laws. It's just as well, as after the burger incident the CCTV showed you pissing in your hands and throwing it on a homeless man.

You really must lay off the alcohol, everyone likes a drink, no one likes a drunk. The best action now is to check into Betty Ford to detox and appear repentant to the press. I know it will be through gritted teeth as you can't feel empathy or guilt but it's a necessary action. You only just survived your last binge when you lost control and battered Pudsey the bear at the *Children in Need* event where Gove was doing a sponsored 'Snortathon'. No idea how he came up with snorting sherbet dip for charity. Richard Branson nearly ended up bankrupt after sponsoring him one pound a line.

This is your last chance, Priti. Sober up, attend your anger management class I'm booking you on and say three hail Barbara's.

Blanche

From: Sophie McBride
To:Blanche
Subject Therapy
7th July 2020

Dear Blanche,

I did it, I went to a therapy session. I'm so glad I did. It was nice just to be around other like-minded people. It's not called therapy though, it's a *support group*. It lived up to its name. It made me realise that it wasn't my fault that Marcus turned gay. I think the group was a little taken aback when I got talking. I didn't want to at first, I was shy and let everyone else speak. Then when I got started, I couldn't stop. All the anger that I had inside just come spewing out. I didn't know I had that much venom and resentment in me. I realised there are many people in my position and there are many reasons why people get married and then come out later in life. There were seven of us in the group:

• Trisha had suspected her husband was having an affair with another woman. They'd been married thirty-five years. She followed him one evening to a bar in town and was shocked to see him kiss another man on entering the pub.
• Donna, a great tall young lady who works in social services, went to check the time on her boyfriend's phone and found a gay dating app on his mobile. She threw him out immediately and hasn't spoken to him since.
• Lindsey, a middle-aged child-minder. Her husband had sat her down and told her that he no longer wanted to be called Michael and instead she should call her Michelle. I don't think I could do it but she's sticking with him and supporting him through a sex change.
• Craig is a man in his mid-forties. His wife has buggered off with

another woman and left him with the kids.

• Shane was a man in his late fifties. He had come home early one day to find his wife in bed with another woman. Initially, he thought it was a valentine's gift but soon cottoned on when he wasn't allowed to join in.

Then there was a lovely woman called Rebecca, a doctor from Peterborough. She's known for two years that her husband was sleeping with his Portuguese assistant but stayed with him because she couldn't face a divorce. Her husband and his lover have been driving around Europe selling poppers. Her husband came home on the day she'd planned to have a big BBQ and he served her divorce papers. What's made it even worse is that they're both staying in the house until the sale goes through. Rebecca has come south to stay with her parents for a couple of weeks to get away from it all. We went for a glass of wine after the meeting and really hit it off. She's quite funny when she's not crying.

She came into my salon this week and I gave her a complete makeover. She said she hadn't been paying much attention to herself with the stress of everything that's been going on. Her split ends could tell you a whole story. She spent the day being pampered. By the time she left we'd cut her hair into a lovely bob and give her some blonde highlights to soften her cheekbones. She also had a manicure and pedicure from our beautician. I didn't charge her, she insisted on taking me out for dinner to say thank you. We went to Nando's, it's unpretentious and you always know what you're getting. I don't think either of us could cope with any more surprises at the minute. There's another week before she must go back to Peterborough. We've arranged to meet up tomorrow to go for a walk along the seafront, socially distanced of course. I think we'll probably go out a few times before she goes home. It's just nice to be with someone who understands.

I was intrigued by the story of your neighbour who could tell your fortune. I've often thought of having mine done but have always been a bit too scared and a little too sceptical. On impulse the other day I had my cards read by Mystic Peg, she has a little tent on the end of Brighton pier. It was just big enough for a table and two chairs. The pier was really busy as it was a scorching hot day and the tent was really stuffy, the smell of a tuna sandwich lingered. Peg asked me if there was anything specific I wanted to know. I said I'd like a general forecast. Peg shuffled the cards and then I split the pack. The first card turned over was the death card. I was assured by Peg that it didn't mean anyone would die, she must have seen the panic on my face. It means new beginnings, the end of one thing and the start of another. I suddenly started paying more attention. The next card was the strength card, it was upside down, that means I suffer from self-doubt and insecurity. I thought that will be the gay husband. Next was the fool card, this stood for innocence and being a free spirit, that will be the divorce. The last card was the lover's card, I stopped listening then as I just thought she was taking the piss. To sum up I'm to embark on a new journey as a free spirit who is innocent yet foolish and may or may not get lucky between the sheets along the way.

Marcus has been very quiet since the dinner party. Not that I'm bothered, I think I'd rather it be communication on a need-to-know basis. He's had the kids a few times, they've not stayed overnight yet though. I'm not ready for Tilly to start asking questions about why daddy is kissing Nathan. John, my eldest, came home after a visit to tell me all about Nathan's blog. It's one of the most influential ones in Brighton apparently: SleepingWithTheProfessor.com. I couldn't believe it. The absolute fucker has been writing all about his love affair with my husband for the past two years. There was detail after detail about how I found out and my reaction. He manages to make himself out to be the innocent party and me to be a boring housewife who's kept his lover captive. I did the only rational thing you can do in that situation, I got pissed and phoned Marcus. I told him that if he wanted to see his kids again that his cunt of a boyfriend better delete his blog before I tell the board of governors he's been shagging a student. It's not been deleted and I haven't called the board of governors, a more sober and understanding me decided it wasn't really Marcus's fault. I might start my own blog, NathansATwat.com

Thanks for listening,

Love Sophie.

P.S wouldn't it be great if we could actually meet up face to face?

From: Blanche
To:Sophie McBride
Subject Re: Therapy

Dear Sophie,

I think we'll see each other face to face sooner than you think. I'm very much looking forward to it. I'm glad you've been able to talk to someone, sounds like you've made a lovely friend in Rebecca. It's always nice to have some mates to fall back on. I used to be thick as thieves with Cilla and Di. I couldn't see them both at the same time though, they bloody hated each other.

In the middle of my daytime duties as a nanny to the Princes in '87, I was just finishing off playing hide and seek with them (I was hiding in the wine cellar), when Eamonn Andrews came in with a film crew. I was mid gulp when he said, 'Blanche, star of the West End and patron to the Bingo Callers' Union, *This is Your Life.*' I only had time to grab two bottles of wine before I was shimmied away by Eamonn's crew to the Thames TV studios. I had no idea that the tension was mounting backstage as the famous theme tune started. Cilla was furious that Princess Di had been billed as the final guest, closing the show and not her. The champagne was flowing, Cilla was already pissed by the time Eamonn introduced my friends from my old Tiller Group, 'Six days a week you danced onstage with your beautiful co-stars, The Tiller Girls. Here they are tonight, with a special performance just for you.' Whilst they tapped away onstage Cilla squared up to Di in the green room and was shouting, 'OH-Aye Di, you could have made an effort. You look like something me mam's cat dragged in.' Di laughed in her face which made Cilla go psycho. The thing with Cilla was that she was like a ticking bomb. As she was on stage next, she didn't have time to react to Di.

'You met in Blackpool after an unfortunate incident with a Blackpool tram brought you both fame and fortune. She's sang her way to the top of the charts and is now one of the UK's top paid television entertainers, Cilla Black.' I knew instantly something was wrong, I could tell by the demon look in Cilla's eyes. When she came on, she staggered over to me, gave me a hug and kiss and whispered in my ear, 'How could you Blanche, I'm the star.'

It had clearly escaped Cilla that this was a *Surprise, Surprise* for me and I had no idea who the producers had kept till last. Eamonn announced, 'Blanche, we've saved your biggest fan until the end. In between Royal duties and talking to her husband's plants, she's here for you tonight. Her Royal Highness, The Princess of Wales.'

Di looked stunning when she walked on set. I almost didn't recognise her as I was so used to seeing her lounge around in her scruffs. No sooner had she walked on and given me a kiss on the cheek than Cilla was tear-arsing it over the stage and rugby tackling Diana to the ground. She was screaming like a scouse bitch possessed. Cilla took her heels off and was just about to plant one in Diana's forehead when the BBC doctor came running behind Cilla and sedated her with an injection in her arse. On her way across the stage Cilla had managed to knock down the *This is Your Life* set which had landed on Eamonn Andrews. It was the only episode of *This is Your Life* to never make it on screen.

Whilst I don't condone violence, it's always good to have a friend who's a little bit psycho and will fight till their last breath for you. Even if it is unwanted at times. Perhaps Rebecca will do that for you. I'm also a great believer in revenge. That blog of yours sounds like a fantastic idea. You can use some of the pictures that Nathan left for you on the doorstep all those months ago to show who the nasty swine is.

Keep safe. I'll continue to plan our meet-up,

Blanche.

Matt Hancock MP
House of Commons
Westminster

19th July 2020

Dear Blanche,

Our *Track & Trace* app doesn't work. We drew straws in the COBRA meeting to decide who would do the press conference. Priti lost but she threatened to happy slap me again, I don't think her anger management course is working. I did the brief instead. We decided not to take responsibility for the track and trace apps failure, we blamed Labour for being in power 12 years ago.

We ran out of time setting the app up properly, we got carried away on the new crazy golf course we've had installed in the Downing Street garden. We've got a league going, the winner gets to decide which hospital to close next. Not all is lost though as the app tells you how close you are to telling the truth so you can avoid it at all costs. We've all downloaded it in the cabinet.

What matters is what works, what works saves lives, we don't work and that's a record we're very proud of. Boris is still in the fridge with a *Do Not Disturb* sign. He said he's hiding from Trevor. Priti has gone back to Israel & Rees-Mogg is working nights as Ann Widecombe's pimp, Farage is his number one client. Blanche, I'm quite lonely at the minute in number ten, all my colleagues are away. What can I do to pass the time and make new friends?

Enjoy your day,

Matty

Blanche
Boadicea Manor
Salford 6

Dear Matt,

Do not worry. There was no expectation for you to deliver on a promise. I fear for the health of the UK if you did, there would have been shock-induced heart attacks across the nation.

There are many opportunities for you to fill in the time, you could borrow Boris's plane and take yourself on a trip to Chernobyl, Alcatraz is equally as nice. I have no problem arranging the trip for you. Don't worry about any travel bans, they don't apply to runts.

If you prefer, I can get you a part-time job as a lab rat. You'd be perfect. I'll get the scientist to put you in the cage next to Raab. We're conducting an experiment to see if an amoeba can develop empathy. We've tied Raab to a 5G mast and read him a list of 42,288 names of people who've died of Coronavirus. He didn't blink. We sent him to a morgue the day before, he just called Theresa in working pensions and told her to cross another ten off the list.

Have a lovely weekend wherever you decide to go,

Blanche

From: Jessica Watkiss
To: Blanche
Subject Holiday from hell

20th July 2020

Hiya Blanche,

I've just got back from the worst bastarding holiday I've ever fucking had. I used the money I had set aside from the holiday vouchers you bought from me and booked a last-minute trip to Corfu. I thought it would be nice for us to get away as a family before I go back to work next month. Big mistake.

On the way out the airport was deserted. People still won't travel because of Covid. Although the restrictions are ridiculous. I can't go to Liverpool but I can go to Greece. The flight was only half full, one of the first ones out since lockdown has eased. We had to wear a mask for the whole flight. It was so uncomfortable that it almost wasn't worth the effort of having to keep moving it up and down in between mouthfuls of vodka and coke. And fuck me did I need a drink.

As God is my witness, I will never take an infant with me on holiday ever again. The little shit did the biggest turd you've ever seen as soon as the aircraft pushed back from the gate. The seatbelt sign was on preventing me from getting up to change Fido's arse until twenty minutes after take-off. By that time the whole cabin stunk. I was mortified, I could feel the eyes of other passengers looking at me disgustedly. I was already having hot flushes as the air hostess came to us before departure and gave me an infant seatbelt and lifejacket.

She asked me if I knew how to use it, I just said yes. She must have been able to tell from the expression on my face that I didn't have a bastard clue. She said in one breath, 'What you do is push your buckle inside the loop then wrap the baby belt around the baby and then it clicks around him at the front if we crash then you just need to undo your belt and baby will be free from his also I'm going to put the baby life jacket in your seat pocket just in case we land on water but don't worry we won't be doing that today.' Then she was off to deliver the same speech to a woman sitting in 3D. It took me a minute to punctuate what she said. All I could remember from it was crash and water. She had her name on a chain around her neck, *Chantelle*. I wrote it down to write a nasty tweet about her when we landed but I'd calmed down by then and didn't bother. I'm not a great flyer at the best times and I was already flustered trying to get Fido to sit still on my lap long enough to restrain him. Why do infants have to sit on your lap for the whole flight, especially when they've done a great big shit? You should be able to put them in a cage on the wing. That *bastard* sat in the window seat and just stared out, listening to his headphones whilst I tried to entertain Fido and not vomit from his stench.

As soon as the seatbelt sign was switched off, I raced to the toilet to change his nappy. I double bagged it and put it in the bin. I swear every now and then you got a faint whiff of it from the air vents. No sooner had we sat back down than Fido started to scream his head off. That bastard just turned the volume up on his audiobook. I spent the rest of the flight trying to get Fido to be quiet, I was scared he was going to burst a lung. I wound the bobbin up, I incy wincyed and I peekabooed, all whilst downing three mini vodkas, nothing worked. As soon as the wheels hit the tarmac he shut up. I could have cried in frustration. When we stood to leave, I looked back at where we'd been sat and it looked like the remains of Aleppo. Pringles crushed into the carpet, inflight magazines and safety cards thrown on the floor, and a selection of empty miniatures from the bar. I couldn't look the cabin crew in the eyes through shame as we left.

The hotel was beautiful, but my heart stopped beating as soon as we got to the reception and I read a sign telling me, *DUE TO CORONAVIRUS, WE REGRET TO INFORM YOU THAT THE KIDS CLUB AND NURSERY WILL REMAIN CLOSED*. That *bastard* turned to me and said, 'Don't worry love, I'll help out with the little one.' As if he was doing me a favour for looking after his own son. I decided not to let it bother me. As soon as I put on my all-inclusive wrist band I went straight to the bar and left Fido with his dad for a couple of hours.

It wasn't as bad as I thought it would be for the first few days. I managed to put in some serious sunbathing hours whilst *he* looked after Fido. There was a little play centre in the hotel, I don't know who was more amused, Fido or his dad. On the fourth day, I took Fido to the baby pool. I don't know what I was thinking but I stupidly took him in without a nappy. With perfect timing, he did the runniest green poo you've ever seen in the middle of the baby pool. I didn't know what to do. I was mortified. Stood knee-deep in sewage water whilst the sun was so hot it made me sweat my suntan lotion into my eyes. Other parents looked on, half in pity and half relieved it wasn't their little cherub who'd forced the lifeguard to announce in broken English on the tannoy, 'Baby pool now closed due to shitty baby.' I was humiliated for the rest of the week. I would have given anything to be back on a hen weekend with the girls.

On the last night, we didn't go down to the hotel restaurant, we stayed in our room to have a romantic evening sitting on the balcony and having sundowners. Fido fell asleep early. It was actually nice just being with *him*. I'd forgotten what that was like. We had a giggle and played some music and even had a little dance. We ended up snogging like teenagers and made love for the first time since I'd given birth. I don't know if it was the vodka that tasted like petrol or the Mediterranean Sea breeze which gave me the confidence to be completely naked in front of him again. You were right Blanche, he didn't care what I looked like. He was dead grateful the next day that I'd let him *park his banger in my garage*, to use your phrase. To be honest I'd forgotten how good it could be. I felt like we reconnected a little bit.

The flight home was more relaxing. Fido must have sensed he was on his way back to his daily routine of watching CBeebies. He slept peacefully the whole way. I was busy doing the washing two days later when I got a phone call from test and trace to say that someone had tested positive for Covid who was on our flight home. Now we've got to isolate for ten days. I'm stuck in this house with *him* and Fido clearing up after both of them. *He* keeps following me around the house thinking I'll drop my guard and reopen my garage. It's well and truly closed in daylight hours without vodka to lubricate the hinges.

Three weeks to go Blanche and I'll be back at work, I can't sodding wait.

The end is nigh,

Jess x

From: Blanche
To: Jessica Watkiss
Subject Re: Holiday from hell

Dear Jess,

What on earth were you doing taking a baby on a plane? It's against every rule of social conduct. There's nothing worse than being stuck on a metal tube with somebody else's screaming runt. Children should be seen only in absolute necessity, never should they be heard. You should have sedated Fido with a bottle of Night Nurse.

I'm glad you managed to have a good bonk. It can make you feel like a new woman can't it. Don't go giving it to him all the time, you want him to work for it. Don't let him think that you enjoy it, or he'll be at you morning, noon and night. Dianna made that mistake with Charles. He was a sex pest. She couldn't handle his libido, she was quite happy to send him round to Camilla's at the weekend.

I don't like the sound of that flight attendant. Is it too late to put a complaint in about her? She doesn't sound fit to be around people. Imagine saying that to a new mother. Best to really ham the complaint up or they won't take it seriously. Perhaps say you saw her hit a child with the aircraft fire axe or that you saw her come out of the flight deck without wearing any knickers.

Do keep me updated with your return to work. I hope it goes well.

Blanche

From:Randy Mottershed
To: Blanche
Subject Queen of the Dogs

25th July 2020

Dear Blanche,

We did it! Our Doggers Picnic was a huge success. There were at least five thousand people who turned up: a mixture of singles and couples. All in their cars, flashing their headlights and beeping their horns. Mel did such a brilliant job at organising it all. She didn't join in with the dogging itself as she was so busy signing t-shirts near the main stage. People were queuing for an hour just to have a selfie with her. It was all caught on camera for a new Channel 5 documentary, *Queen of the Dogs*. They filmed the whole event. I constantly had a camera shoved in my face.

I didn't really get a chance to join in with the dogging. Mel had me on the souvenir stall. Three hundred t-shirts I sold and nine hundred car stickers that read, *We've Bonked in Balmoral*. Mel blew an air horn to signal the end of the first session of dogging and that it was time for the entertainment to start on stage. The stage was illuminated very sophisticatedly with a single spotlight. It was raised high enough off the ground that everyone could see. We were all clapping like the clappers when Jane McDonald stepped on stage. She looked amazing Blanche. She wore a blue figure-hugging catsuit which sparkled every time the spotlight caught a sequin. She fashioned it into a dog suit by adding a matching tail and puppy ears. She greeted the crowd by saying, 'You're barking mad you lot.' She then went into a lively rendition of Donna Summer's *Bad Girl*. The doggers joined in at the chorus, '*toot toot, hey, beep beep.*' Body parts were jiggling everywhere in time to the beat. Just think how boring my life was when I first wrote to you Blanche and how much it's changed. I've changed. I don't wear any brown now.

By the time Jane had finished her second song, *It's Raining Men,* the doggers were dancing and singing along, scantily clad in gay abandon. Jane addressed us all again, 'There are some right special people out there tonight and I just want to say a huge thank you to the three people who made this all possible: Mangled Mel, Randy and Her Royal Highness, Princess Ann.' I've got to admit, I got right choked up when the crowd cheered for Mel and me.

'Right, you gorgeous people, I've been working on something right special for you all. But you've got to join in and help out. It's me new single and I'm releasing it just for you.' There were whoops and cheers from men and women as they waited for big Jane's big surprise. The music started and everyone was soon joining in with Jane's cover of Black Lace's *Gangbang:*

'*We're having a gang bang,*
We're having a ball,
We're having a gang bang,
Against the wall....'

On the second day of the picnic, Jane joined me on the stall and sold thirteen-hundred bottles of her perfume, *Northern.* Mel got 5% of her takings. It was nice spending time with Jane. She said she had a brilliant time and that she was sorry that she couldn't stay for the clearing up, she had a cruise to catch.

Mel and I were talking, we'd like to give you some money as a thank you. It was really all your idea and Mel's made an absolute fortune. It's more money than we ever dreamed of making in a lifetime. We're going to reinvest some of the money in an even bigger event and call it *#DogFest.* You just say the word Blanche and whatever you want, it's yours.

I did ask Alex if she'd like to join us for the picnic as a voyeur, sadly she couldn't make it. I spoke to her just a few days ago, she's been dating a foreigner she met online.

With sincere gratitude,

Randy

From:Blanche
To: Randy Mottershed
Subject Re: Queen of the Dogs

Randy,

It's my absolute pleasure cocker. No need for the cash, you save it for a rainy day. I don't know how your Mel copes with all the social media. My flatmate Fergie is very sensitive when it comes to any form of communication that could be infiltrated by her ex-in-laws. Her paranoia is getting out of hand. We've spent a full week in the pitch black as she thought a passing drone was spying on us through the window. She covered every pane of glass in newspaper so no one could see in. I ripped them down when I saw it was an old copy of the *Daily Mail*. I'm not having anyone think I read that shite.

You are right though Randy, one good deed does deserve another. I'm sure they'll come a time in the future when I can rely on you in my hour of need. Can't I, Randy? Think of us as friends, after all, I find nothing but delight in all your success.

To say you're the husband of the *Queen of The Dogs*, it doesn't sound like you're getting much time with the old bitch yourself. Don't be such a pushover, Randy. You deserve happiness too.

I'm really looking forward to seeing your documentary and seeing what Mel looks like in the flesh. In my head she's a right ugly bitch, it will be good to see if I'm right. I'm glad you got to spend some time with Jane McDonald, I've been listening to her new song on the radio all week. It's not normally the sort of thing they play on Radio 2 but I find it's a much more liberal station since Sara Cox joined. I've been humming about gangbangs all week. I'm delighted with Jane's number one.

You keep doing what you're doing Randy. You're a very special man.

Love,

Blanche.

From: Alex Huntington
To: Blanche
Subject EuroDate

28th July 2020

Dear Blanche,

What do you reckon to this? I'm in love. He's absolutely drop-dead gorgeous. I'll tell you all about him in a minute, I've got to tell you this first. Dr Altman is back at work after the disaster of the BBQ. She seems much happier after spending two weeks down at her parents' house in Brighton. She's got the spring back in her step and has stopped crying at work. She told me she went to a support group and met people going through the same as her. She's been talking about a woman called Sophie who found out her husband was seeing one of his male students. Unbelievable, isn't it? *Nothing as queer as folk*, as my mother used to say. I'm just glad she's made a friend as work has been a much happier place to be now that she's smiling. Even the patients have noticed how lovely she's been. They no longer come out of her surgery looking like they've been told they're terminal.

Dr Altman's finishing early on Friday to go back to Brighton and spend the weekend with Sophie who runs a salon. Dr Altman is going to get pampered and then they're hitting the town.

Now for my news. I think I've met *the one*. I came across a new app called *EuroDate*. It matches you with men from all over the continent. I thought, why settle in the UK when there are millions of men across the world who could be waiting for someone like me. Their face appears on the screen with a little bio of them and if you like them you click on a little love heart which is coloured in blue with the yellow stars of the European flag. If you both press it, you match and you can send each other a message. I clicked the heart on everyone as I think it's important you get to know what's on the inside. My picture was of me in a wedding dress. I think it's important to make your intentions clear from the start. Dr Altman, I mean Rebecca (I can't get used to calling her that), gave me her dress as she said it was nothing but a curse. I thought it would be really good for the men of Europe to preview what they'd see on their wedding day.

Anyway, he's gorgeous: short, fat and ginger. He smokes twenty a day and lives in Sofia, Bulgaria. We've chatted for hours on end on the phone and a few hours on Zoom. I shouldn't say this but, we got a little naughty. I didn't know long-distance sex was a thing until now. It was just like the real thing, only on my own. At one point I thought he had friends there watching as I heard voices in the background, he assured me it was just the radio. He's a real gentleman. I can't wait to meet him in person, SO I'M FLYING OVER TO SOFIA NEXT WEEK! Sorry for the caps, I'm just *REALLY* excited. He's promised to wine me and dine and treat me like a princess. He lives on a farm in the middle of nowhere. He's going to pick me up from the airport.

He's called Viktor. I know I shouldn't get ahead of myself, but I've been practising my signature *A Viktor* all week.

Wish me luck Blanche,

Alex Viktor

From: Blanche
To: Alex Huntington
Subject Re: EuroDate

Dear Alex,

There's a word for women like you, desperate. Don't be so bleeding stupid as to travel to the other side of Europe for a man who you don't know. Normally I wouldn't care but I've become quite fond of you since you started sending me letters. You remind me of a young Cilla, fucking stupid. For heaven's sake don't do anything in haste. If you've already gone, let me know you get back safe.

Somewhat concerned,

Blanche

Boris Johnson MP
10 Downing St
Westminster

31st July 2020

Dear Blanche,

It's been quite a week. I've been busy asking my Magic 8 Ball to make all my decisions for me. I've given away vouchers for bikes to be fixed. I was first in line at Halfords to have my stabilisers oiled and my *Dora the Explorer* basket installed. Dom and I are going to ride into the countryside together. He offered me a lift in his sidecar, but I prefer to go solo. I'm going to put some Dairylea Dunkers in the basket and Panda Pop in my water holder. Dom said if I behave, he'll treat me to an ice cream cone with a flake and raspberry sauce. I just hope I don't fall off again as last time I scraped my knee. Theresa cleaned it with TCP, it stung yet I didn't cry. I was rewarded with an ice-pop for being brave.

I asked my Magic 8 Ball, *should I lock down another city to look like I know what I'm doing with this blistering virus?* The ball replied *Yes*. I ran into the games room and picked up my Red Arrow dart and threw it at my wall map. It landed on Manchester. I've never heard of it. It's in a faraway land they call *The North*. Gove warned me never to go there. Apparently, the people are poverty-stricken, have rickets and call lunch, dinner and dinner, tea. Ludicrous. Most disgusting of all, they put curry sauce on their chips. I want to build a wall like Trump to keep them out of the south. I don't have enough Lego.

I've done the only sensible thing I could and gave everyone three hours' notice of the regional lockdown. I won't allow family gatherings in houses; everyone can go to the pub together to *eat out to help out*. It just makes sense. I've allowed the pubs to remain open as I believe people take more care when lubricated with their favourite tipple. I got Hancock to make a statement, well why have a dog and bark yourself? It blames the lockdown on the Mancunians for not social distancing and sticking to the very clear rules. I just hope no one discovers the email I received from The World Health Organisation. I deleted it four months ago, it recommended that we should all wear face masks.

The press is at me again Blanche, they're saying I couldn't organise a piss-up in a brewery. It's a complete lie, I'm always tipsy in The Wacky Warehouse. Carrie makes me take the baby once a month. I do love the ball pit.

I bet Sir Trevor McDonald is behind the press onslaught. Trying to submit me into paying him the money that I owe him. Well, he doesn't scare me, not anymore. Oh, who am I kidding? Blanche, I'm terrified. Last night Larry the cat knocked over the empty milk bottles on the front step. I couldn't sleep all night thinking it was Sir Trevor coming for me. Please ask him to leave me alone.

The only job I've enjoyed these last few weeks is interviewing cabin crew for my new jet. There was a lovely young lady who seemed eager to please, she was called Chantelle. She had her name on a necklace. She sadly informed me she'd been fired from her current airline after a passenger had written in to complain about her. They said she had a very aggressive sales pitch and forced them to buy four sets of airline-exclusive gift sets. I think she's marvellous, we could use some of that spirit in the Brexit negotiations. I've given her the job. I can't wait to see her in uniform.

Kind regards,

Boris

Blanche
Boadicea Manor
Salford 6

Dear Boris,

That Tory Magic 8 Ball has a lot to answer for: section 28, tuition fees, claiming that two gloves don't make a pair, police cuts, NHS cuts, knife crime, Priti's maths, Gove's drug addiction. Maybe you should bet the future of the nation on something more reliable, Pooh Sticks for example. I believe Theresa has been taking the guidelines of wearing the face mask whilst shopping very seriously, she's been on eBay all week wearing a muzzle.

Do be careful when you're out on your bike. It would be awful if someone were to cut the wires on your brakes. Could you describe in detail to me which bike is yours and where it can be found?

Don't worry too much about the press, I'm sure Sir Trevor will get to you before they do. Unless they find the explicit videos of you and Dominic pleasuring yourself over the austerity figures. Please tell him not to send me any more DVDs.

Regards,

Blanche

P.S Don't be fooled by that Chantelle, she's just as aggressive as Priti. If you think you can try your luck with her whilst Carrie isn't looking then think again; Chantelle doesn't sleep with anything with less than four stripes.

AUGUST

Diane Abbott MP
House of Commons
London

1st August 2020

Dear Blanche,

I understood all from your last message and I have a plan. I've entered into the next series of *Britain's Got Talent*. They're doing the pre-auditions next month before filming starts next year. According to Google, one of the TV judges will be there to allow the production team to rehearse camera angles. I'm hoping it will be Amanda. I don't plan to do anything just yet, as you know I'm a stickler for details. I want to have everything meticulously planned before I stumble into action. I still don't understand what Cilla has to do with Amanda.

I've not had so much fun since the 10th May 1990 when I told Thatcher the best that she could hope for was to be elected mayor of Dullage. It's riveting all this espionage. I'm becoming rather mediocre at it. I can't wait to carry out my mission and get into the rehearsal studios. I think you'll be very impressed.

Yours in action,
Diane

Blanche
Boadicea Manor
Salford 6

Diane,

I'm sure you've got everything in hand. I just wanted to drop you a line of encouragement. Don't fuck up! And try not to send some other poor bugger to jail. Including yourself. If you do need anything, let me know. I have people now.

Blanche.

Blanche
Boadicea Manor
Salford

2nd August 2020

Dear Vicky,

I haven't heard from you in a while cocker. I hope you're keeping well and had a right knees up in Santorini. Looking forward to hearing all about it. Everything is well here. My flatmate Fergie is still driving me up the wall. She's a mucky cow. I'm forever cleaning up after her.

Write soon,

Blanche

Blanche
Boadicea Manor
Salford 6

4ᵗʰ August 2020

Cilla,

Stop the shite you dead old trout. I know you're still sending letters to Labour MPs. Well, I've got news for you, they never made their final destination. I warned you Cilla, help the Tories and you'll be pissing sorry. Do it again and I'll have that body you've possessed on a IV drip in seconds, and you'll be off Saturday night tv and spending eternity as a cold white mist.

I wouldn't mind but what are you helping the Tories for anyway? You're as common as muck like the rest of us. You always thought you were a cut above, yet it was you who flashed your knickers to any TV executive who'd look. You bonked your way to the top. You might have helped me with my first break in the West End but don't ever pretend you weren't jealous of me.

What happened Cilla eh? You were bringing people together from all over the world on *Surprise Surprise,* you stood for doing good for people. What on earth would make you want to support a party that would cause poverty for so many? This isn't the Cilla I know. You had a heart.

Remember that weekend when we both decided to get away from it all and you called me and said, 'Pack your bags Blanche, we're going on us hols.' You whisked me away to Jersey. Wasn't a bleeding holiday in the end though was it? You bumped into a scabby looking donkey on the seafront. For the next twenty-four hours you were trying to rehome it and find a blacksmith to give him a pair of new shoes. You gave that donkey the best five months it ever had before it was turned into glue.

You were devastated when he died. You cried every time you saw a Pritt-stick. What happened to that mad old donkey loving cow? Come on now Cilla. Time to pack it in.

Blanche

Blanche,

The date didn't go well. He took my money when I fell asleep and abandoned me in a hotel room. I'm just in Serbia. I've managed to hitchhike my way here. I'm hoping I'll be able to get all the way back to the UK by Christmas. I'll write when I'm home.

Alex

Blanche

Boadicea Manor

Salford 6

England

From: Jessica Watkiss
To: Blanche
Subject Fat cow

7th August 2020

Dear Blanche,

I'm beside myself. My plan of eating nothing but dust for the past two months didn't work. I had visions of going back to the office looking like a different person and getting compliments from all my colleagues. I'd planned to buy a whole new wardrobe and turn heads when I walked back in. I wanted them to think, bloody hell, she looks good considering she's just had a baby. Instead, they'll think I'm an asteroid when my fat arse blocks out the sunlight from the floor to ceiling windows. I've tried hard to squeeze into my pre-maternity clothes, I had to lay on the bed to fasten one skirt. I thought it was going to cut the blood supply off to my toes. The only way I'll get in any of them is if I button them up first then catapult myself inside. I really wanted Katie in HR, who's a size six, to be pig sick when she saw me. I look like I've fucking eaten her. The only thing that fits me is a face mask.

I did really well the first few days on my diet: after I fed Fido in the morning, I'd leave him in his highchair whilst I did one of Joe Wicks' workouts on YouTube. Later I'd put Fido in his pram and join the other mummies in the park for a 5km walk. By the end of week two, I thought I'd nailed it. However, after an overly enthusiastic 15km walk I had a blister the size of Wales on my left foot. I declared myself disabled and I've not left the sofa since. I don't know why but I thought that one walk would cancel out any calories I consumed for the next few weeks, including the past ones I stuffed in my gob on the all-inclusive holiday. Why the fuck did that *bastard* not tell me I look like a beached whale in my costume. I'm surprised I didn't get harpooned when I went into the pool. When I was looking through the holiday pictures I thought, who's that fat bitch. It was me.

I tried filming a Tik Tok video to make my friends think I was an amazing, yummy mummy who had not only lost a few pounds but could perfectly juggle a newborn and housework. I didn't bother though as the light kept reflecting off my triple-chin. Instead, *he* filmed me trying to pole dance around the bookcase after three bottles of wine on Saturday night. I fell asleep with a half-eaten pork pie stuck to my face. I could have killed him when I saw he'd put it on Facebook. I'd been boasting that morning about my new vegan blog and how I plan to raise Fido on an all-organic diet. I'm going to have to style out the shame and say it was ironic and I was in on the joke. I did the only logical thing to cope with the embarrassment, I poured a large glass of Chardonnay and ate a Terry's Chocolate Orange. Does that count as one of my five a day?

Even Fido says, 'Moooooo' when I walk to the fridge. I still can't stop shovelling shite into my fat gob. I've had the shopping delivered for the last few weeks. I have food shame. Tesco delivers my wine on a Monday, Morrisons bring my Gin on a Tuesday, chocolate and crisps on a Wednesday from Sainsbury's, and Thursdays is a fruit and veg box from the farmers market which I then put in the bin on Sunday. On Friday and Saturday, we treat ourselves to a JustEat. I'm never going to shift this baby weight.

I'm going to have to wear my onesie to work. What the hell can I do Blanche? You're always the voice of reason.

From fatty of the year,

Jess.

From: Blanche
To: Jessica Watkiss
Subject Re: Fat cow

Dear Jess,

Have Fido adopted and get yourself to bootcamp. I'm sending a crane round this very minute to winch your fat arse off the sofa. I don't want you going back to work and being mistaken for a people carrier.

Nil by mouth is the way forward. Wire your jaw shut or use a nail gun from the shed to save time. I can get you a very good deal on cosmetic surgery. In the early 90s, me and Cilla went in for a little nip and tuck before it was fashionable. I had a hand transplant, I'd always wanted hands that are *as soft as your face* like Nanette Newman in the Fairy Liquid adverts. Cilla had a boob job, only when she ran up the stairs the silicone moved and she ended up with her tits in her stomach. Her belly button started lactating Strongbow.

Stop putting pressure on yourself. Every mother gets a free roll of fat they can never return with every child they have. Besides, everyone has been in lockdown for the past four months and is now either a raging alcoholic or three stone heavier, or both. You could try wearing a muzzle instead of a face mask at your desk. That should stop you from scranning any shite out the office treat draw.

Don't go trying to post any more inspirational videos, it's a well-known fact that people who do that spend their days crying into a tub of ice cream. It's all bullshit that's designed to make you think you're failing at life. Look behind that quote and Instagram video and you'll find a teenage pregnancy, a cannabis addiction, a marriage where the husband is out playing 'golf' with his secretary four nights a week, and worse of all, a Tory membership. Social influencers are the lowest of the low. Hard-faced bleeders who couldn't influence their way out of a paper bag, which is where I'd like to put them, with the opening glued shut. Imagine phoning companies and having the gumption to ask for freebies in exchange for a review on their platform. I'd push them off the bloody platform. You had to work for things in my day. I was down that precinct in all weathers saving up to buy the latest trends. I wouldn't have dreamed to ask for a freebie. Never mind the fear of missing out, they should have the fear of my bleeding fist if they ever ask me for a freebie. Don't go down that route, I'll have you disowned.

Anyway, as long as you brush your hair and teeth and wear a nice black top to hide the flab, you'll be fine. Your colleagues will just be glad to have you back. Enjoy it. You're fabulous.

With friendship,

Blanche

Cilla
Dressing Room 3
ITV Studios
London

12th August 2020

Oh Blanche,

Of course, I remember Scotty the donkey. He was a scabby mess, but he was my scabby mess. Every time I sang *Liverpool Lullaby,* I'd think of him.

Oh you are a mucky kid
Dirty as a dustbin lid
When he hears the things that you did
You'll get a belt from yer dad
Oh, you have your father's nose
So crimson in the dark it glows
If you're not asleep when the boozers close
You'll get a belt from yer dad

I'm skriking now just thinking of him. I always kept a tube of superglue in my handbag to remind me of him.

Blanche, I have to keep writing to the Labour MPs. I need them to make as many mistakes as Boris. He has to stay the Prime Minister, Blanche. He has to. Oh God, Blanche, I made such a mistake... Boris is the father of my child.

I don't know how it happened. I thought I'd had the menopause. I was forty-seven and he was twenty-six. I was doing an interview for *The Daily Telegraph* and he was there on the writers' desk. I wasn't thinking straight. I'd just filmed two shows back-to-back and had a bottle of cider on the way to the office. He said he could give me exclusive coverage. Before I knew it, I was in the cubby hole doing disgraceful things I'd not done since my time working the Blackpool prom. Blanche, it was bloody awful. When he dropped his pants the smell of pickled eggs hit the back of my throat. I was about to tell him to stop when I had a moment of clarity but he'd already finished. I was pregnant by the time I pulled my knickers back up. He's not got sperm, he's got torpedoes.

I called the baby Brian, after Epstein. My Bobby was ever forgiving, he said he'd love the baby as his own. We ended up having Brian adopted. Boris promised to stay in touch with him and look after him forever. That's why I need Boris to stay Prime Minister. For my little Brian. I'm sorry Blanche. I hope you understand. I can't stop writing to Labour MPs, if they're stupid enough to take my advice then they shouldn't be in government.

With regret, and hope.

Cilla

Blanche
Boadicea Manor
Salford 6

Cilla,

You fame hungry bitch. You made your Tory bed, you can lay in it.

Blanche

From:Randy Mottershed
To: Blanche
Subject #DogFest

20th August 2020

Dear Blanche,

Things have been manic since the Doggers' Picnic, I've not stopped replying to Mangled Mel's fan email. She's too busy filming her videos to reply. She ran a competition to see who could guess correctly the number of Maltesers she could fit in her mouth at once. Her fans went mad over it. The person who came closest was a man from Oxford who guessed 103. She actually managed 422. The stunt gained her another three thousand OnlyFans subscribers.

There have been many emails of thanks and three inform us the Doggers' Picnic has resulted in a conception and they're going to name the baby Jane, after Miss McDonald. I can't keep up with the orders from the online shop. Mel launched a new t-shirt last month, printed on the chest it reads *Eat Out to Help Out*. Underneath is a burger in a bun, only it isn't a bun, it's a.... well, you can imagine. It's been our best seller.

We went to preview the Channel 5 documentary, *Queen of the Dogs*. It was an enlightening and educational look into our community. They used Jane's new single as the soundtrack. I was a bit disappointed that I'd been edited out. It would have been nice to have my fifteen minutes of fame. It's been good exposure for Mel, she's making money hand over dildo. I think I might have created a monster. I'd like it to be just Mel and I again before all this craziness started. Mustn't grumble though Blanche, not every man can say their woman is *Queen of the Dogs*.

It means a lot to hear you say you think of us as friends. Whatever you need, say the word and you'll have it. We've got the money to do almost anything now Blanche. #DogFest is going to be much bigger and better than the Dogger's Picnic. Princess Ann is even helping us organise this one. The thought of a long weekend dogging has really captured her imagination. She's suggested getting a huge inflatable bed in the shape of a crown with handcuffs built into the frame. Ann's ideas are wild, Mel is all for them. We're getting around the socially distanced guidelines because of Ann's influence on the authorities. She's told them she can organise a peerage for those in charge if they leave us alone.

Mel's planning on getting a whole line-up of pop stars to attend this event, I don't really know why we need anyone other than Jane. Tickets are selling fast even though they're £120 each. You of course can have one for free if you would like to attend. It's from the 6th till the 9th of November. It might be chilly, but Mel's already thought of that and hired thirty outdoor gas heaters. I think I'll ask Alex to come. I've still not seen her since our trip to London. It does brighten my day when I talk to her.

Take care, Blanche. See you soon, and don't forget, we're here whenever you need us,

Randy

From:Blanche
To: Randy Mottershed
Subject Re: #DogFest

Randy,

I'd love to attend the #DogFest event, but I don't want to. Besides, you don't want to be looking after me, you should be out there getting your end away. If Mel tries to put you on the stall again tell her to sod off. You can hire some staff to help out. Sounds like you'll need it with such a huge turnout. I hope it doesn't rain, you don't want to be ankle-deep in a sea of sperm. You'll have to hope Boris doesn't lumber us with any more restrictions, your whole event would have to be cancelled. It would bankrupt Mel. Just think, when you first wrote to me you were worried about finding another couple to go dogging with. Now you've got a dogging family as big as the Royals.

Have you thought of inviting the Tory MPs to your event? Some of them are right dirty bastards by all accounts, they'll be there like a shot. If you get Ann Widecombe, Gove, Farage and Rees-Mogg will be sure to follow. I don't know how she does it but they throw themselves at her like lemmings.

I'm sensing you've got a little soft spot for Alex. I'm sure Mel would understand if you offered Alex a bite of your Bonio. Be warned, she gets a little clingy.

Keep me updated with everything.

Blanche.

Rishi Sunak MP
The Treasury
Westminster
London

25th August 2020

Dear Blanche,

I didn't realise that my initiative, Eat Out to Help Out, would backfire so spectacularly. Last night I took the cabinet to Nando's for our cheeky 90% off, we're Tories so we get more, and Boris created a scene that would embarrass a corpse. He's on a diet so he didn't eat as much as he normally does, he only ordered Halloumi Sticks & Dip, Wing Platter, Peri-Peri Whole Chicken, Chicken Burger, Chips, Spicy Rice, Macho Peas & a Salted Caramel Brownie. He was showing off in front of Gove and used the Extra Hot Peri-Peri sauce on everything. Despite sweating, burping and gasping for water he insisted on eating every last crumb. He chews his food like a trash compactor. This was all washed down with two gallons of bottomless Coca-Cola which resulted in a belch the sound of an exploding atomic bomb. Gove was in hysterics.

Theresa sat at the head of the table constantly on the lookout for an approaching waiter to keep her vodka topped up. She's an annoying drunk who craves attention. When we got a taxi back to Parliament, she was giving a two-finger salute to the people who stood in the queue at the food bank. I don't understand why those people can't use my vouchers for a decent meal out. The working-class are very stubborn.

Back in the restaurant, Priti kicked up a fuss when the bill came as Boris insisted on splitting it equally. He's one of those people who drinks Champagne whilst everyone else is on tap water and charges them for the pleasure. Priti refused and called him a tight-arsed bastard. Boris started to sob and throw the little crayons the waitress had brought over for him. Cummings took him out of his booster seat and marched him outside to calm down. He only came back inside on a promise of a scoop of vanilla.

Blanche, what am I to do? I cannot surround myself with these people all day every day for the next four years.

Yours sincerely,

Rishi

Blanche
Boadicea Manor
Salford 6

Dear Rishi,

There is nothing worse than being embarrassed by one of your friends. Cilla showed me up something chronic when we were flying to Thailand. She was always a nasty bitch to the cabin. I think she was jealous of how glamorous they looked stepping off the aircraft after a long-haul flight. Cilla could only leave the aircraft after nipping to the toilet and grouting her smoker's lines to look presentable in case of any press. On one particular flight, she'd had too many ciders. When the aircraft landed, she jumped up and ran over to the main door, mistaking it for the toilet she pulled the handle and set off the emergency shoot. She catapulted herself all the way to Phuket. I had to apologise to the captain, it was lucky he'd brought his spanner to restow the slide.

It took me three weeks to find Cilla. She was working for a pimp in the main resort. He said she was the hardest working girl he's ever had. Cilla received a parting gift of a silver phallus. A symbol of how many men she'd bedded in one afternoon. She boasted about it for months but said she nearly come a cropper after catching her fluffy handcuffs on a rotating fan. She was with a punter called Nigel from Wolverhampton. He gave her a fifty-dollar tip and said he'd never seen such elasticated breasts. He used her left one as a blanket.

Rishi, I do feel your pain, but don't worry. I very much doubt you'll last four years.

Regards,

Blanche

September

Blanche
Boadicea Manor
Salford

1ˢᵗ September 2020

Victoria,

What are you playing at? I've not heard a peep out of you since you buggered off to Santorini. Have you done a Shirley Valentine and found yourself a Greek hunk? I don't bloody blame you. Write and tell me all about it. I want all the juicy bits.

Blanche

From: Alex Huntington
To: Blanche
Subject I'm home

3rd September 2020

Dear Blanche,

You won't believe what happened. What do you reckon to this? I flew over to Sofia to meet Viktor and he was exactly how he was in his pictures, short and fat. I was so sure he'd be the one. I thought I could end up living on his farm and working as a milkmaid.

When I walked through the sliding doors of immigration at Sofia airport, he stood waiting for me with a huge bunch of flowers. I was going to book us into the airport hotel as Viktor said his farm was a three-hour drive away, however, he'd booked us in a motel halfway. He drove us there in his rusty old wagon, it was like something out of an old western movie. The rust was the only thing holding it together. There was a small café in the motel where we had goulash for dinner. It was a lovely evening. He showered me in compliments and took my hand to kiss it. What he lacked in looks he made up for in manners. In broken English, he told me he'd booked a twin room as he said he'd like to get to know me before we shared a bed. I thought was *really* sweet. In the room, we sat on our opposite beds chatting to each other about all kinds. We were listening to some local radio station, I didn't know what they were saying but I thought it was an excellent way to learn the local language. Then he started pouring this spirit. I can't remember what he said it was called but it was made from potatoes, 'good for the digestion'. It isn't good for the head though, that I can confirm. He said the way to do it was to knock it back in one. I did it five times.

I woke up the next afternoon when the maid came in to clean the room. I could barely open my eyes my head was throbbing that much. I went to tell the maid not to bother cleaning the room but when I tried to open my mouth to speak, I realised I couldn't, it had been taped up. Panic ran through my body. I couldn't move, my arms and legs were taped up too. The maid pulled a knife out of her belt. I thought I was a goner. She moved very slowly over to me. I was wiggling to try and escape, turns out she was the nice one. She cut through the brown tape that was holding me hostage, freeing my limbs. Everything was gone: money, passport, suitcase, everything. The maid took me down to the café and made me a coffee until I'd calmed down. It wasn't until I'd hitchhiked halfway home that I suddenly thought, why did that bitch have a knife? She told me, no police. I didn't even question it. She just threw me into the first lorry heading west.

The lorry driver was a lovely Slovak man named Marcel. He was transporting goods for Tesco across Europe. I thought I must be in safe hands with him as *Every Little Helps*. He had pictures of his family in his cabin and he let me share his sandwiches. It took four days to drive back to England. The journey was broken up as we called into Kosice, Slovakia, for five days so I could meet his wife. She was lovely and fed me up like you wouldn't believe. I've never tasted food so good. She took charge of getting me an emergency passport from the embassy to get me home. She even introduced me to her brother Jakub. He was very handsome and took me out one night to show me the town. It was *really* small, we were back in an hour.

I'm sorry I didn't write sooner. You must have been worried sick. It completely slipped my mind as ~~Dr Altman~~ Rebecca has had me working overtime rearranging patients' appointments. She doesn't work Fridays anymore as she goes to Brighton every weekend to see Sophie. I find it very unusual that she'd go to all these lengths for a friend, then again, they both know what each other is going through. It must be a comfort. Sophie is actually coming up here next week as we're all going to a funfair.

I don't know how you can be socially distanced on the dodgems but it's worth finding out, I'm going stir crazy sitting in this flat.

One thing is for sure though Blanche, I'm off men for life. There is no way I would so much as look at one now. I reported the crime to the police. They took it very seriously but said they didn't have much to go on other than they were looking for a man who may or may not be named Viktor and who may or may not be a farmer in Bulgaria. I admit it wasn't the brightest decision I've ever made. I'm OK though, feeling a bit lonely if I'm honest.

Best wishes,

Alex x

From: Alex Huntington
To: Blanche
Subject Re: I'm home

Alex,

If I knew where he was, I'd rip his head off and shit in his neck. But I don't unfortunately. Let that be a bloody lesson to you, you don't travel across Europe for a man you haven't met. Not unless you can be completely certain of the circumstances and know of his character. When I went to Cliff Richard's villa in Spain it was only on the account that he'd been vetted by our Cilla. The villa was lovely, but it was the most boring weekend of my life. I was expecting sex, drugs and rock n roll. I got yoga, green tea and canapés. Never again. I would have been grateful for someone to tie me up and drag me out of there.

It's scandalous the police won't do anything to help a tragic spinster. You only had to post dog shit through someone's letterbox in Langworthy Road when I was a teenager and the police would be there in a shot. She was a right loopy bitch four doors down, she thought she could see dead people. She could see stars by the time me mam had finished with her. I suppose these days she'd get an ASBO and an ankle tag. Back then being shamed by the community was a far worse punishment. The mad cow had to get a bus to the other side of Salford to be served in a corner shop.

I blame Tory cutbacks: 23,500 fewer police officers on the streets since 2010. No wonder they don't have much hope of finding Viktor.

Meanwhile, Boris is sitting in number ten doing bugger all apart from giving cash to his friends. Makes my blood boil. Doesn't it yours?

I think it's absolutely right that you stay off men for a while, though something tells me it won't be for long.

Kind regards,

Blanche

Diane Abbott MP
House of Commons
Westminster

15ᵗʰ September 2020

Blanche,

I'm so sorry. As you put it, *I fucked it up.* I promise you, Blanche, I had everything planned. I was going to go down to ITV studios for the pre-auditions to *Britain's Got Talent* and audition in disguise. I wanted to see how close I could get to Amanda. I was then going to go away and put a plan together. I didn't get that far. I don't really know how to tell you. I've enclosed a press cutting which explains it.

Daily World 13th
September 2020

TV JUDGE IN MASKED PANDA 999 CALL

Britain's Got Talent judge, Amanda Holden, was rushed into hospital last night after being involved in a serious incident involving a talent hopeful. An unknown contestant auditioning as a roller-skating, fire-eating panda, caused untold damage to the studio after setting it ablaze.

The contestant, nicknamed Blue Panda, was wearing a full panda costume with a Tory rosette, when they skidded and fell in a puddle left behind by the previous act, Rupert the flying pug. Audience members reported the panda communicated by a series of hand gestures which left them bemused.

Amanda, who was the sole judge on the panel for the pre-recording rehearsal was said to be reaching for her red buzzer when tragedy struck.

'Panda had just lit a fire stick when it skidded on that pug's p*ss and crashed to the floor. The stick went flying through the air and landed on the golden buzzer. It released Confetti which rained down everywhere like a golden shower,' said Daniel from Birmingham. 'I'm not sure what happened next Bab, everyone was clapping and screaming as they thought it was part of the act. It wasn't until a producer was slapping Amanda on the back that we realised she was choking on confetti.'

Further eyewitness reports suggest that Blue Panda set the stage alight whilst trying to reignite another fire stick to carry on their routine. A stray spark ignited the confetti which soon engulfed the studio.

'It was proper lush until the fire alarms went off,' said Soumia from Newport.

The hunt is now on for the Tory supporter who was hiding behind the mask.

Commenting from Downing Street last night regarding the rumours that Blue Panda is a substantial Tory Party donor, Prime Minister Boris Johnson said, 'We may or may not have a Panda who is a member of our party. There is no suggestion that a party donor is involved in any wrongdoing. As a gesture of goodwill, we have made a large donation to the Panda Project.'

A show insider has confirmed Amanda was taken to St Thomas's Hospital where she remains in a medically induced coma. It is thought Amanda will remain in the hospital for the foreseeable future.

I panicked Blanche. When the stage went up in flames, I had flashbacks to that day in 1990 in Trafalgar Square when the African Embassy was set ablaze. I skated out of the studio and all the way back to Hackney as quick as I could on my skates. I didn't talk to anyone, and I only stopped for a Greggs' iced bun for my sugar levels. I've burnt the costume in a bonfire in the garden. I don't think anybody saw me.

What should I do Blanche? I'm panicking.

Desperately seeking advice,

Diane

Blanche
Boadicea Manor
Salford 6

Diane,

You're a bloody genius, but choking is a nasty way to go.
Don't do anything yet. Standby to take over Number Ten.

Blanche.

From: Sophie McBride
To:Blanche
Subject Rebecca

17th September 2020

Dear Blanche,

I can't believe it's been two months since I last wrote. Time has gone in the blink of an eye. I barely know where to begin. I'm almost embarrassed to tell you what's happened, I hope you won't judge me too harshly.

Remember I told you about that blog that Nathan had written about his affair with my husband, SleepingWithTheProfessor.com. Well, he must have thought he was a right Carrie Bradshaw writing those columns. You should have seen all the comments of support he had. Well, I had one too many glasses of wine one night and left a comment saying he must think he's very clever writing about a woman who has done nothing to him and in fact, though he has painted himself to be the victim, he is the one who has destroyed a family and left a photo album on my doorstep for me to find. He omitted that from his own blogs. His followers read my comment and have called him every name under the sun. He's since deleted the whole website. A victory for wives who have been cheated on everywhere.

I've continued going to the support group. I've been to every session actually. Rebecca (Dr Altman) has come with me. She's been staying at her folks every weekend so she can attend. We've become very close. Closer than I could ever have imagined. We've been out most Saturdays since we met and even had a picnic on the beach. We've laughed so much, I think that's what I've missed the most these last few years, just letting your hair down and being silly. Rebecca had ice cream with a flake on the beach and a seagull came down and took it out of her hand. She sat in shock whilst I giggled like a teenager. We treated ourselves to some nice munchies from M&S and got a couple of G'n'Ts in a can each too. We had the food laid out on a little blanket and we just grazed all afternoon on a little tapa. I even tried olives to look sophisticated, they're like little pellets of vomit. Then I thought, why am I trying to impress her? Why do I care if Dr Rebecca Altman thinks I'm sophisticated? And it hit me Blanche, I fancied her. Me, whose husband has just run off with another bloody man was sitting here looking at a woman thinking, I'd quite like to kiss you. She must have sensed it. I don't even know how it happened, we kissed. It was soft and lovely. I couldn't tell you the last time I kissed someone and felt those butterflies. It must have been all those years ago snogging Marcus at the bus stop on Friday nights.

It wasn't awkward after. We kissed a few more times before we went home. That was about a month ago and we haven't stopped kissing since. We stop Monday to Thursday when she goes back to Peterborough for work. We've been sending each other silly messages like lovesick teenagers. Not that I'm saying it's love, it's just different. Exciting. I've been reading up on it, there are thousands of us. They call us *late-blooming lesbians*. I quite like that term. We haven't told anyone yet and I won't be telling the kids until I'm sure it's right. I almost can't wait to tell Marcus just to see the look on his face.

Can you imagine if the fortune teller was right, that I am about to embark on a new journey as a free spirit whilst getting shagged. I do bloody hope so!

Love Sophie (the late-blooming lesbian)

P.S I can't believe Cilla did that when you were on *This Is Your Life*. It's always the quiet ones.
P.P.S Would love to meet up anytime. Just need enough notice to get cover at the salon.

From: Blanche
To:Sophie McBride
Subject Re: Rebecca

Sophie,

I'm surprised you think of me as judgemental. I don't know what I've done to give you that impression. I think a lesbian experience can be very freeing. I myself was a *late-blooming lesbian*. Looking back on it now, it was probably just boredom. I've never forgotten Jacqueline, she was my one big disappointment in life. I always thought I could tell a Conservative voter a mile off. She had me fooled, easy to do when you're mute I suppose. She was the only lesbian lover I ever had. I'm glad I tried it, I couldn't have done it full time.

It will be a very modern family sitting around your table this Christmas. The kids won't care, just means they'll get even more presents in future. Don't rush into telling them and don't give any signs like investing in Dolly Parton's back catalogue or suddenly chopping off all your hair. I apologise, that's a very stereotypical view of lesbians, they come in all shapes and sizes since they relaxed the membership rules.

I would plan very carefully how you're going to tell Marcus. Maybe repay the favour and hand him and Nathan a photo album of you both in compromising positions. Some may say that's a little childish, I say if you can't beat them, twat them. Maybe the four of you can go out for a socially distanced picnic and break the news. I think it's quite cosmopolitan really what's happened. You should join some other support groups and take in a few gay bars, there are lots of them in Brighton as you know. I used to frequent them myself in the late 90s after I'd run Tony's election campaign. I ended up putting a Tiller Girl drag queen tribute show together. It was marvellous. They had thirty-five costume changes in two and a half minutes. They built up to a finale where fireworks would shoot from their bosoms to the soundtrack of *The Sound of Music*. It was one of my mum's favourites and I was willing to put my own history with Julie Andrews behind me.

Embrace your new sense of self. I'm very happy for you Sophie.

Blanche

P.S I'll consult my diary and let you know when we can meet up. I think a trip to Westminster would be wonderful, don't you?

William Townsend
29 Hellbourne Close
Salford

19ᵗʰ September 2020

Dear Blanche,

I found the letters which you wrote to my mum, Victoria. She kept them in a little box in her bedside drawer. I found them when I was arranging her things. I'm sorry to have to write and tell you this way. Mum passed away in late July.

If I had a contact number, I would have called you sooner. You weren't in her book. I read over the letters you sent her and hers to you. She kept copies in the envelopes of your responses. Your friendship must have meant a lot to her. Her letters were brave and honest. I'm glad she had someone to share that with. I know it was short-lived, but you gave her fight. She kept that fight until the end.

I know you helped her pay for Santorini. It was very kind of you. She didn't make it there. She had every intention, her suitcase was packed on her bed ready to go. Her passport is still on her dresser — untravelled. I don't know what to do with it.

She was taken to hospital two days before she was due to depart. She didn't tell any of the three of us, her children I mean, that she wasn't well until she was already in the hospital. It was Covid. She caught it from my dad. He recovered.

Mum was brave and strong. She fought to the end. We weren't allowed in to see her, we could FaceTime her every day and we were on FaceTime when she passed. A nurse held her hand. I can take comfort that she wasn't completely alone. I would have gone if they let me, virus or not. I would have sat with her. I wanted to sit with her. I wanted to protect her as she protected me. From him. From dad.

He said he'd never let her go. He didn't.

We had to wait a month for the funeral, only us three children and my dad were allowed. She would have hated him being there. How could I have stopped him? We brought flowers and we spelt her name *Vicky*. I think she would have liked that. I hope she's free now to be who she wants. I hope she's at nursing school in the sky. And I hope she's laughing. That's what I hope most of all.

I didn't say goodbye, that was too hard. You can't say goodbye to your mum. I got to tell her, 'I love you, Mum.' The easiest and hardest words I've ever said. I hope she heard. I hope she knew. I hope she knows.

Thank you, Blanche, for giving her strength.

Maybe she went to Santorini after all.

With sincerest sympathy,

William

Boris Johnson MP
10 Downing Street
Westminster

20ᵗʰ September 2020

Dear Blanche,

I fear Sir Trevor McDonald is closing in on me. He will stop at nothing to torment and submit me into paying for the protection of Meghan and Harry. How do I even know he's providing the security I asked for? I heard a rumour he had a contract with the palace to provide security for the Duchess of York, he just provided a swan and a corgi until the contract was prematurely ended. For all I know he's just given them a poodle and pigeon for protection. Why did I not check the small print? Is there someone I can fire who can take the blame? Maybe I will write to Sir Trevor and tell him I'm protected by Carrie, she's bloody terrifying.

I've been caught in a blasted media storm caused by a fire-eating, Conservative voting panda. Well, that is what the media thinks. I know the man behind the mask is Sir Trevor. He will stop at nothing to belittle me and get his money. Well, it backfired on him, I've been forced to make a payment to the Panda Project. I have even less money than usual to pay for his services. It's almost impossible to pay for the essential items once I've paid the money to my friends for bogus services. I'm fed up with it all Blanche, I just want a damned holiday. Even Dom has been distant from me recently. I long to be with him. To feel his warm protective embrace. All I've got at the moment is Carrie giving me earache about how I need to do more around the house. She doesn't appreciate I am dealing with a pandemic. How do I stop having more children? There's even talk of a new strain of them in South Africa. I don't remember ever having a woman there.

How simple life used to be. I wish I had time to chase you around the house again my little Maid Marian. Dom dressed up in the outfit for me as a special treat last week, I must admit, his legs looked rather fetching but his breasts were not as magnificent as yours.

I long to leave this all behind me, number ten and the decisions and the constant squabbles in the cabinet. I haven't been in since last week. I couldn't face it. I'm not really needed at the moment as Dom is still making all my decisions. What a splendid job he's doing of it too.

Blanche, please talk to Sir Trevor for me, ask him to leave me alone. I live in constant fear.

Sincerely yours,

Boris

Blanche
Boadicea Manor
Salford 6

Boris,

What a daft apeth you are. You've made a right bloody mess of everything. I will not speak to Sir Trevor for you. I warned you, Boris, he's a very powerful man and he isn't to be messed with. I fear the repercussions you'll face when he catches up with you. He'll be there when you least expect it, lurking over your shoulder, in your reflection, breathing on your neck. Try not to think about it. Did you hear how he once crushed one of the world's most wanted men with his bare hands? He ground their bones until there was nothing left but a fine powder. It's a good job Gove didn't find it.

Just try and enjoy what time you have left in Downing Street. I have a feeling it won't be very long. Then you can go back to your daily play dates with Dom and get journalists beaten up.

Have you ever thought of just paying Sir Trevor for the service you hired him for? If you can pay your friends for bogus contracts, surely you can pay for something which you've signed for?

Blanche

From:Randy Mottershed
To: Blanche
Subject Mel & Alex

23rd September 2020

Dear Blanche,

I have been thinking about Alex a lot recently, we've continued to Zoom every week. She's had it rough these last few months. I can't believe what she's been through. I find her very brave, how she puts herself out there. She's like my Mel in some ways, only she doesn't video her private parts and put them online for a fee. Alex told me she's off men now, which is a shame as I'd like to have taken her out. I love my Mel, even though she's very much a control freak these days. It would just be nice to be listened to from time to time.

Mel's going to great lengths to make #DogFest a huge event, she's advertising it as the Dogger's Glastonbury. Instead of camping in a tent, you sleep in your car and put your headlights on if you fancy a bit of action. Mel wants a funfair there this time, she's arranged for me to go to view one and sign a contract if I feel it's right. It's a travelling fair and they're passing through Peterborough in a couple of weeks. I'm going to visit them and Alex at the same time if she's free.

You wouldn't believe the organisation that goes into something like this. From portable toilets to stages and dressing rooms. I'm glad I just do as I'm told to be honest. Jane McDonald is obviously headlining after her new album — *Songs to go Dogging To* — reached the top of the charts. Deposits have been paid for the entertainment, it's left us with hardly anything to live off. Mel says you have to speculate to accumulate. Two-thousand t-shirts got delivered yesterday to sell on the souvenir stall. They have a new design, they say *Top Dog* across the chest with a picture of Princess Ann riding a Corgi underneath. Ann's not been off the phone with Mel, she's asked if she can set up her own stall selling sexual aids. Ann designed all the toys herself and gave Mel exclusive rights to promote them on her OnlyFans account. She's been trying them all week; I don't know if she likes them as she won't let me in the room to help. At one point she was screaming as I've never heard before. I don't think they're very good.

Kind regards,

Randy

From:Blanche
To: Randy Mottershed
Subject Re: Mel & Alex

Randy,

You best hope Boris doesn't tighten the Covid restrictions again now you've spent all that money. You'd bankrupt yourselves and be back to bonking in a layby on the M1. I used to think being poor was a terrible thing, I see now that money doesn't buy you happiness, does it? It certainly doesn't buy you class. You only have to look at a Tory MP to know that. The poorest of folk tend to be the most caring, 'salt of the earth,' as me mam would say. I think I forgot that somewhere along the way. Maybe being friends with Cilla rubbed off on me a little, all champagne and no compassion.

You know, when I lived in that terrace in Langworthy Road, I didn't know we were poor. I thought every family had a damp patch on the ceiling, an outdoor toilet, hung their tea bags on the line and a useless man of the house. And you know what, they did where I came from. It was nowt to be ashamed of because we had pride. We looked after each other, kept an eye out, and would rally around when things went wrong. A lot of people have lost their pride through no fault of their own. It's hard to stay dignified when the system is set up to make you fail. It's difficult to keep your head high when you're queuing up at the food bank or deciding whether to put your last fifty pence in the electric meter or spend it on three tins of savers beans. Keep it high you must, only those with privilege will tell you it's your fault.

Try to keep your pride, Randy. By all means, help Mel, but don't be a mug. Know this, if it does all go to pot, I'll be there to help.

Keep safe Randy.

Blanche.

OCTOBER

Boris Johnson MP
10 Downing Street
London

1ˢᵗ October

Dear Blanche,

It's been a disastrous time for me this week. I've been forced to close the bars in Parliament at ten pm like the rest of the nation. Rees-Mogg is furious, he's been sending Diane Abbott to Bargain Booze every night to get his fix of Babycham. He gives her a two-pound tip, he's very much an ally to the Black Lives Matter movement.

Dominic and I have been left with nowhere to meet up for our evening rendezvous. Normally we'd burrow into a little corner of *The Famous Cock*, it's the VIP bar in Parliament, and he'd run his fingers through my back hair, and I'd polish his head. Theresa was caught vandalising the sign last week, she stuck a picture of Piers Morgan under the lettering, she's never forgiven him for a difficult interview on *This Morning Britain*. Piers tricked her into dancing to Abba in a swimming costume. It was later reported that Farage uploaded the video to an X-rated social media sight where it gained 3 million likes and crashed the internet. Gove went blind for a week.

Dom and I have been forced to release a new initiative so we can spend time together, *Free Adult Education for All*. We've signed up for an empathy class. We've been separated in class for laughing at videos of the homeless. I've also enrolled in a self-defence course to learn how to protect myself from any surprise attacks from Sir Trevor McDonald, I've been able to use some moves on Priti. I regretted it when she gave me a Chinese burn.

Blanche, I'm fed up with this workload, I just want to be back at *The Times* making up quotes and spending the evenings with Dom trying to light our farts.

Please help.

Boris

Blanche
Boadicea Manor
Salford 6

Dear Boris,

It won't be long, and you can go back to your day job, whatever that is. I promise.

Blanche.

From: Jessica Watkiss
To: Blanche
Subject Bun in over
4th October 2020

Blanche,

I'm fucking pregnant!

That *bastard* has knocked me up again. It must have been the last night of our holiday. It's the only time we've done it since I gave birth to Fido. How can you fall pregnant after doing it just once? I must have more eggs than a bastard hen.

I was made up to be going back to work. I hadn't managed to fit into any of my slim clothes which resulted in me online panic buying some baggy trousers and flowing tops. I actually scrubbed up for my first day back really well. I'd been feeling a bit queasy in the few days before my return. I put it down to nerves. I didn't think any more of it. On my first day back, I went in and did the obligatory hellos around the office and showed off a few photos of Fido. I was met with a few comments, 'What an unusual name'. I just smiled and said I really wanted something fun and modern. I didn't tell them that I panicked and named him after a bastard dog. I'd just sat down at my desk and logged on to my computer when I had to run to the toilet. I vomited my guts up. I still didn't think anything of it until Mandy on the service desk shouted over, 'You sure it's not morning sickness? Imagine that, being pregnant on your first day back from maternity leave.' I didn't take any notice of her until she asked me if I'd been sick before. When I said I had, she told me, 'You best pop out and have a test. They'll send you straight home with this virus going around if you're up the duff.'

I waited until lunchtime and walked to the chemist. I was nearly crying at the thought of it. Mandy came with me to the toilet when I did the test. Those thirty seconds waiting for the results to come after I pissed on the stick were the longest of my life. Sure enough, two bastard blue lines appeared. I cried my eyes out whilst Mandy congratulated me and went and got that skinny bitch Katie from HR. She apologised for not having organised a collection for the baby, as if she had time to do so when the piss on the test was still fresh, then bundled me off home in the back of a taxi to be placed on furlough until my maternity leave starts again.

I told *him* that evening. He was buzzing. Congratulating himself for having the most powerful sperm in the world. I said, 'shut the fuck up, who do you think you are, Boris Johnson?' He said, 'aww, that will be your hormones.' I punched him and confirmed that it was indeed the hormones.

I'm devastated Blanche, I just wanted to be me again for a few hours a day when I'm at work. We've already block paid for the nursery until the end of January. At least it means I get to have some time to myself during the day. I don't think I could manage with a toddler crawling everywhere when I already seem to be ballooning at an alarming rate. No wonder my slim clothes didn't fit. I knew it couldn't be because I'm a greedy cow.

Blanche, what the fuck am I going to do?

With a bun in the oven,

Jess

From: Blanche
To: Jessica Watkiss
Subject Re: Bun in over

Jess,

Calm down. Remember, a baby is a gift from mother nature, or in your case from the bottom of an empty bottle of Chardonnay. It's great Fido will have a little brother or sister to play with. You'll be able to use all the baby stuff you've already bought. You won't have to buy anything new. Princess Di reused all of William's baby items with Harry. She even recycled his cloth nappies, she didn't bleach them well enough to remove William's skid marks. It's wonderful news. Congratulations. It will take a while to sink in. You'll soon be over the moon.

You could start your own blog to pass the time, call it The Joy of Contraception. You can write a true account of pregnancy, childbirth and motherhood. I'm sure Durex would sponsor you. Post unfiltered pictures of you scraping baby shit up off the carpet and retell the tail of your birth. You'd be an online hit. An anti-influencer. My flatmate Fergie tried influencing to promote her old autobiography. She wrote a review and stuck it in her window, being on the 26th floor of a high-rise no one saw it.

Take each day as it comes and just be grateful the nurseries are still open. I've enclosed a book of Royal baby names, it's an old one of Fergie's. I've crossed out all the shite names like Beatrice and Eugenie. Remember, I'm here for you, just as I know you'll be there for me in my hour of need.

With love,

Blanche

Blanche
Boadicea Manor
Salford 6

17th October 2020

Diane,

It's nearly time to move. 1st December. Get your cabinet ready.

Blanche

From: Alex O'Neil
To: Blanche
Subject Happy Ending

19th October 2020

Dear Blanche,

What do you reckon to this? It's the best news I could ever have hoped to tell you. No more lonely evenings sitting in my flat with my cat after a hard day at work. No more dodgy dates or European psychos. No more dating apps. No more climbing through windows, because

ALEX HUNTINGTON GOT MARRIED!!!!

I'm now Alex O'Neil. Blanche, he's proper gorgeous — Conner O'Neil. He runs the Waltzers on a travelling funfair. I'm so sorry I didn't invite you to the wedding, it was all a bit mad and hectic.

Randy called me to tell me all about #DogFest and how Mangled Mel needed to book a travelling funfair for the entertainment. As it happened, the funfair was coming to Peterborough for an illegal lockdown rave. Randy asked me if he could stay at mine for the night whilst he went to meet them and check if they were any good. I didn't have anything else going on so I said yes. He came down on the Friday afternoon in his HGV. He had to park it at the surgery as I don't have any parking spaces at my flat.

It was such a brilliant night. Randy was excited. I get the feeling that things aren't great between him and Mel. He didn't go into details, just said he was glad to be out of the house. Luckily, I was only a fifteen-minute walk away from the rave. I made a real effort. I Googled what to wear, it was totally inappropriate for this time of year. Being of a certain age,

I put my thermals leggings underneath my denim hotpants and wore a gold bikini top over my woolly jumper. I put electric blue mascara on my hair and wore bright pink wellington boots to complete the outfit. I looked *crazy*. I'd bought a couple of glow sticks online to use on the dance floor. Randy wore a blue boiler suit.

I couldn't believe how big the rave was considering everyone was supposed to be social distancing. There was a line of caravans parked up on the field beside the rave that belonged to the workers. Randy had been told to go to the black caravan with two yellow stripes around the centre and ask for B. B, short for Bernard, was a lovely toothless man who led the fair. Randy and B went inside the caravan to talk contracts. B gave me a wristband which allowed me to queue jump and go on all the rides for free.

I felt like a VIP going past all the girls shivering in the queues. First, I went on the big wheel, only it wasn't really that big and it was quite cold when you got to the top as the breeze caught you, I was glad I'd put my thermals on. I gave the dodgems a miss as I thought it might be a bit awkward bumping into people you don't know, plus young drivers these days are lethal. I went on the waltzers next, I used to love going on them as a kid. I sat inside the little cart and that's when I saw him, Conner O'Neil. The most handsome man I've ever laid my eyes upon. He looked so cool in his dungarees, his tight white polo top he wore underneath showed off all his muscles. My heart skipped a beat when he came over to my cart to lower the protective bar ready for the start of the ride. He spun me around that little track until I was that dizzy I could see six of him. I thought I'd died and gone to heaven. When we stopped, he raised the bar and jumped in the car beside me and asked in a sexy gravelly Irish accent if I fancied some company on another spin round the track. We stayed there for another five rides until I was seeing thirty-six of him. As we stood up, he asked me if I was hungry. I wasn't but made a positive grunting sound to say yes. He walked me to a stall to get candyfloss and I don't know whether it was the company or the recipe, but it was the sweetest and most delicious candyfloss I've ever tasted. I would have married him there and then if he asked me.

We ended up spending the next few hours together. I climbed in his sack to go down the helter-skelter with him before we went on the ghost train where he put his arm around me to protect me. I had butterflies so big I thought they were pigeons. He leaned in to kiss me just as a skeleton dropped out of the ceiling. We went back to his caravan after that to warm up with a hot drink. I completely forgot about Randy until he texted me to see where I was. I told him and B brought him to Conner's caravan. It was only next door, turned out B is Conner's dad. The four of us chatted for a while and celebrated with a mug of Jack Daniels each as Randy awarded B's fair the contract for #DogFest. I swapped numbers with Conner before we left. I couldn't believe he'd texted me to make sure I'd got home safely. He's a real gentleman.

I woke up just knowing I'd see Conner that day. I was knocking on his caravan door by 9am. I'd already waved Randy off before he headed back up north. Conner was a bit surprised to see me so early but as I said to him, I needed to strike whilst the iron was hot. It's been a whirlwind ever since. Connor told me how he would like to leave the fair behind and live a more settled life. His parents had been putting pressure on him to find a girl to marry as it was frowned upon to be single at the age of thirty-three in their community. I took five days' leave from work and spent every minute of the next week with him. I even helped him out on the waltzers at the next illegal rave.

We didn't stop laughing all week. On the seventh night, he took me on the big wheel. When we got to the top, we could see the lights of the city centre in the distance. It was *really* romantic. I just blurted it out, 'Will you marry me?' It took him a while to respond but he said 'Yes.' We celebrated with a ride on the waltzers. I'm going to move into his caravan. I've got to work my notice at the surgery, I've already told Dr Altman I'm leaving. She told me to follow my heart. She's much nicer now she's a lesbian. I couldn't believe it when she said she and Sophie from Brighton were now an item. Love conquers all in the end.

Conner's mum and dad were made up and said they could finally hold their heads up high in the community. They said there was no point in hanging around as the man who ran the huck-a-duck stand used to be a priest. We were married three days later on the love train. Conner looked so handsome, and I felt beautiful in ~~Dr Altman's~~ Rebecca's wedding dress. She was my bridesmaid and Sophie was her plus one. I wore the dress with my wellingtons which I'd decorated by putting a veil around the rim of each boot. Everyone had spuds and sugar dummies to eat. We partied all night at the fair. It was perfect.

Do you think I've rushed into it or do think when you know you just know? Can love really last a lifetime?

Sending you all my love,

Mrs Alex Neil

P.S I've enclosed a slice of wedding cake, it was shaped like a waltzer's cart.

From: Blanche
To: Alex O'Neil
Subject Congratulations

Alex,

Congratulations to the bride and groom. May you have many happy years ahead of you. Like a fat lass at Greggs, you've run into it very fast. Yes, Alex when you know you know. The moment I first set eyes on my late husband's Rolex, I knew immediately he was the one for me.

Don't worry about not inviting me to the wedding. I would have had to politely decline. After two of my own weddings and being locked up in the basement for Princess Di's, I come out in a rash at the very thought of them.

I do love a funfair. If I could ever get a Saturday off from the market stall on the precinct as a teenager, me and a few other girls on Langworthy Road would get the bus to Belle Vue Zoological Gardens. It was such a treat going up there and seeing the animals and having a go on Bobs Rollercoaster. Me heart used to be in my gob before the big drop. I used to hate sitting next to Sharon from number five, she would wet her knickers on the climb up.

The animals were always my favourite, giraffes and zebras. I think that's where I must have gotten my love for animal print from. I would never wear real fur; I don't believe in killing animals for clothing, I am partial to a nice leather handbag though. It closed down forty-five years ago. When Blackpool pleasure beach opened the *Big One* rollercoaster in '94, me, Cilla and Di camped out overnight to be the first in line to have a go. Cilla was all for using her star power to queue jump but Di, very much one of the people insisted we waited in line. It was one of the rare moments when Cilla and Di called a truce. We didn't have a tent or sleeping bag, we just huddled up close under a blanket and sang songs with the others waiting in line. No one bothered us for our autographs, we very much blended into the crowd. The three of us were shitting ourselves when we finally got on and we were making the slow climb. When we came hurtling down that first drop Cilla lost her dentures in the wind. The automatic picture that's taken on your way down showed a gummy Cilla trying to catch her overbite whilst Di looked fresh from a photoshoot with not a hair out of place. I looked as white as a ghost.

I believe that love can last a lifetime. It does change though. Lust turns to love and instead of wanting to rip their clothes off, you want to rip their head off instead. But when you'd protect them from anything and anyone, that's when you know it's true love. Hold onto it Alex and enjoy it, you never know when a petrol lawnmower will come and take it all away.

Blanche

From: Sophie McBride
To:Blanche
Subject Coming out

26th October 2020

Dear Blanche,

I really do need your help. Things between Rebecca and I have been great. We decided to tell the kids that mummy and Rebecca were more than just good friends. I spoke to Marcus about it first, he was in shock. He had the nerve to ask me if he'd turned me gay and if it was just a phase. This man who's been sleeping with his boyfriend for years behind my back has the cheek to ask me if I've been lying to him. I was so angered by him I just said, 'Yes, you were that shit at sex, I thought I'd try it with a woman.' His face dropped. Why is he even bothered?

We sat John down first, we thought he'd understand it more or he would be so angry that I wouldn't want his little sister to see his teenage outburst and get upset. Rebecca and I told him we wanted to talk. He said good because he wanted to get something off his chest. I thought he was going to tell me he'd got a girl pregnant or he was trouble at school for smoking cannabis or something. He was shifting in his seat and playing with his hands. Then he came out with it, 'Mum, I'm gay.' Just like that. No warning, no nothing. Peter, who I thought was his best friend who's stayed over a million times is his boyfriend. I didn't know what to say other than, 'well don't think you're staying in the same room again.' He said, 'I know you'd be uncool,' then got up and stormed out.

He's been staying at his dad's all weekend and ignored all my calls and text. I'm worried sick about him. Kids can be cruel, can't they? I don't care what he is as long as he's happy. Do you think we've made him gay, it's possible isn't it with two gay parents?

In shock,

Sophie

From: Blanche
To:Sophie McBride
Subject Re: Coming out

Sophie,

You can't catch gay! Even if it does seem like an epidemic in your house. It's only been one weekend, give him time, he's a teenager. What he's done is really brave and you should be very proud that he won't be marrying a woman and living a lie for twenty years. Kids are different these days, they're out and proud. They don't have Thatcher's Section 28 to deal with. Schools offer support groups now and teachers can help. You can't turn your TV on without seeing a gay character these days, which is brilliant and how it should be, I just wish there were fewer Tories.

The only thing John wants to know is that his mum still loves him. That's all there is to it. It really isn't a problem.

Give him a hug from me (and some Durex),

Blanche

P.S Not letting Peter stay in the same room is a bit like bolting the stable door after the gay horse has buggered off to the drag show.

November

From: Alex O'Neil
To: Blanche
Subject Bankrupt

1st November 2020

Dear Blanche,

Did you see Boris's conference? What did you reckon to it? I can't believe we're going into another lockdown. Randy has called B and cancelled the funfair for #DogFest. Connor said we were relying on that money to get us through the winter. We have no other source of income, and we can't be put on furlough as we're self-employed. I can't believe this Blanche, we're starting off our married life completely skint. I've got savings but they won't last very long. Connor said the community will pull together and there is always the food bank in a worst-case scenario. I never pictured myself queuing up for handouts. What are we going to do Blanche?

Alex

From: Blanche
To: Alex O'Neil
Subject Re: Bankrupt

Alex,

It's time we did something about it and stopped letting Boris and his Tories screw us over. No one should be forced to start married life destitute on the scrap heap. Alex, there is never any shame in doing what you need to do to survive. If you need to go to the foodbank, then go. But I have enclosed a cheque for £2,000 to get you through the month. Don't put it in the bank, cash it in at one of those converter places.

Help me to help you and everyone else who's been screwed over this year. You've asked me several times how you could ever repay me for my support this year, and now I'm telling you how. It's time to bring down this government and stop them from putting money in their friends' pockets and back into the purses of those who need it most, hard workers like you.

Meet me at Euston station at midday on Saturday 5th December. Bring everyone you know, and don't forget your face masks.

Blanche

From:Randy Mottershed
To: Blanche
Subject Not a pot to piss in

1st November 2020

Dear Blanche,

We've had to cancel #DogFest because of the new lockdown. We've lost everything. Princess Ann told us just carry on and have it anyway, but we can't risk everyone attending getting a fine. Doggers are a very law-abiding community.

We've had to cancel all the entertainment and the funfair. I felt awful talking to Alex afterwards knowing she really can't afford to lose out on this money, there's nothing I can do. Mel has already tweeted that it's cancelled to all her followers. She's been working hard trying to attract subscribers to her OnlyFans to raise some much-needed cash.

I'm going to be stuck with a thousand t-shirts and no way to shift them. I'm really not looking forward to cancelling Jane McDonald, she's been so good to us. It really is all a mess. What can we do Blanche, we're going to have to sell the house to refund everyone.

Kind regards,

Randy

From:Blanche
To: Randy Mottershed
Subject Re: Not a pot to piss in

Randy,

Don't panic. We won't take this laying down. We have to stand up to the government for doggers everywhere. It's your right to go dogging and no one should take that away from you. If the virus was handled properly in the first place, we'd be back to normal by now. You know me, Randy, I'm a pacifist, but it's time we took back control for doggers everywhere. Help me to help you.

Be at Euston station at midday, Saturday 5th December. Get Mel to tweet it to all her followers and give instructions on her OnlyFans. It will only work if you bring everyone! Don't forget your face masks.

Blanche

P.S Don't cancel Jane, just tell her there is a change of venue

From: Jessica Watkiss
To: Blanche
Subject Bastard Boris
7th November 2020

Blanche,

Have you seen the bastard news? That incompetent twat Boris has closed the nurseries except for key workers without childcare options. I'm not like him, I can't go around popping out kids all day and just forget about them. Some of us have got to accept responsibility, no matter how much it drives you bastard mad. I bet that Carrie will still have a nanny helping her out. Just because I'm at home all day doesn't mean I don't have things to do. Now I'll have to do it all with a fucking toddler around my feet. I wouldn't mind but I should be at pissing work. I'd be able to go if Boris hadn't handled this pandemic as shit as one of his own marriages. That *bastard* thinks I'm overreacting, he still gets to leave the house as he's a key worker. I'm absolutely furious Blanche, first I can't work and now the nurseries are closed. I'm not standing for this anymore.

What the fuck am I going to do Blanche?

In complete hysteria,

Jess.

From: Blanche
To: Jessica Watkiss
Subject Re: Bastard Boris

Jess,

I know exactly what you mean. I couldn't be looking after snotty nose little brats all day, not without being able to dump them in a park or nursery for a few hours respite. And you're right, Boris certainly won't know what it's like to look after his own kids. He's never changed a nappy in his life, except for his own.

Help me to help you. You can bring Fido if you like, it will be a nice day out for him, just strap him on your back. Tell the mothers at the nursery group you're not taking this Tory shambles anymore. Invite them all along with you. Tell them you're demanding childcare for all and free milk for schools.

Meet me at Euston station, midday, Saturday 5th December.

Blanche

P.S Don't forget your face mask

Carrie Symonds
10 Downing Street
Westminster

10ᵗʰ November 2020

Dear Carrie,

I take no pleasure in telling you this and believe me, I'm not one to cause drama. I think you should know your boyfriend is having a homosexual relationship with his chief advisor. As you're aware, Dominic is currently living in your abode pretending to look after Boris. Perhaps you don't realise that Boris has passed all decision-making duties over to Domonic, leaving Boris powerless.

I've enclosed a copy of the correspondence from Boris and Dominic which will make the situation clear.

Best wishes,

Anonymous

Boris Johnson MP
10 Downing St
London

14ᵗʰ November 2020

Dear Blanche,

I hope you can still read this letter despite the tear stains on the paper. It's happened, my apocalypse! Dom left me to govern by myself. It's awful, preposterous. I feel like a doughnut missing its hole.

Dom sat me down at the dining room table and told me 'Boris, I'm leaving. I'm off to work as a full-time tour guide at Barnard Castle.' The news hit me like an angry HS2 protestor. I'm man enough to say I couldn't quite control my bottom lip. He is my world, my Bob to my Marley, my Wallace to my Gromit, my jam to my toast. Someone very vindictive wrote to Carrie and told her all about our bromance. I know exactly who it is. This time Sir Trevor McDonald has gone too far. I'm not scared of him anymore. He can do what he wants to me, but he can't take away my Dom. Carrie has turned psycho and threatened to castrate me with a pair of safety scissors if I didn't get rid of him. I'm rather fond of my scrotum. I do potato prints with it with Gove to pass the time before PMQs. I hate her Blanche, but she is so very scary.

Number ten feels so empty. Who will make my decisions now? Who will lead this country? I spat out my Coco Pops when Carrie suggested I fire him. We're not talking, she said, 'I never like that bald-headed, lanky streak of piss.' I fear what she will do when she realises I gave Dom our baby as a parting gift. He carried it away inside a little brown box.

Blanche, what can I do, how can I fill this empty feeling? My heart is in pieces.

Despairingly yours,

Boris.

Blanche
Boadicea Manor
Salford 6

Dear Boris,

Boris, it's time to put on your big boy pants. Choose another advisor to help you make some disastrous choices. Prince Andrew is available and cheap. I hear his going rate is a packet of Haribo Star Mix. I'm not sure what he uses them for, one mustn't question the Royals.

You're on your own now.

Blanche

From: Sophie McBride
To:Blanche
Subject LGBT Bullying
20th November 2020

Dear Blanche,

You were right, John needed me to tell him I loved him, that was all. He's back at home now. I made his dad give him a lecture about being *safe*. I don't know what sex education is like these days in school but if mine was anything to go by then it will be non-existent for gays. I told him about me and Rebecca, he wasn't fazed, said he already knew and then went back upstairs to play on his X-Box. He's a 'gaymer', whatever that means. There's a big community for them on Twitter apparently.

I thought long and hard about what you said about Section 28. Disgusting that the Tories did that. I thought, maybe if Marcus was able to talk to someone all those years ago then he wouldn't have felt forced to marry me and live a lie.

Did you see the BBC yesterday? The Government have pulled the funding for projects tackling LGBT bullying in schools. It's really made my blood boil. All I want is for John to be able to be who is and go to school without fear of being bullied. I hate to think there will be no one for him to talk to at school because of those cuts. I've written to the school governors to see if there's anything I can do. I just feel so helpless. Not every little boy or girl is going to have parents as understanding as John and they should be able to talk to someone. I really am angry about this. What can we do Blanche?

Lots of love,

Sophie

From: Blanche
To:Sophie McBride
Subject Re: LGBT Bullying

Dear Sophie,

You're absolutely right. Lesbian, gay, bi, trans, pansexual, genderqueer, queer, intersex, agender, asexual and straight allies should all be able to be who they want. I may not know what all the words mean, it doesn't really matter does it? All are people at the end of the day.

Live and let live. None of my business what people get up to, besides, the queers know how to throw a bloody good party.

Such a shame all the Pride events were cancelled this year because of the virus. I think it's about time we reminded the Conservatives of the Stonewall Riots. Help me to help you and your child Sophie, and all the other John's out there.

Meet me at Euston station, midday, Saturday 5th December. Be there. Bring all your LGBT+ friends and allies. Don't forget your facemasks and your rainbow flags.

Your LGBTQIA+ sister in arms,

Blanche

The Coup

I squeezed Fergie's body into a green camouflage full-length dungaree that she had crammed into the 'slim draw' of clothes she very rarely ventured into. I paired it with a matching duffel coat for the train trip down to London. I placed a hip flask in the inside pocket to sip at intervals to keep Fergie at bay. The last thing I bleedin' needed was her taking control of the body. I must say, it's a very surreal experience staging a coup whilst possessing a duchess. I did do her hair in my style to give me confidence on the way down, I could get used to a ginger beehive.

No one on the train recognised her so I was safe to travel pretty much incognito. I couldn't help but feel a little sadness for her that not a single person so much as glanced over. A far cry from the 500 million people who tuned in to watch her get married. But fame is so fickle: one day you're the toast of the Royals and the next you're living in a high-rise in Salford.

The train on the way down from Manchester Piccadilly to Euston was bursting at the seams. Not a single person social distancing, but not the space to either. I was pressed up against a young man named Jason who had biceps as big as Fergie's head. He was travelling down from Kendal to take part in the riots. He said he had nothing else to do since the gyms were still closed. His speech wasn't very clear due to not having seen a human face to face in months.

The carriage was a rickety old rust bucket on wheels. Although the chairs had been refurbished, sadly the smell they contained hadn't. The heating was on full blast causing the windows to steam up. A young woman with a nose piercing and pink streaks in her hair was sitting next to the window. She drew a scene of Downing St in flames with her finger in the condensation. Elsewhere people were reading the front pages of the news headlines and frantically refreshing their smartphones for the latest breaking news. Tory hypocrisy and their incompetence scandal. I was bloody delighted knowing I'd been the cause of it all.

4th December 2020
The Daily Fail

CABINET MELTDOWN AS SENIOR ADVISOR LEAKS DOCUMENTS

A red-faced Boris Johnson was last seen in public scurrying back into the protection of number 10 Downing St last night. Refusing to answer any questions, a clearly dishevelled Prime Minister lowered his head as he rubbed his Spider-Man face mask and barricaded himself behind the famous black door.

The Prime Minister was expected to make a statement in the early hours of this morning; however, sources close to Boris Johnson say he is unable to make any decisions since his senior advisor who goes by the name of Blanche, has been uncontactable for several days.

It's now known an anonymous figure has collected confidential correspondence from Boris Johnson's ministers sending copies to the offices of the national press. At this moment we cannot be certain who has sent the documents but can reveal the correspondence has been sent with a Salford postmark. The letters dating back to January this year reveal:

• The world-famous test and trace system was initially used to track down the Prime Minister's unidentified offspring.

• The Prime Minister hoped for a Royal scandal to divert the attention of the press away from his policies.

• The Prime Mister wasted **millions of taxpayers'** money on bogus schemes, a new landscape garden for number ten and personal holidays for himself and his ministers.

• Sex and violence have infected parliament, particularly the offices of the Home Secretary.

• Brexit negotiations have been influenced by the trade of football stickers whilst the most important decisions were made via consultation with a Magic 8 Ball.

Labour MP for Hackney North and Stoke Newington, Diana Abbott, was the first member of the opposition to respond to this leak and tweeted earlier today, 'Shocked at the inadequate reaction from this corrupt Government. Boris must resign along with all the MPs who have deceived and let down this great country. #Borishasfailedthenation.' Labour leader Keir Starmer, is reported to have been in meetings all morning ready to put a government in place should Boris

Johnson's government fail and be invited by HRH The Queen to form a new government.

Yorkshire singer, Jane McDonald, who is currently riding high at the top of the charts after releasing a cover of Black Lace's *Gang Bang*, which has become an anthem for doggers up and down the country, released a video message to her fans earlier today. Urging her fans to join the protest march against the government through the city of London, Jane confirmed she would herself be in attendance.

Crowds have been gathering in large numbers since yesterday morning when news of the government leak first broke. Protestors have been camping in Trafalgar Square where the Poll Tax riots took place some thirty years earlier. Many have been wearing t-shirts adapted from those original riots, the wording 'Drag Out Boris' captured the image of an unknown woman wearing a platinum beehive.

Amongst the crowd is Brenda from Bristol who told our publication, 'The lot of them want stringing up. I'm sorry but no, that is not how a government should behave. I'm not leaving here until the whole stinking lot of them are gone.'

She called for ministers to 'learn the lessons' of previous scandals, claiming the Government was too slow to react to the expenses scandal. She urged the government to 'listen to the people.'

Deputy Labour leader, Angela Raynor, condemned the Tory government earlier this morning as she stopped to talk to the press on her way into the House of Commons. 'Like so much of what this government does, they will try and distract from the truth and turn this into an expensive PR stunt. Passing the blame to hard-working individuals who have had enough of Boris's bumbling incompetence.' A short while later, Home Secretary Priti Patel, responded to the Deputy Leader of the opposition: 'Migrants have been filling central London, setting up camp in Trafalgar Square. I am streamlining extradition arrangements to have them forcibly removed.'

Turn to page 4 for full coverage and contents of the leaked correspondence.

I arrived at Euston and made my way to the departure screens where I'd arrange to meet my loyal four. As I got near to the information screens, I realised I hadn't a pissing clue what any of them looked like. Nor would they be expecting Fergie to turn up. The concourse was heaving with stationary bodies wearing *Drag Out Boris* t-shirts. They stood collectively like a small army, chattering amongst themselves with an air of excitement and determination. I hadn't seen a group more determined since the Bingo Callers Union collectively went on strike. They were against the proposal for the number of balls in a standard game to be raised to 200. I needn't have worried about recognising my gang, I spotted a short woman the size of small bungalow grazing on a KFC bucket. She stood ankle-deep in her own perspiration. A dent had been made in the concrete concourse from her heavy frame. I instantly knew she was Mangled Mel. A tall slim man stood beside her, nervously fidgeting and shuffling his feet. He was looking down at the poisoned munchkin, waiting for her approval in life. A middle-aged brunette who was stood within the small circle was announcing to anyone who would listen, that the man whose fingers she was interlocked with — and turning white with her vice-like grip, was her husband. 'We work on the waltzers at a travelling fair.' The husband had a look of regret in his eyes and was spinning the wedding band on his index finger. He was wondering how quickly he could remove it and try it on with the two lesbians who were smearing war paint onto each other's cheeks. From the side of the circle a pregnant woman called out, 'Bastard hell, is that who I think it is?' The odd tribe looked as threatening as a summer fruit trifle. They appeared more ready for a family day out than creating the historical chaos I had planned.

I explained to them that I, Fergie, had come as Blanche's replacement. If only they knew it was me under this ginger bonnet. Luckily, after the year of drama they'd all had, they'd believe any old shite. It takes a lot to take my breath away, but I was completely flummoxed when Alex stood forward, dragging her husband with her, and questioned, 'What do you reckon to this Fergie? We've brought the whole funfair with us, they're all furious they weren't able to get any government support during the lockdown. Jacqueline has had to give up her lions.' I gasped at the site of my old lesbian jailbird. The years had not been kind to her. She moved with frailty and remorse. I imagined that was caused by having Thatcher as her pinup. She appeared proud to have shared a kiss with the woman whose portrait she had printed on her t-shirt. For a split second, I wondered what our lives would have been like if I hadn't turned on my heels all those years ago. Would we have lived happily ever after, probably not.

My attention returned to the congregation of funfair workers who wore face masks advertising their various rides. You wouldn't want to come across them on your own on a dark night. They all looked like they'd been born on top of the ugly tree and battered every branch on the way down. I'd written them off as brutes, which is very useful for the plan I had concocted when one of them stepped forward and said, 'It's a pleasure to meet you, Ma'am.' He gave a curtsey. I was just about to tell him to not be so bleeding soft when I remembered all he could see was a Duchess and not a Salfordian with a master plan.

The lesbian couple, Dr Altman and Sophie, stood forward and indicated the sea of fifty rainbow flags held by members of their support group. They all wore matching rainbow face masks. The lesbians were bursting with pride that so many of their friends had turned up to march against the budget cut for anti-LGBT bullying education. They held placards high that read *DON'T BULLY POOFS, BULLY BORIS*. I was delighted. I was about to thank them when the pregnant woman shouted, 'What time will this be done with? I've left Fido at lost luggage and they close at eight.'

The trains kept arriving at Euston delivering masses of pissed off regular folk from the West Coast Main Line. The advertising screens had stopped showing the Queen's Tena Lady advert with the slogan: *Now the Corgis are the only thing to piss on the carpet*. Instead, they displayed rolling news of London at a standstill. The queues to get into Trafalgar Square were longer than the ones to get into Barnard Castle on New Year's Eve. The crowds were all chanting a mixture of slogans from the hundreds of groups that had united in their disgust at the Government, all affected in different ways by Boris's policies. The butchers from Essex chanted, *Beef up Boris*. Lead Butcher Barry had given a brief interview to Piers Morgan that morning. He expressed his anger at having to sell his sausages at half price every time his shop was forced to close in lockdown. Members of The Bingo Callers Union held placards that read, *Two Fat Tories, 88*. Whilst the mothers' group, who'd united after having to home school their kids, held signs that said, *WE'RE KNACKERED, LET US SLEEP*. Boris was about to find out there was nothing a mother wouldn't do when pushed to the edge of sanity after being forced to spend a year with her own kids.

I led the crowds along Tottenham Court Road and down towards Trafalgar Square. The police had cordoned off the traffic earlier in the day when protesters had started to arrive. The shops had closed and shut their doors; some had boarded up their windows in case of opportunistic looting. They needn't have bothered; the crowds were well behaved. All united in anticipation that something momentous was about to happen. One singular sly old man tried looting Boots for a packet of extra small, ribbed condoms. He was caught by Barry and the rest of the Butchers from Essex who marched him down to the Thames. They threw him in over one of the Golden Jubilee Bridges. Film crews captured the action and beamed it live to the nation. A soggy Jacob Rees-Mogg was pixelated onto the famous Piccadilly screens crawling out of the river. On seeing the news unfold from her budget hotel room, Ann Widecombe, who was dressed in red Marks and Spenser lingerie, crossed out Jacob's name from her little blue book. She turned to the next page, then using the budget hotel room's phone, she gave Farage a booty call.

At Trafalgar Square, the front of The National Art Gallery had been made into a makeshift stage. Taking centre of it and working the crowd into a frenzy of excitement was Jane McDonald. 150,000 voices sang back to her the words of her hit, *Gang Bang*. The police who had been sent to oversee the day stood at the sides of the square joining in. They were flirtatiously waving their batons and swinging their helmets in front of their privates. As the impromptu concert arrived on television sets across the continent, a choir of arm-chair observers joined in the chorus. Sixty million downloads of the song were made by the end of the week, making Jane's cover version the best-selling single of all time, overtaking Bing Crosby's *White Christmas*.

As I stepped on stage the crowd silenced, waiting in anticipation of every word I, or to them, Fergie, said. The paparazzi's long-focus lenses captured every moment. Realisation dawned upon them that there stood the body of Sarah Ferguson, Duchess of York. Newspaper editors were already creating headlines for the following day's print. *The Daily Mail* ran with 'DUCHESS OF COURAGE,' 'FERGIE, THE PEOPLE'S VOICE' dominated *The Mirror* whilst, 'Fergie, where've you BUSTY been,' spread across the *Daily Star*.

In the sitting room of Buckingham Palace Liz had just sat down in front of the TV with a microwavable fish pie for one. Upon catching sight of her ex-daughter-in-law on the TV she turned to Philip and said, 'Golly, how awful. I do hope she's not going to announce she was at Pizza Express in Woking. I fear the crown can't take another hit, Philip.' With a point of Liz's finger, Vulcan, the Queen's corgi, took direction from her master. Vulcan jumped up from her cushion and elegantly raised her front paws to the TV, increasing the volume of my historical speech.

Fearing Fergie might come back into control of herself, I took two huge gulps of gin from the hip flasks to keep her at bay before making my way on stage. I allowed the crowd to lean forward as if they were ready to receive a secret from a duchess before I began. 'I've had enough, have you had enough?' The crowds erupted. 'Just like a prostitute's knickers, a Tory MP will never change. From Thatcher taking away free milk for our children to Boris spending your hard-earned tax on holidays to the Balearic Islands for his pals.'

In the palace, Liz placed her microwave meal to her side on the sofa and invited Vulcan to take its place on her lap. 'Oh, dear Vulcan, this just will not do. She sounds positively... Northern.'

I continued to address my baited audience, 'Never has such a shower of shite held such high office. As useless as a condom with a hole. They wouldn't know how to tell the truth even if they wrote it down and leaked it to the press themselves. No more are we going to take this hypocrisy laying down.' The crowds' cheers turned into continuous thunder as my famous four made their way to the front, ready to lead the rebellion to our next destination. 'No more will we do as they say and not as they do. No more will we stay at home whilst they fuck off to Barnard Castle. No more will we accept bullies in our Government. No more will we live in a kingdom where feeding kids becomes a job of a fucking footballer and not those in power. No fucking more!'

The masses started to chant, *Fergie, Fergie, Fergie*. I can't deny I was a little put out they weren't shouting my name, at least they were hearing my words and wearing my face on their t-shirts. I wasn't finished yet, 'Are we going to accept this? Are we going to allow these perverse elitists to control us any longer? Isn't it time we stood up and regained control from these fuckwits who lead us? Isn't it time we expect more from our Government? To expect them to turn up to work when there's a fucking pandemic? Not to slouch on the sofas of Parliament and to cheer when they vote down a pay raise for our nurses? No more hiding in fridges. No more dividing the nation. No more turning up to work looking like *Stig of the Dump*, and no more fucking "NEXT SLIDE PLEASE."' The crowd went wild. A sea of placards raised up as my fantastic four led the crowds out of the Square and down Whitehall towards the boundaries of Downing Street. Jane McDonald provided a soundtrack of *Things Can Only Get Better* as the crowd marched onward intime to the beat.

Downing Street was surrounded on all sides. Thousands of people were rocking the railings that protected number 10. Larry, the Downing Street cat, looked down amused from the rooftop. He'd wanted Boris out since Carrie had started to use the laser pen, which normally kept him entertained for hours chasing the red light, on Boris instead. Carrie used it nightly to distract Boris from intimacy.

Inside, Boris hid underneath the kitchen table frantically shaking the Magic 8 Ball, asking it for guidance. He was soon joined by Patel, Raab, Hancock and Sunak. Hancock's lip trembled as Patel slapped him and told him, 'Get a fucking grip, child.' Raab and Sunak stared at their leader waiting for orders to follow. Gove stood in the hallway behind the door to number 10, plotting his next move. He debated joining his colleagues he couldn't stand under the table or immediately announcing his bid for the new leader of the Conservatives. He'd never liked the word loyalty; he found the concept restrictive. In a split-second decision, Gove opened the door to number ten and walked into the flashing lights of the world's press. Striding over to the locked security gates, he looked at me directly on the other side. I was waiting patiently for his next move.

Once a snake, always a wanker. I'd met many a power mad man back on Salford precinct and knew exactly how he'd react after our last letter.

Gove paused, took out his phone and tweeted, 'I stand with the people and I'm delighted to announce my bid for the new Conservative party leadership.' Sliding his phone back into his jacket pocket that contained more personality than he did, he indicated to the police guards to open the doors to the socially distanced protestors. I walked calmly through the opening gates as hundreds of hard-working folk swarmed into Downing Street knocking Gove off his feet. He retreated and crawled into the guard's shelter where he smiled smugly, planning what he'd do if he were to become Prime Minister.

I didn't get my hands dirty, that's what my loyal four was for. They each led a team of revellers through the doors of number 10 and straight through to the kitchen where Boris and his Tory quartet were hiding. Each of them was dragged out leg first from under the table. As Boris was carried out of Downing Street above the heads of the revolutionaries his Magic 8 Ball fell from his grip along with the power of being Prime Minister. As he was carried past the press, he gave a conference to himself, 'I will go out of the Street but remain firmly in the house. As we walk through these shadows of the valley of death, we have the light to continue into the darkness. I will remain as I depart through the gates of West...' Boris was silenced by the stray fist of Sir Trevor McDonald. The cameras zoomed in on Boris as he was hooded and thrown into the back of Sir Trevor's van which was last seen heading south out of central London over Westminster Bridge.

The rest of the quartet were paraded back up Whitehall and into Trafalgar Square to be strung up to the top of Nelson's column. For the next forty-eight hours they remained there, serving as target practice for passers-by who catapulted offal at them supplied by Barry's Butchers. They were eventually let down and set free to scurry away like rats. Priti was last seen in a migrant boat heading towards Calais.

The crowds dispersed shortly after the civilian invasion of Downing Street and buggered off home. The lesbians waved their flags all the way back to Brighton. Mangled Mel and Randy headed back up north via a lay-by on the M6 where Mel found more subscribers to her OnlyFans.

Alex was last seen searching for her husband who had escaped her in the crowds and disappeared with the rest of the travelling funfair on a ferry across to the Isle of Man. Jess had got halfway home before she realised that she hadn't collected Fido from lost luggage. Fergie and I headed back up to Salford, me still very much in control.

The next day Fergie had awoken in charge of her body. Normally she reaches for the gin she keeps beside her bed before she turns off her alarm, but today was different. When we got back from London, I placed a glass of water beside the bed instead of a pint of Gordon's. She might be a swindling Royal outcast, but I'd grown rather fond of Fergie. I wanted her to have a moment to see what we'd done yesterday. There was already banging at the door before Fergie woke properly. She answered the knocks and was greeted by the press who had followed us home the night before.

Bewildered, Fergie shut the door and headed to the sofa and turned on the news channel. She was in disbelief when she saw the continuous coverage of the events of the previous day. Images of her leading a large crowd through London, addressing the nation and dancing to Jane McDonald filled the screen. Seemingly idolised by all those who were in attendance a tear came to Fergie's eye as she recalled her wedding day, the last time she felt the nation's love. Although she could only remember yesterday in a haze, as if an out-of-body experience had occurred, she could feel the warm from the crowds. We sat watching the news all morning, well I was forced to as I couldn't take control whilst Fergie was completely sober. Unfortunately for me, Fergie vowed a life of sobriety there and then. Whilst the nation loved her, she was going to give herself to them completely.

Turning our attention back to the news, Sir Trevor McDonald came on screen with the breaking headline rolling across the bottom of the screen, 'Sir Trevor McDonald interviews HRH The Queen from inside Buckingham Palace.'

'Your Majesty, what were your thoughts yesterday when you saw your ex-daughter-in-law addressing the crowds in London?' Trevor respectfully asked Liz, knowing this interview would be repeated the world over and could possibly open up many links to the underworld.

'Philip and I were delighted at seeing our favourite Duchess recapture her free spirit which made us fall in love with her all those many years ago.' Liz replied with ease after years of media training.

'Ma'am, some may say you are capitalising on the love of the nation for the Duchess of York at a time when the Royal family have been through a year of division and recklessness?'

'Like many families in 2020 we faced unprecedented challenges, and like any family, it is the love you hold dear in your heart that propels you through those challenging times.'

'Ma'am, there are reports that the Duchess of York has been living as a recluse in appalling conditions since being expelled from the Royal family?' Trevor probed Liz.

'Truths are many and that is the problem with the truth.' Liz quoted a line from Sir Trevor's autobiography back to him.

'Is it true, Ma'am, that the Duchess of York has rekindled her romance with Andrew?

'Who?'

'Your son, Ma'am.'

'Oh no, we don't talk about him, do we, Phillip?'

'And finally, Ma'am, can the public expect to see the Duchess of York back within the palace grounds?'

Liz finished by looking directly into the camera and giving the public and Fergie the news they wanted. 'Oh yes, the Duchess of York will be in attendance at our socially distanced Christmas gathering. I imagine she will be life and soul of the party.'

Fergie couldn't believe what she'd heard and sat there in stunned silence for several minutes. If I was able, I would have given her a good slap to bring her round. Then like a Duchess who had been outcast from the Royal family and invited back in, she jumped up and ran to the wardrobe to find something to wear which would announce her return. There was sod all appropriate. She'd only been able to afford to shop at the seconds stall in the precinct since she'd been living off benefits. There was a bag in the corner of the bedroom filled with clothes that were too small for Fergie. I'd been meaning to take them to the charity shop when I was in control. Fergie ripped at the bag like it was a packet of ready salted. She pulled out clothes from her bygone public appearances: a black naval all in one suit she'd worn for an ITN interview in '86; a black and white polka dot dress from an unmemorable engagement; and a light brown skirt suit she'd worn for her interview with Oprah in '96. Holding her breath and her stomach in, Fergie stepped into the cotton dress. Closing her eyes, she pulled it up to her waist and zipped it up with ease. A diet of gin and custard creams clearly works wonders for the figure. As soon as she'd finished smearing her mug with Sacherelle skin preparation foundation, a hefty-looking man barged through her front door wearing a muscle-tight dark suit with the Royal Arms embraided over his right peck. Before she had time to think, Fergie was in the back of a blacked-out Range Rover on her way to Buck House, and I was going along for the ride.

On arrival at the palace, Fergie was ushered into Liz's living room. For all their wealth the room was *baltic*, dimly lit and smelt damp. Recalling her Royal protocol training, Fergie approached the Queen and gave a curtsey. Liz responded, 'Sarah, how nice. What a pleasure you've been able to find the time to visit. One can scarcely believe where the time has gone since our last meeting.'

'Your Majesty, thank you for inviting me, I'm...' Fergie didn't a get chance to finish her sentence before Liz interjected, 'Yes, well that's enough of that. Now do tell me, what's your secret to connecting with the masses as you do?'

I wished Liz could have seen me roll my eyes underneath Fergie's. In all my living years in which I'd befriended royalty, Liz was the one who seemed even less human than my dead self. As cold as a Salford ghost. I was dying for Fergie to pick up the glass of gin that Liz had got one of her butlers to put on the coffee table and quench my thirst. I noticed there was no slice of lemon.

'Ma'am, there is no secret. I just listened, I think.' Fergie, not quite being able to remember told the truth.

'Yes, well, perhaps we'll discuss it later. You must be tired after travelling for such a long journey. We prepared a banquet for you.' Liz indicated to a beige buffet that had been placed on the popped-up wallpaper pasting table. Vulcan sat upright underneath ready to catch any stray crumbs. The table was symmetrical in its layout of crab paste sandwiches, mini sausage rolls, and bowls of crisps. A single portion of red jelly made a calorific centre piece to brighten up the feast.

Throughout the brief exchange, a butler had topped Liz's glass up twice with a supermarket sherry that had been poured into a crystal decanter. She'd already had three before our arrival, exclaiming to Philip, 'Dutch courage was needed for the duchess.'

Not wanting to appear rude, Fergie lifted a paper plate off the wallpaper table and began to fill its circumference with bland delights. The atmosphere in the room was still as cold as ice but Fergie was warmed by the thought of being back within the royal circle. The Butler was once again filling Liz's glass when a stray chipolata which was placed high up Fergie's mound of sandwiches, lost its balance and somersaulted in what appeared to be in slow motion down towards the floor. Quicker than a flash of lightning, Vulcan was on all fours running from underneath the table, through Liz's legs and diving up to catch the meaty treat between his gnashers. Fergie stood in shock at another one of her faux pas as her ex-mother-in-law was knocked to the floor, sherry glass in hand, not spilling a drop.

The butler ran to Liz who was lying on the floor looking like a tweed mess pile. Fergie's wrist went limp losing her grip on the plate, Vulcan wasted no time in consuming the food which crashed onto the priceless Persian carpet. Fergie dropped to Liz's side; we were both now looking directly into the Queen's glazed eyes. 'Unconscious but breathing.' The butler announced to the room as if announcing the arrival of a foreign dignitary. Fergie stayed hovering over the Queen, looking for signs of life. An image flashed through my spirit as I stared into Liz's eyes from behind Fergie's. I had a split-second thought, what would Marilyn do?

13th December 2020
The Daily Star

A BIT OF A HEIRDO

Her Majesty the Queen was seen out for her first official engagement since the government coup last week. The Queen was attending the reopening of Randy's Royal Passage at Balmoral, the UK's first official dogging site. The Queen sported a white beehive similar to the one worn by The Duchess of York at the Trafalgar Square rallies last week. We ask, WHO REINED IT BEST?

Blanche
Buckingham Palace
Westminster
London
SW1A 1AA

10 Downing Street,
Westminster
London
SW1A 2AB

Dear Diane,

Cheers!

Love Blanche

ABOUT THE AUTHOR

Mike Lawson grew up in Manchester binge watching Victoria Wood and eating biscuits. Working as cabin crew for some rather dubious airlines; stories collected at 36,000ft made their way into the popular Biscuits with Blanche Facebook blog. Mike spends his days dreaming of becoming a Strictly Come Dancing contestant and pretending he's vegetarian. A second novel is in the works.

Twitter @WriterMike85

Facebook.com/BiscuitsWithBlanche

Printed in Great Britain
by Amazon

12434447R00167